THE SIRENS
SANG
OF
MURDER

THE SIRENS SANG OF MURDER

Sarah Caudwell

Delacorte Press

Published by
Delacorte Press
Bantam Doubleday Dell Publishing Group, Inc.
666 Fifth Avenue
New York, New York 10103

Each character in this novel is entirely fictional. No reference to
any living person is intended or should be inferred.

The trademark Delacorte Press® is registered in the U.S. Patent
and Trademark Office.

Library of Congress Cataloging in Publication Data

Caudwell, Sarah.
    The sirens sang of murder / Sarah Caudwell.
        p.   cm.
    ISBN 0-385-29784-X
    I. Title.
PR6053.A855S54   1989
823'.914—dc19   89-31335
                                                            CIP

Manufactured in the United States of America

Published simultaneously in Canada

November 1989

10 9 8 7 6 5 4 3 2

BG

To Billee,
for putting up
with the writing of it

THE SIRENS
SANG
OF
MURDER

Prologue

There will be much disappointment, I fear, among my fellow scholars. From the Senior Common Room of St. George's College, where anxious colleagues ask daily, "Finished yet, Hilary?" to the far distant lecture halls of Yale and Columbia, where I understand that the phrase "In Professor Tamar's forthcoming publication" is constantly to be heard, the world of learning waits with impatient eagerness for my long-promised work on the concept of causa in the common law. How then am I to admit that I have yet again allowed myself to be led astray from the true path of Scholarship and that what I now offer my readers is no more than the chronicle of my defection?

Would it not perhaps be more seemly to refrain from publishing any account of my investigation of the Daffodil affair and to allow the whole matter to rest in obscurity? The mere facts of the case, after all, are hardly in themselves of sufficient importance to warrant publication. The reason for the high mortality rate among the advisers to the

Daffodil Settlement; the identity of the white-robed figure seen on the cliffs on Walpurgis Night; how Julia Larwood came to be arrested in evening dress one morning on a beach in Jersey—of what serious interest or value can it be to my readers to be informed of such matters? And yet the case provides so striking a demonstration of the methods by which Scholarship, when applied even to such trifling questions, may dispel Error and reveal Truth that it will perhaps afford not only instruction to the public but much needed encouragement to other scholars. I have accordingly been persuaded, despite my misgivings, that it would not be right to withhold an account of it.

It was far from being my intention, when I made my way to London shortly before Easter, to permit myself to be distracted from the labours becoming to the Scholar. My former pupil, Timothy Shepherd, now in practice at the Chancery Bar, finding himself obliged by a combination of his professional commitments and his arrangements for the Easter vacation to be absent from London for a period of some three weeks, had invited me to make during that time such use as I might wish of his flat in Middle Temple Lane. Happening to have reached a part of my researches which required frequent visits to the Public Record Office, and which therefore could not conveniently be pursued in Oxford, I accepted his invitation with alacrity and gratitude. I regretted, naturally, that Timothy himself would be absent, for I have always found him a most generous host; but the friendship I had long enjoyed with other young members of his Chambers at 62 New Square assured me of agreeable company when I sought respite from my labours.

There was nothing to forewarn me, on my arrival in

the capital, of the dark and sinister events in which I was shortly to become embroiled. The sun was shining on Lincoln's Inn Fields; the azaleas were blooming in the gardens at the edge of New Square; the barristers hurrying in wigs and gowns across Carey Street were exchanging seasonable gossip about who was going to get Silk—it is on Maundy Thursday, as my readers are doubtless aware, that the Lord Chancellor announces which members of the Junior Bar are to be elevated to the eminent and lucrative rank of Queen's Counsel.

My young friends in 62 New Square, when not engaged in deploring the inadequate remuneration negotiated on their behalf by their Clerk, Henry, with their instructing solicitors, were innocently employed in activities befitting to the Chancery Bar: Selena Jardine, if my memory serves me, in a lengthy and acrimonious piece of litigation relating to the rights of the debenture holders in a public company; Desmond Ragwort in advising on the construction of documents affecting the title to certain land in the West Country; Michael Cantrip in sundry possession actions in various county courts. In the Revenue chambers next door, Julia Larwood was peacefully studying the latest Finance Bill.

Everything, in short, was proceeding in a manner appropriate to its nature and the season, with no such departure from the natural order of things as might be expected to be the portent of hidden danger and mysterious death. Or so, at any rate, it seemed to me. I did not realize, of course, how odd it was for Cantrip to be sent to the Channel Islands.

CHAPTER **I** ═══

"**N**o, no, let me go or I'll scream," cried the lovely Eliane, her beautiful eyes filling with tears and her bosom heaving under the delicate silk of her blouse as she struggled to free herself from the vile embrace of the brutal Barristers' Clerk.

"Scream all you like, you little fool," snarled the Clerk, his hideous features twisted in a vicious leer. "There's no one left in Chambers to hear you."

But at that very moment there appeared in the doorway of the Clerks' Room the suave and aristocratic figure of the brilliant young barrister Martin Carruthers.

"That's where you're wrong, Toadsbreath," he drawled with suave contempt. "Take your vile hands off Eliane this minute. She may be only a temporary typist, but she is too rare and fine a creature to be touched by the likes of you."

"Mr. Carruthers, sir, I thought you'd gone home,

sir," stammered Toadsbreath, cringing like a whipped cur before the young barrister's contemptuous suavity. Eliane gazed at Carruthers with adoration in her lovely eyes.

Cantrip and Julia were collaborating in the composition of a novel, based on their experiences of life at the Bar and to be entitled *Chancery!*, which they confidently expected to earn them wealth beyond the dreams of avarice and so free them from the tyranny of their respective Clerks. It had fallen to Cantrip to write the first instalment.

Offered the signal privilege of glancing through the opening paragraphs, I was reading them by candlelight in the Corkscrew, the wine bar on the north side of High Holborn which is the customary resort of my friends in Lincoln's Inn when the long day's work is done. Cantrip sat watching me with the anxiety characteristic of the aspiring author. It occurred to me that at least in appearance he was a not unsuitable model for the hero of a novel—the blackness of his hair and eyes combined with the pallor of his complexion to suggest a certain romantic quality which I supposed might appeal to the more susceptible portion of the reading public.

"What do you think of it, Hilary? Pretty hot stuff, wouldn't you say?"

I answered, well knowing the sensitivity of the creative temperament, that I could scarcely contain my impatience to read further.

"May I infer," I continued, "since you tell me that your narrative is based on real life, that you have a new temporary typist in Chambers?"

"That's right," said Cantrip. "Lilian's her real name. Pale and blonde and sort of wistful-looking. Makes you feel she's probably an orphan, going out to work to support her aged parents."

"So touching and unusual a predicament," I said, "cannot fail to engage the sympathy of your readers. And is it indeed the case that you have discovered your Clerk making unwelcome advances to her?"

"Oh, absolutely. Not exactly like I've put it in the book, of course—you've got to ginger things up a bit, haven't you? But I went into the Clerks' Room the other evening and Henry was sort of leaning over her and she was saying, 'Don't be silly, Henry, someone might come in.' So I gave him a quizzical sort of look and asked if I was interrupting something."

"And Henry cringed?"

"Well, not exactly. He said no, not at all, sir, he was just going to take Lilian for a drink in the Seven Stars, and shouldn't I be reading the papers for my possession action in Willesden County Court? That," said Cantrip with a certain vindictiveness, "was when I decided to call him Toadsbreath."

The proposed collaboration, though I wished it every success, seemed to me to be fraught with difficulties. The difference in educational background—Julia was educated at Oxford, while Cantrip, poor boy, through no fault of his own, spent his formative years at the University of Cambridge—would lead, I feared, to an irreconcilable disparity of style. Moreover, I had difficulty in seeing how the labour of composition was to be divided between them.

"Oh, that's easy," said Cantrip. "We've done a lot of research, viz read a lot of these books that people make

pots of money out of, and what we've noticed is that some
of them have heroines who are sort of fragile and waiflike,
like Lilian, and some of them have heroines who are more
sort of regal and imperious. So to be on the safe side we're
going to have one of each. I'm doing the Eliane bits, and
Julia's doing the bits with the regal and imperious one. Her
name's Cecilia Mainwaring, and she's at the Tax Bar."

"Dear me," I said, "does Julia intend a self-portrait?"

"Well, not exactly. Cecilia's what Julia'd be like if she
wasn't Julia, if you see what I mean—tremendously cool
and poised and well groomed and never getting ladders in
her tights or spilling coffee on her papers or anything. Oh,
there's Julia now—be frightfully nice to her, she got
roughed up a bit in court this morning."

Julia showed at first sight no manifest signs of ill treat-
ment. Her hair was no more than usually dishevelled, her
clothing no more than normally disordered, and she stumbled, in her progress towards the bar, over no more than
the customary number of briefcases; but it was with fever-
ish urgency that she purchased a bottle of Nierstein and
with pitiful weariness that she sank at last into her chair. I
enquired cautiously if she had had a difficult day.

"I suppose you could put it like that," said Julia. "In the
same sense that I suppose you might say that the early
Christians had a rather trying time with the lions in the
Colosseum. I have been appearing against the Revenue
before Mr. Justice Welladay."

"Come now, Julia," I said kindly, "Mr. Justice Welladay
couldn't eat you, you know."

"So I tried to persuade myself, but I found that I had
grave doubts about it. It is a matter of observable fact that
Welladay has twice as many teeth as anyone else, all of

enormous size. He also has eyebrows which gather in a continuous line across his forehead, like some savage beast of the primeval jungle waiting to spring on its prey." Despite the risk of learning a good deal more about some obscure provision of the Taxes Acts than I had any desire to know, I thought it right to enquire upon what issue she had found her views at variance with those of the learned judge. Though I have the honour to be a member of the Faculty of Law, I am happy to confess that I am an historian rather than a lawyer, and there is little in the English law of taxation after the year 1660 which I find of absorbing interest; but it would have seemed unkind—and since she had purchased the wine, ungrateful—to deny poor Julia the consolation of giving a full account of her misfortunes.

"My client," said Julia, "a simple, innocent property developer, had entered into a perfectly straightforward transaction which happened to involve a bank in Amsterdam and one or two companies in the Netherlands Antilles and which therefore happened to result in his having no tax to pay. Or rather, that's how it would have resulted if the case hadn't come before Welladay, who considers it the duty of every citizen to arrange his affairs in such a way as to maximise his liabilities to the Inland Revenue, and of his professional advisers to assist him in achieving that result. When I pointed out that the *Duke of Westminster's Case* is a decision to the contrary effect and according to accepted rules of precedent still binding on him, he gave a most disagreeable laugh and asked if I didn't happen to have heard of a decision of the House of Lords called *Furniss v. Dawson.* I have spent the day explaining, with the utmost respect, that the facts of *Furniss v. Dawson* were in no way similar to those of the case before him, and the words 'Oh really, Miss Larwood' and 'Miss Larwood, are you seriously suggesting . . . ?' have been constantly on his lips, accompanied by ever more menacing movements of the eyebrows. The woman you see before you, Hilary, is not the Julia of former days but merely the mangled remnants which my instructing solicitor was eventually able to scrape up from the courtroom floor."

A deep draft of Nierstein seemed to revive her spirits. "Vengeance, however, will in due course be mine. The day is not far distant when the evil Mr. Justice Heltapay will find himself confronted by the proud and imperious Cecilia Mainwaring, and little his teeth and eyebrows will avail him then. She will wither him with a scornful glance of her magnificent eyes, denouncing him as an oppressor of the widow and orphan and perhaps adding a few disdainful comments on his failure to follow long-standing decisions of the Court of Appeal."

"I gather," I said, relieved that the conversation had turned to happier matters, "that your novel is to have two heroines but only one hero. Are Cecilia and Eliane to be rivals for the affections of Carruthers?"

"Certainly not," said Julia. "Cecilia, by reason of her cool and disdainful exterior, is widely supposed indifferent to the gentler emotions, but she secretly nurses a passion, of the most noble and spiritual kind, for the aloof and elegant Dominic Ravel. Fearing to be rebuffed, however, she is too proud to tell him of her feelings." I had no difficulty in recognizing Ragwort as the model for Dominic Ravel, though Julia in expressing her regard for him had never shown such reticence as she imputed to her heroine.

"I don't mind Dominic being aloof and elegant," said

Cantrip rather anxiously. "But he's not allowed to be suave. Carruthers is the one that's suave. Did that come across, Hilary, that Carruthers was a tremendously suave sort of chap?"

I assured him that this characteristic of his hero had been most admirably established.

"And who," I asked, "is the principal villain? Toadsbreath or Heltapay?"

"Both of them," said Cantrip. "Eliane's really an heiress, you see, but Heltapay's the executor of the estate and he wants to keep it all for himself, and Toadsbreath doesn't want her to get it so she'll go on being at the mercy of his vile lusts, so they're in cahoots to stop her finding out about it. In the end, of course, they're foiled by Carruthers and Cecilia, so Eliane gets her inheritance and marries Carruthers and they all live happily ever after."

I gathered that the joint oeuvre was designed to be in the romantic rather than the realist tradition.

"It's designed to make us pots of money," said Cantrip. "You can't do that if you don't ginger things up a bit."

"We are of course anxious," said Julia, "to appeal to as wide a public as possible, and it seems to us that the readers who want fiction to be like life are considerably outnumbered by those who would like life to be like fiction."

"But that doesn't mean it hasn't got verysmellitude," said Cantrip. "It's all based on real life, so it's going to have verysmellitude in bucketfuls."

"It is only in respect of the most trifling details," said Julia, "that we depart in any way from the purely factual. The idea of Eliane being unjustly deprived of her lawful inheritance and restored to it by the efforts of our hero is based entirely on actual events."

I expressed a measure of scepticism. Delightful as the company is in 62 New Square, it seemed improbable that any young woman who had inherited a substantial fortune would choose to remain employed there in the capacity of temporary typist.

"The size of the inheritance," said Julia, "is a matter of mere detail. Lilian is the specific legatee, under the will of her deceased uncle, of a complete set of the works of the late Captain W. E. Johns. The executors, Messrs. Stingham and Grynne, have failed and neglected to hand it over to her."

"I don't suppose," said Cantrip, "that they actually wanted it for themselves. But let's face it, if you appoint a snooty firm like Stingham's to be your executors and then go and die leaving an estate worth twelve hundred quid, they're not exactly going to give you top priority. If they get round to applying for probate by the turn of the century, you can think yourself jolly lucky."

"The poor girl first sought advice from Henry, who told her that the matter wasn't worth fussing about. He would naturally be reluctant to antagonise a leading firm of solicitors. In her despair, she turned to Cantrip."

"Well, not in despair exactly," said Cantrip, "but jolly miffed. She hadn't actually seen this uncle of hers since she was a kid—he was one of those chaps who are always going off to make their fortune and turn up once in ten years or so to borrow a fiver—but she thought it was frightfully nice of him to have wanted to leave her these books and pretty rotten that she wasn't getting them after all. It made a sort of bond between us, because that's how I felt about the air gun my Uncle Hereward gave me on my fourteenth birthday, and it got taken away from me just because I broke a few windows."

"And were you," I asked, "able to assist her?"

"Oh, rather," said Cantrip. "There's a bird at Stingham's called Clemmie Derwent who's an old mate of mine—we were at Cambridge together. So I rang her and told her to get a move on, as a favour under the Old Pals Act, and they're going to hand these books over any day now. So Lilian thinks I'm the greyhound's galoshes, and Henry's as miffed as maggots."

"That," I said, "must be extremely gratifying."

"Well, in a way," said Cantrip, with a look of sudden doubt. "The trouble is, though, that when Henry's miffed he can make life a bit difficult. You suddenly find you haven't got any fees coming in and the only work you're getting is Legal Aid cases in Scunthorpe. What he's done this time is put the kybosh on a rather jolly little spot of holiday I thought I'd got fixed up in Jersey. Clemmie Derwent wants me there on the Friday after Easter to advise the trustees of some settlement thing, and she wants me to stay over until the Monday, so I thought it would be a sound scheme to stop on for the rest of the week and sit on the beach and build sand castles. But Henry's gone and accepted a brief in West London County Court on Tuesday afternoon, and he says he can't give it to anyone else, so I've got to come back. I bet you anything he did it on purpose."

"Are you saying," said Julia in a curious tone, "that Clementine Derwent has instructed you in connection with a case in Jersey?"

"That's right," said Cantrip. "I haven't the foggiest what it's about."

"I see—how nice," said Julia, imparting to these words

a degree of coldness which one might have supposed sustainable only by some more polysyllabic observation.

I was perplexed. Unless she had decided in the cause of Art to rehearse *in propria persona* the icy disdain which characterised her heroine, I could think of nothing to account for her sudden change of manner. Her tone had unmistakably been that used by a well-bred Englishwoman to indicate that if she were not well-bred, or not English, she would be making a scene. Had I not known how long it was since she and Cantrip had been on the terms sometimes productive of such a sentiment, I would almost have suspected her of jealousy.

"I say," said Cantrip, "are you miffed about something?"

"No," said Julia. "Of course not."

"Yes, you are," said Cantrip. "What are you miffed about?"

"My dear Cantrip," said Julia, "I have already said that I am not miffed about anything."

"All right then, what aren't you miffed about in particular?"

"Since you ask, I am in particular not miffed about Clementine Derwent sending you instructions in connection with a case in Jersey. Clementine is entitled to send instructions to anyone she pleases, and I hope her clients will be as impressed as I am by the originality of her choice of Counsel."

"Look here, Larwood," said Cantrip, "what's that supposed to mean?"

"You will forgive my saying, I hope, in view of our long-standing friendship, that you are not universally regarded as an expert in Revenue matters."

"No, of course I'm not. Whenever I try to read a Finance Act I come over all wobbly and have to lie down, like you with a first-aid manual. What's that got to do with me going to Jersey? No one's said there's a tax angle."

"My dear Cantrip, in Jersey there's always a tax angle. It's the whole *raison d'être* of the place."

"Just because it happens to be a tax haven—"

" 'Offshore financial centre' is the expression generally preferred in polite circles."

"Just because it's an offshore what's-it that doesn't mean they can't have cases about anything else. They have cows there, don't they? It's probably a claim for possession of a cow shed."

"That would be governed by the law of Jersey, that is to say by the ancient customary law of the Duchy of Normandy, and would be dealt with by Jersey advocates. The services of English solicitors or Counsel are required in Jersey only in those cases where fiscal considerations are of major importance. That is why it is usual, you see, to instruct in such matters Counsel believed to have at least a nodding acquaintance with the Taxes Acts. Miss Derwent, in her less original moods, would normally instruct . . . myself, for example."

My perplexity vanished. The chagrin of a woman displaced in her lover's affections is as nothing compared with that of a barrister superseded in the favour of a leading firm of solicitors. Cantrip, now likewise perceiving what was amiss, made haste to soothe Julia's wounded feelings with all the eloquence of which he was capable.

"Look here, Larwood, I've heard you talk a lot of bilge in my time, but the bilge you're talking now just about takes the biscuit. Have a bit of sense, for heaven's sake—

even if Clemmie'd gone off you for her tax stuff, you don't honestly think she'd send it to me, do you? Clemmie's not an idiot—she'd go to someone else at the Tax Bar."

"I suppose," said Julia, beginning to be mollified, "that there is something in what you say."

"What I think is that Clemmie's going to land me with something so frantically boring, she can't get anyone else to do it—going through two hundred files of correspondence in somebody's beastly office or something like that. Let's face it, I owe her a favour on account of her helping over Lilian, and when a solicitor you owe a favour to sends you to Jersey for four days, there's got to be a snag somewhere. I mean, there's nothing wrong with the place itself, is there? I don't have to learn that funny Frogspeak they talk there?"

Julia confirmed that it would be unnecessary for him to master the local patois and that there was no other feature of the island which might be regarded as a drawback. She spoke, indeed, with such enthusiasm of its golden beaches and picturesque valleys, its imposing castles and charming manor houses, its abundant dairy products and tax-free wines and tobaccos as to present a picture of something little short of an earthly paradise.

"Unless," she added, apparently as an afterthought, "you happen to be frightened of witches."

"I say," said Cantrip, "do they really have witches?"

"Oh, certainly. I speak, I may say, with some authority on the subject, having once been fogbound for four hours at Jersey airport with nothing to read but a book about witchcraft in the Channel Islands. In ancient times, we are reliably informed, Jersey was the centre of certain mysteries in honour of Demeter and Persephone similar to those

THE SIRENS SANG OF MURDER

practised on the island of Samothrace in the Aegean. We may assume, of course, that they were also in honour of Hecate, Queen of the Witches, who is invariably associated with those two goddesses as the third member of the celebrated triad of maiden, mature woman, and crone. The priestesses of the cult were believed to have power by their singing to control the winds and sea, so that it was prudent for seafarers to the harbour of Le Rocq to pay them their required tribute, and similar powers were imputed in later folklore to the Jersey witches."

"I'm going by plane," said Cantrip.

"There are one or two stories, however, which suggest that the witches do not always confine their attentions to those travelling by sea. You would do well, perhaps, to avoid wandering after dark anywhere near Roqueberg Point in the parish of St. Clement, at the southeastern tip of the island. That, according to tradition, is where they gather to sing and dance in the moonlight and lure young men to their doom."

"What kind of doom?" said Cantrip.

"The authorities are not entirely clear about that, but you would be unwise to assume that it was very agreeable. You should also remember that the witches have the ability, like the goddess Demeter herself, to transform themselves at will into beautiful young girls or hideous old hags. I would not wish, my dear Cantrip, in any way to inhibit your enjoyment of your time in Jersey, but I think I must advise you, just to be on the safe side, to steer clear of young girls, mature women, and crones."

Ragwort feared the worst.

On the evening of Cantrip's departure I once more found myself sitting with Julia in the Corkscrew, at the same candlelit table and in the same convivial shadows. The absence from our table of Cantrip was made good by the presence there of Selena and Ragwort. Selena, who had spent the previous few days sailing in the Solent, was in blithe and springlike spirits—the sparkle of seafaring was still in her eyes, and the sunlight still gleamed in her hair. Ragwort, on the other hand, had composed his features in an expression of such marmoreal gravity as one might see in the monument to some young man of saintly character martyred in the reign of Domitian.

Despite every effort to attribute the desire of Miss Derwent for Cantrip's presence in Jersey to some proper and decorous motive, Ragwort had been unable to think of any. He was compelled, with the utmost reluctance and distaste, to conclude that her motives were improper. He did not think it right to specify further.

"I thought," said Selena, "that Clementine Derwent was engaged. To another solicitor."

"So I believe," said Ragwort, "and would naturally wish to draw the inference you suggest. I understand, however, that her fiancé is at present on six months' secondment in Hong Kong, and she does not strike one as a young woman of ascetic temperament."

"No," said Julia, "she doesn't, does she? The impression she gives is of robust health and vigorous appetite, like an advertisement for cornflakes. One doesn't feel that she would take kindly to six months' deprivation of the pleasures of the flesh."

"You confirm my fears," said Ragwort.

"A girl in Clementine's position," continued Julia, "would no doubt reflect that there are two kinds of young men. On the one hand, there are those, such as yourself, my dear Ragwort, to whom the least one could offer would be the devotion of a lifetime and a profoundly spiritual regard almost untainted by the grossness of carnality. From the pursuit of young men of that kind Clementine is plainly debarred by her existing obligations. On the other hand, there are young men who might be persuaded to settle for something less. Young men—how shall I put it?—young men of obliging disposition. It is pretty generally known, I believe, that Cantrip is one of the latter sort."

"It is distasteful to think," said Ragwort, "that a fellow member of Chambers is regarded as available on demand to gratify the baser appetites of any woman who happens to be temporarily short of a husband or fiancé. Knowing, however, that that is the case, I fear there is little doubt that

Miss Derwent has resolved to take advantage of the position."

Selena was unpersuaded. Though aware that a number of intelligent and otherwise discerning women had from time to time considered Cantrip attractive—at this point she looked rather severely at Julia—she saw no reason to suppose him an object of universal desire or, in particular, of Clementine Derwent's desire.

Ragwort, happy as he would have been to do so, was unable to share this sanguine opinion. Selena, he supposed, must have forgotten the sordid episode which had occurred some eighteen months before, when Cantrip had escorted Miss Derwent home from a party given by a mutual friend.

Having heard nothing of the incident, I sought particulars.

"Alarmed," said Selena, "by the increase in crimes of violence in central London, Clementine had very sensibly undertaken a course of lessons in the art of self-defence and was anxious to put her training to some form of practical test. She accordingly made a bet with Cantrip that she could successfully defend her virtue against the most vigorous and determined attack on it."

"That," said Ragwort, "was the ostensible contract. In substance, I fear, it was neither more nor less than a sordid and degrading bargain for the provision of services of a most personal nature for the sum of five pounds—a sum, I should have thought, which even Cantrip would consider humiliatingly modest."

"But if that was indeed the contract," said Julia, "then Clementine must have underestimated the effectiveness of her newly acquired skills. She laid poor Cantrip out cold, and when he came to he had lost all enthusiasm for the intended ravishment. It is fair to say, however, that Clementine behaved much better than solicitors usually do in their financial dealings with the Bar—she applied her winnings in taking him out to lunch."

"And if," said Selena, "she does have designs on Cantrip's virtue, and he finds them unwelcome, he can always say no." An upward movement of Julia's eyebrows, a downward movement of Ragwort's lips, signified disbelief in Cantrip's ability to pronounce the word. "Oh well, perhaps not. But even if he can't, it still seems to me to be of no undue concern."

"No undue—My dear Selena," said Ragwort, "reflect on what you are saying. Of no undue concern? Any attempt by a member of the Bar to ingratiate himself with a solicitor, whether by gifts or by offers of hospitality or by favours of any other kind, is grave professional misconduct. And even if the matter can be kept from the Conduct Committee of the Bar Council, it can hardly be hoped, though of course none of us here would dream of mentioning it to anyone except in the strictest confidence, that it can be kept entirely secret—people in Lincoln's Inn are such dreadful gossips. If poor Cantrip should happen in future years to achieve any measure of professional success, malicious tongues will all too readily attribute it to his willingness to oblige his instructing solicitors in a manner unbecoming to Counsel."

Selena remained unmoved. If we were to worry about anything, she said, it should be the possibility, unlikely as it was, that Clementine required Cantrip's presence in Jersey in the misguided confidence that he was versed in fiscal matters. What was he to do if someone asked him to advise on Section 478 of the Taxes Act or construe a double tax treaty?

"For that," said Julia, "we have a contingency arrangement. He's meeting the lay clients tomorrow to hear what their problem is and he's expected to give them the answer on Monday. If there turn out to be any fiscal implications, he'll send me a telex on Saturday and I'll telex back the best answer I can think of."

"Tell me," said Selena, for the first time looking a little anxious, "do you think that Cantrip will be able to obtain ready access to a telex machine?"

"Good heavens, yes," said Julia. "Any offshore financial centre, such as Jersey, is always amply equipped with such things. I told him to explain to his hotel that he might have to send urgent telex messages at some time when their operator was not on duty—I'm sure they won't object to him sending them himself."

"Oh dear," said Selena. "You do know, don't you, Julia, what Cantrip's like about telex machines?"

The proposal to instal a telex machine at 62 New Square had been thought, after long months of debate, negotiation, and intrigue on the part of its supporters and opponents, to have been finally disposed of at a Chambers meeting which had taken place in the preceding January. Greatly assisted, no doubt, by the always persuasive advocacy of Selena, who was one of its most resolute adherents, the pro-telex party had appeared to be gaining the day until Basil Ptarmigan, the senior, most eloquent, and most expensive Silk in Chambers, began—not precisely to address the meeting, but rather to muse mellifluously aloud that change was not always for the better.

It was frequently said (Basil had reflected) that one must move with the times. Might it not be prudent, before doing so, to ascertain the direction in which the times were moving—whether towards triumph or disaster? He had been told that the telex machine was the latest thing in modern technology; but they would not, he supposed, be so childishly excited by mere innovation as to purchase it on that account. He had been told that "everyone else" had a telex machine—an expression apparently denoting in this context the Revenue Chambers next door; but he believed that he himself might claim to enjoy, without the benefit of such an appliance, as extensive an international practise as any of the members of 63 New Square. He had been told that clients expected telex facilities: a time would come perhaps when clients would expect to find Coca-Cola dispensers and computer games placed in the waiting room for their refreshment and recreation, and it might well be that Chambers would have to bow to their wishes, but he could not help hoping that that day would be deferred to some time beyond his own retirement.

The pro-telex party sighed and mutely conceded defeat, agreeing that a final decision on the project should be postponed to some future, uncertain, and, it was assumed, infinitely distant date.

In the following month Basil received several telephone calls in the early hours of the morning from an eminent American attorney, associated with him in a case of some magnitude, who appeared unable to understand the nature of the time difference between London and New York and evidently believed that in the absence of telex facilities this was the only reliable means of communicating with him. (Selena, my principal informant on these

Sarah Caudwell

matters, had heard of this not from Basil but from the New York attorney—who happened, she said, with the expression of a Persian cat disclaiming all knowledge of the cream, to be an old friend of hers.)

At the Chambers meeting in February, Basil began again to muse gently aloud. It was extraordinary (he reflected) that they always seemed to have such difficulty in Chambers in reaching any positive decision about anything: one almost felt that there was some truth in the accusation, so often levelled at the Chancery Bar, that they were slow, reactionary, and out of touch with the modern world. Take, for example, the proposal to acquire a telex machine: it was now several months since the matter had first been raised; many valuable hours had been spent in discussion and investigation; the few trifling difficulties had been shown to be easily resolved, and it was surely beyond dispute that such a machine was nowadays indispensable to successful practise at the Bar. Yet still they had taken no active steps to acquire one—why ever not?

A week later the machine had been installed in the Clerks' Room. (The advantages of this location were considered to outweigh the minor inconvenience of incoming messages sometimes being read by casual visitors to Chambers before being seen by the intended recipient.)

The members of Chambers had for the most part treated it with circumspect awe, as an object whose arcane mysteries were known only to the temporary typist. They would no more have thought of transmitting a message themselves than a suppliant at Delphi of consulting the oracle without the intervention of the priestess.

With Cantrip, however, it was otherwise. He had watched its installation with keen interest and had succeeded in obtaining from the engineer in charge some elementary guidance as to its use. Permitted to run his fingers over its chaste ivory keyboard and to discover with what exquisite sensitivity it responded to his lightest touch —deleting here, inserting there, amending elsewhere— the poor boy fell victim to as fatal a fascination as that exerted by Isolde over Tristan or Lesbia over Catullus.

He had spent the next three days in a delirium of telex-sending. The medium seemed to have a strangely liberating effect on his creative powers, enabling him to express his thoughts and feelings with a freedom and fluency which he had never before experienced. His messages, covering a wide range of topics and sometimes employing various ingenious noms de telex, were addressed not merely to his friends, acquaintances, and enemies in every corner of the world but often to total strangers whose telex number happened to become known to him. Could he have contented himself with mere composition, no harm would have come of it, but seldom if ever was he able to deny himself the ultimate rapture of pressing the key marked "Enter" to transmit the message to its destination.

It could not continue. After a perplexed inquiry from the Lord Chancellor's Office about a message purporting to be from 10 Downing Street, but readily traceable to 62 New Square, and consisting of the peremptory command "Give Cantrip Silk," strict instructions were given to the temporary typist to permit none of the members of Chambers to have direct access to the telex machine: from these, despite all Cantrip's blandishments and the regard in which she held him, Lilian had conscientiously refused to depart.

* * *

On the morning following the day on which Cantrip left for the Channel Islands I found in Timothy's letter box a communication of apparent urgency from the London Electricity Board, and knowing that he had made some arrangement with Henry for dealing with such matters, I turned aside on my way to the Public Record Office to deliver it at 62 New Square.

Though Henry himself had not yet arrived, the Clerks' Room was uncustomarily crowded. Interest appeared to centre on the telex machine, round which were gathered several members of Chambers, the senior partner in a leading firm of solicitors, three or four articled clerks in a state of high amusement, and a slender, fair-haired girl whom I took to be Lilian, the new temporary typist. The message which engaged their attention had evidently been transmitted in Jersey earlier that morning.

To the Senior Clerk 62 New Square
Absolutely private and tremendously
confidential

Dear Henry,

As per your esteemed instructions I have started negotiating with your deserted wife re her claim for increased maintenance. She says with five children fifty pence a week is not enough. Have pointed out that as you never divorced your first wife in Singapore or the one in Buenos Aires she has no legal rights and is lucky to get anything, but she seems to know about the money in your Swiss bank account and how you got it, so you may want me to offer a bit more to keep her quiet. The children do look rather hungry. Awaiting your instructions

Your sincere friend and well-wisher,

Titus A. Newt

The pseudonym deceived no one. The question whether it would be proper, as it would plainly be politic, to remove and destroy the message before it was seen by Henry was still under discussion when his arrival rendered it academic. Thinking the moment unpropitious to my errand, I joined Selena and Ragwort in seeking shelter from his rage in Basil Ptarmigan's room—a room of such serene and elegant distinction, its walls lined with centuries of legal learning, that Henry would not venture, it was felt, to give rein there to his indignation.

We found Basil in consultation with Julia, who had persuaded her instructing solicitors that for the purpose of the appeal from Mr. Justice Welladay's recent decision it was essential to engage the services of leading Counsel: she and Basil were now deliberating the grounds of the appeal. The eminent Silk accepted our apologies for the interruption, courteously implying that company so agreeable and distinguished could never be considered intrusive. Selena explained why we were obliged to seek refuge.

"As you know," said Basil, "I have always had grave doubts of the wisdom of installing a telex machine. Technology is responsible for much that is wrong with the modern world—now we are going to have Henry in one of his difficult moods, and we all know how tiresome that is for everyone."

"I'm not sure," said Julia, "that it's the existence of telex machines that's wrong with the modern world—I'm inclined to think it's the existence of Cantrip. He's sent me a telex as well, and its contents are rather disturbing. Perhaps the rest of you would care to read it while Basil and I finish drafting our notice of appeal."

TELEX M. CANTRIP TO J. LARWOOD TRANSMITTED GRAND HOTEL ST. HELIER 9:00 A.M. FRIDAY 27TH APRIL

Yoo-hoo there, Larwood, me here. All right so far advicewise, but thought you ought to know about chap here called Edward Malvoisin casting vile aspidistras on fair name of J. Larwood. Don't worry, I got him sorted out all right—jolly lucky I did, bet you'll never guess who was listening.

This Malvoisin chap is the Jersey lawyer for these characters I'm meant to be advising. Seemed like a pretty good egg to start off with—met me at the airport yesterday P.M., whizzed me off to the Grand Hotel, and began pouring booze down me like there was no tomorrow, so I took a pretty genial view of him.

I suppose you know the Grand Hotel—all potted plants and wickerwork, with the waiters still getting over the excitement of Queen Victoria's Jubilee. It's the sort of place where you'd expect to find my Uncle Hereward, sitting on the veranda chatting with his ex-army cronies about the great days of Empire. That reminds me, I meant to tell you—the old boy's been

threatening to come up to London for a few days. If he
turns up before I get back, don't let him get into any
trouble. He's fairly harmless really if you know how to
handle him.

Where was I? Oh yes—me and the Malvoisin chap
in the bar of the Grand Hotel. It was fairly early still,
and we had it pretty much to ourselves. No one else
around except a chap reading *The Times* in one corner
and an old biddy all wrapped up in black shawls doing
her knitting in another—probably got lost on the way
to the guillotine.

The way your name cropped up was because I was
telling Malvoisin I was in 62 New Square and he said he
knew a bird in 63, and I said I knew a bird in 63 as well
and they both turned out to be you. So of course we
wittered on about you for a bit and to start off with he
seemed to have pretty sound views on the subject, viz
that you were hot stuff on double tax treaties and fanciable with it.

Only then he gave me a funny sort of look and said
something like what a pity it was about you being the
way you are. At first I thought what he was talking
about was just your general sort of goopiness, and I
pointed out that one didn't mind it once one got used to
it and anyway it wasn't your fault. Then he gave me
another funny look and said something about people in
London being very broad-minded, and it turned out
that what he thought was that you were like those
ancient Greek birds who fancied other birds instead of
chaps.

I don't know how he got the idea, I expect it's
because you're always talking bits of Latin. Anyway, I
told him he was talking codswallop and you were one of
the keenest chap fanciers I knew. He wouldn't believe

it at first but I told him I was talking from firsthand experience, nothing hearsay about it. He still looked as if he didn't a hundred percent believe me, so I told him all about what happened after you won that case about goldfish in front of the Special Commissioners. It's not the sort of thing I'd usually go into a lot of detail about to a chap I'd only just met, but the way I see it is that if you find someone casting aspidistras at an old mate, you've jolly well got to spring to the defence—I mean, you'd do the same for me, wouldn't you, if you came across some bird saying "Nice chap, old Cantrip, pity about his cootlike tendencies"?

You might think it doesn't matter a lot what someone says about you in the bar of the Grand Hotel because of there being no one to listen, but that just shows how wrong you can be. I'd just finished putting Malvoisin straight when the chap who was reading *The Times* got up to go and I saw who it was. Bet you'll never guess, not in a million years.

All right, I'll tell you, it was old Wellieboots, large as life, teeth and eyebrows included. Gave me a nasty shock seeing him there, all unexpected. Don't know what he was doing there or how much he heard, but the point is that if he heard what Malvoisin said about you, he heard what I said as well. So it's jolly lucky I was there, because you wouldn't want old Wellieboots getting funny ideas about you, would you?

Have just sent frightfully witty telex to Henry. Don't let on it was me—bet he's as miffed as maggots.

Must dash off now and advise these trustee bods.

Over and out—Cantrip

There was some curiosity about what had happened after the case about goldfish, but Julia, though willing to explain in some detail the interesting questions of law raised by the case itself, declined to give particulars of its sequel. The first significant victory of her forensic career, the goldfish case had occurred at the time when she and Cantrip were on those terms conventionally described as closer than mere friendship. She had celebrated her triumph in his company, and with an exuberance more unrestrained than it might have been, she said, had she known that in future years it would be made the subject of a public proclamation to the senior judiciary.

"Oh dear," said Selena. "I hope that isn't going to cause you any embarrassment."

"I suppose," said Julia, "that when I next appear before Mr. Justice Welladay, the thought of his having quite such a detailed knowledge of what I had previously regarded as my private life may indeed be a trifle disconcerting. That, however, isn't actually what I'm worried about. The thing that's worrying me—"

"How fortunate," said Basil, "that the judge in question was Arthur Welladay. Other judges, perhaps, might be distracted by the idea of you engaged in youthful dalliance from the learning and gravity of your arguments, but since Arthur never in any case pays any attention to any argument addressed to him on behalf of the taxpayer, it will make no difference. I wonder what he's doing in the Channel Islands. Making sure they exist, perhaps—on the last occasion that I appeared before him, he seemed to be accusing me of inventing them as part of a tax avoidance scheme. So I offered to put in evidence of their existence, and he became rather cross with me."

"Basil," said Selena with gentle severity, "you really ought not to tease him, you know."

Sarah Caudwell

"My dear Selena, I've been teasing Arthur Welladay for twenty-five years, and it's far too late to break myself of the habit. He was just the same at the Bar—wherever the Revenue position was most plainly indefensible, there was Arthur defending it. And he wouldn't touch anything that looked like an artificial avoidance scheme—not even the innocent little discretionary settlements that the rest of us were earning our living from in those days. Poor Arthur, it's really very sad—if it hadn't been for that, he might have been quite a good lawyer. He is a member, as of course you know, of a distinguished legal family and has a by no means contemptible intellect, but I'm afraid this obsession with tax evasion has seriously impaired his judgment. He's really hardly rational on the subject."

"To return," said Julia, "to the matter of Cantrip's telex, the thing that's worrying me—"

"Have you any idea," said Ragwort, "why this Jersey advocate should suspect you of unorthodox tastes?"

"Possibly," said Julia, "because I have been to some trouble to persuade him to. Edward Malvoisin is apparently under the impression that every woman he meets is secretly yearning for him to make advances to her. If his advances are rejected, he regards this as merely confirming that the yearning is indeed secret. So far as I'm concerned he is mistaken—if I'd known him when he was twenty-five or so, I daresay I might have thought him quite good-looking, but he has the kind of looks which tend to become rather fleshy and florid by the late thirties. Not my sort of thing at all. On the other hand . . ."

"Yes?" said Ragwort, raising an eyebrow.

"On the other hand, Stingham and Grynne use his firm for most of their work in Jersey, and quite often instruct me in connection with the same matters, so I was reluctant to express myself with the degree of rudeness which would evidently be required to persuade him of his error. I thought the tactful thing would be to give the impression that my repugnance was general rather than particular."

"That was very sensible of you," said Selena. "How thoughtless of Cantrip to spoil it."

"Isn't it?" said Julia. "But that isn't what I'm worrying about, either. The thing about Cantrip's telex that I find really disturbing is the threatened arrival of his Uncle Hereward."

Colonel Hereward Cantrip had served his country with great distinction in the Second World War, having twice been awarded the DSO, and now lived in well-earned retirement on the South Coast. On those happily infrequent occasions, however, when the widowed sister who kept house for him decided for some reason of her own to dispatch him to London for a few days, he was considered by the rest of the family to become the responsibility of his nephew. Julia had once or twice at such times been prevailed on to assist in his entertainment, and would have been content to do so again. It was, she said, no more than one friend might reasonably ask of another. To undertake the task, alone and unaided and for some indefinite period, of keeping him out of trouble was quite another matter. Trouble, so far as Julia had been able to discover, was what Colonel Cantrip had spent a lifetime of more than seventy years getting into. To keep him out of it, she felt, would require a woman of sterner resolve than herself.

"I don't think," said Ragwort, "that you should allow yourself to become unduly anxious. After all, there's no sign of the old gentleman so far, and we know that Cantrip is appearing in West London County Court on Tuesday afternoon. So he can't be away for more than four days."

Ragwort has a touching confidence that things will turn out as they ought.

CHAPTER 3

EXTRACT FROM *THE GUIDE TO COMFORTABLE TAX PLANNING*

Jersey: The largest and most southerly of the Channel Islands. Lying off the Cherbourg Peninsula and geographically forming part of France, the Islands were included in the dominions of William of Normandy at the time of his invasion of England in 1066. His successors to the English crown, though compelled to relinquish their possessions in mainland France, retained suzerainty over the Islands in their capacity as Dukes of Normandy. In recognition of the Islands' independent status, and of their vital strategic importance during periods of conflict with the Continent, they have always enjoyed immunity from all forms of United Kingdom taxation. In the Second World War they were the only British territory to suffer occupation by the Germans.

Population: 80,000. Area: 5.5 miles by 9.5. Capital: St. Helier. Principal industries: Agriculture, tourism, and financial services. Access: By air 1 hour from London or Paris; by sea 1 hour from St. Malo, 8 hours from Southampton. Recommended season for meetings: April to September.
Note 1: An unsuitable choice of tax haven for those who have been advised to avoid rich foods. . . .

(The Guide to Comfortable Tax Planning, which contains much invaluable advice on such questions as where to stay in Vaduz, eat in Gibraltar, or buy a novel in the British Virgin Islands, which flights to Luxembourg offer free champagne, what to see in Nassau, do in Vanuatu, wear in Panama, drink in the Netherlands Antilles, and on no account do in the Turks and Caicos, is unfortunately not available to the general public: it has been compiled by certain members of the Tax Bar for the benefit of no one but themselves, and the few copies in existence are subject to constant revision by means of notes circulated among the contributors. I have the kind permission of the editors, however, to quote those passages which may be of assistance to my readers in connection with my present narrative.)

Having devoted the following Monday, almost without interruption, to my researches in the Public Record Office, I was by evening in much need of refreshment. It was a few minutes after half past five that I made my way to the Corkscrew, expecting it to be some time before I was joined by any of my friends. I found Julia, however, already there, though she claimed to be still working. She had thought that a glass of wine would prove an aid to the construction of a particularly opaque provision of the new Finance Bill. She could not permit herself, therefore, to engage in any immediate sociability. In the meantime, she suggested, it might amuse me to read the telex messages which she had received from Cantrip in the course of the weekend.

TELEX M. CANTRIP GRAND HOTEL ST. HELIER TO J. LARWOOD 63 NEW SQUARE TRANSMITTED 6:30 P.M. FRIDAY 27TH APRIL

Look here, Larwood, what I want to know is why everyone here thinks I'm so frightfully witty when I haven't made any jokes. Is everyone loopy in this tax-planning business?

The thing I'm meant to be advising on is a thing called the Daffodil Settlement—don't ask me why it's called that, it's some sort of code name. If you think that's peculiar, wait till you hear the rest of it.

The trustee of the thing is a Jersey trust company which is owned by a Swiss outfit called the Edelweiss Bank. The bods actually running it are an Irishman called Patrick Ardmore, who's the top man in the Jersey company, and a French bird called Gabrielle di Silvabianca. She's in charge of the Edelweiss office in Monte Carlo now, but the thing was set up fifteen years ago when she was working at the Jersey office and she's gone on looking after the investments.

We all got together this morning in Edward Malvoisin's office and it looked at first like being a pretty genial sort of gathering, with Clemmie and Malvoisin being frightfully chuffed about seeing the French bird and the French bird and the Irish chap being frightfully chuffed about meeting me and a general spirit of chuffedness all-round.

The French bird is rather good news. I don't mean fanciable exactly—must be fairly ancient, and she's got one of those squashed-in-looking faces, with sort of mud-coloured eyes not leaving much room for anything else—but the sort of bird that livens things up somehow. Edward Malvoisin says he fancies her like mad, but it doesn't do him any good because she's batty about her husband. She's married to an Italian—he's a count, like Italians mostly are, so that makes her a contessa.

The Irish chap is all right as well—bit of a smoothie, but sound views on getting through the heavy stuff in plenty of time for drinks before lunch.

Then the accountant turned up, long stringy chap by the name of Gideon Darkside with a face like a skull and crossbones, and lowered the geniality level by about 90 percent. He spent twenty minutes explaining how his plane had been held up and it wasn't his fault he was late and another twenty telling us how important it was to get down to business and not waste time on gossip, so it wasn't till nearly half way through the morning that anyone thought of showing me a copy of the settlement.

There were pages and pages of stuff about the trustee's investment powers and that sort of thing, but the gist of it was that it was a settlement made by a chap called Philippe Alexandre, who lived in Sark, for the benefit of the descendants of some chap called Sir Walter Palgrave. At least that's who it said it was for the benefit of—when I looked at the bit about discretionary powers it turned out that the trustee could give the loot away to anyone it liked, and these Palgrave characters would only get what was left over.

The first thing that got me worried was that it said the trust fund was one hundred pounds sterling, and I pointed out that wouldn't go far towards paying our expenses, let alone any fees that anyone might be thinking of charging. They all thought that was tremendously witty, even old Darkside. They said there was actually a bit more than that, and when I asked how much they said nine and a quarter million quid, give or take a hundred thousand. So we should be all right for our fees.

So I said all right then, if that wasn't the problem, what was? They all looked a bit embarrassed and not awfully keen to explain, but in the end Clemmie said the problem was that they sort of couldn't find their beneficiaries. What I thought she meant was that all these Palgrave characters had gone off to America or somewhere leaving no forwarding address, the way beneficiaries do sometimes, and I said the best thing would be to hire a private detective to track them down.

They all thought that was frightfully witty as well. They don't know a thing about the descendants of this Walter Palgrave chap and they don't give two hoots what's happened to them, because the last thing they're going to do with this trust fund is give a penny of it to these Palgrave characters. The idea of having a settlement where the people named as beneficiaries are the ones that are actually going to get the money didn't seem to be one they'd ever heard of before, and they weren't too keen on it. "Prejudicial to confidentiality and fiscal effectiveness" was what they thought it would be—I suppose they meant it would make it more difficult to keep things dark from the Revenue.

So I said all right, if they weren't going to give the money to the Palgrave characters, who were they going to give it to? So they said what they wanted to do was give effect to the wishes of the settlor. I asked if there was any chance that that meant the Philip Alexandre chap, who was supposed to have made the settlement, and like I was rather expecting by this time, they thought that was so witty they nearly fell off their chairs. What they meant by the settlor, they said, was the chap who'd actually put the money in in the first place, and it certainly wasn't Philip Alexandre.

So I said fine, who was the chap who'd put the money in and how were they going to find out what his wishes were if there wasn't anything in the settlement to tell them? That's when they started looking as if they'd definitely rather be talking about something else. According to them, the usual thing with this sort of settlement is to get a separate letter from the settlor telling the trustees what he wants them to do with the cash. No deed or witnesses or anything, just a few notes scribbled out on the first bit of paper they've got handy —back of an envelope or something like that. I said all right then, where was the envelope that the settlor's wishes were written on the back of?

So, bearing in mind that this is a nine-million-quid settlement run by a top-class international bank with high-powered professional advisers, what do you think they've gone and done with the envelope? Absolutely right, Larwood, lost it is what they've gone and done.

Well, the line they take is that they haven't lost it exactly, because so far as they know it's still sitting on some file or other in somebody's office somewhere. It's just that they've all got thousands of files and they don't know which one it's on. It's not on any of the ones to do with the Daffodil Settlement so what they reckon is that it must have been filed under the name of the settlor. But there's nothing in the Daffodil files to say what the name of the settlor is, because that would be prejudicial to confidentiality and fiscal what's-it. And they've just tumbled to the fact that none of them actually knows who he was—the only one who did was a chap called Oliver Grynne, who was the senior partner in Clemmie's firm and kicked the bucket some time last year. The only thing the rest of them know is that the settlor snuffed it a few weeks before that and that means it's time they started doling out some loot.

I pointed out that strictly speaking there wasn't anything for them to get in a tizz about, because according to the settlement the trustee could give the trust fund to anyone it liked, so there was nothing to prevent the Edelweiss outfit from trousering the loot and saying no more about it.

Gabrielle thought that was the wittiest bit of all and laughed like a drain. Well, not like a drain really, because she actually sounds rather nice when she laughs, sort of bubbly but not squeaky, like champagne coming out of a bottle. Anyway, she laughed a lot.

The rest of them didn't think it was witty at all, they all looked a bit shocked, and Darkside made a face like a corpse sucking a lemon, as if I'd made a joke in the middle of a funeral service. The way they saw it, trousering the loot wasn't on. Inconsistent with the bank's international standing and reputation for unblemished integrity was what they said it would be—I

suppose they meant it would look bad if anyone found
out. So they wanted to know what else they could do.
Sweet suffering swordfish, Larwood, what do they
expect me to do about it? Pull the beneficiaries out of a
hat for them? Send me a swift telex if you've got any
bright ideas.

Over and out—Cantrip

"To such innocent minds as Cantrip's and my own," I
said, "the arrangements which he describes appear bi-
zarre. I assume, however, that to one versed in Revenue
matters they are entirely normal and commonplace?"

To my surprise, Julia seemed hesitant.

"Up to a point," she said at last. "That is to say, the
settlement sounds for the most part like the sort of thing
everyone was doing in the late sixties and early seventies—
Basil must have drafted dozens of them. The basic idea was
that the trustees wouldn't be liable for U.K. income tax or
capital gains tax because they were nonresident and the
intended beneficiaries wouldn't be liable because they
weren't legally entitled to income or capital—they
wouldn't get anything except in the exercise of the trustees' discretion. And it was standard practice, in that kind of
settlement, to avoid any mention of the real settlor or the
persons he or she really intended to benefit. What I don't
understand is this reference to the Palgrave family—I'd
have expected a disposition in favour of the Jersey Lifeboat
Fund."

"Perhaps," I said with incautious naiveté, "the settlor
had no desire to benefit that institution."

"Oh," said Julia, "it wouldn't actually get anything, you

know. But it's indisputably charitable by the law of both England and Jersey, so it's convenient from the tax point of view to make it the default beneficiary. I don't say that was the invariable practice—sometimes there was a provision that in default of appointment the fund should be held on trust for the Chairman of the Board of Inland Revenue. Or the Chancellor of the Exchequer, or someone like that."

"In the hope of engaging their sympathies?"

"Not exactly. The Revenue used to contend, you see, that the default beneficiaries under this sort of settlement would be liable for tax on capital gains realised by the trustees even if they never actually received a penny of the fund. So some people liked to draw settlements which on that view would impose the liability to tax on the Chairman of the Board—you know how people in Lincoln's Inn enjoy teasing the Revenue."

"Perhaps Sir Walter Palgrave," I said, "held some similar public office—the name seems faintly familiar."

"I thought so too," said Julia, "but I don't know in what connection—he certainly wasn't Chairman of the Board of Inland Revenue. Well, whoever he was, it looks as if his family may receive a rather pleasant little windfall if Cantrip's clients don't manage to identify their settlor."

"But, Julia," I said, "the position is ridiculous. They must have some way of finding out who he was."

"Oh no, I shouldn't think so," said Julia. "If they had, you see, it would mean there was some loophole in the arrangements they'd made to protect the confidentiality of their client's affairs, and that's not at all what one expects of a Swiss bank—the Swiss are very serious about that sort of thing. I rather wish I'd warned Cantrip about that—if his clients knew he'd been mentioning the name of the settlement in an uncoded telex, they might be rather upset about it."

"Were you able to offer him any advice?"

"I sent him a telex suggesting that his clients should apply to the Royal Court of Jersey for directions. But, as you will see, he feels that the idea will not appeal to them."

TELEX CANTRIP TO LARWOOD TRANSMITTED 10:30 P.M. SUNDAY 29TH APRIL

Yoo-hoo there, Larwood—thanks for the telex, but not ruddy likely. My clients go waltzing along to the Royal Court to get directions and who's that sitting at the back of the courtroom with his notebook out and his ears flapping? The chap from the *Financial Times,* that's who, Larwood, the one who's always chatting up Selena and wanting to do exposés of things. If you were a Swiss bank that had lost its files and didn't know what to do with nine million quid, would you want a half-page spread in the *F.T.* about it? You bet you wouldn't.

Not to worry, though, it doesn't look as if giving legal advice is mostly what I'm here for. I've found out what Clemmie wanted me for, and it's not because she thinks I'm the world's greatest tax lawyer and it's not for what Ragwort thinks either. I got her to come clean about it after dinner on Friday evening.

We'd been having dinner at Patrick Ardmore's place at Gorey, which is a rather jolly little fishing vil-lage at the eastern end of the island—all of us except for Darkside, who said he'd got work to do even if no one else had. We had a lobster each and lots of wine and everything was pretty bonhomous until someone said

something about the Cayman Islands. I didn't hear
what it was exactly, because I was having a cosy chat
with Ardmore's wife—rather fanciable blonde doctor,
who thinks all tax planners are more or less round the
twist. I just heard someone say "last year in the Cayman
Islands," and then everyone not saying anything for a
bit, and then someone else talking about something
completely different. But it definitely seemed to cast a
blight, and we never got properly bonhomous again.

So the party broke up quite early after all, and
Edward Malvoisin drove us all home—viz me and
Clemmie to the Grand and Gabrielle to a tremendously
smart-looking place about halfway between Gorey and
St. Helier. On the way there Gabrielle said she'd hired
a car for the weekend and would Clemmie and me like
her to drive us round a bit? To which Clemmie said that
she, i.e. Clemmie, couldn't make it, because she'd got
to work on some papers, but Cantrip, i.e. me, would
love to, wouldn't I? She kicked me on the ankle and I
said yes, rather, because no one can say I don't know a
subtle hint from my instructing solicitor when I get
one.

Pretty peculiar was what I thought it was, so when
we got back to the Grand I hauled Clemmie into the
bar and got her to spill the beans about why she was so
keen on me going driving with Gabrielle. And the gist
of it is that what she wants me for is to be a sort of
bodyguard.

The Daffodil crowd get together twice a year, once
here and once in the Cayman Islands, and at all the last
three meetings before this one Gabrielle's had the feeling that someone's following her. Clemmie says she
pretends to treat it as a sort of joke, but she's really
pretty rattled about it. Clemmie was getting worried

about her, being rather a fan of hers, and she reckoned it would be a good idea to have someone around this time who could make themselves useful if there was any trouble. But she didn't want Gabrielle to know she'd fixed it up on purpose, in case Gabrielle thought she was fussing and got miffed.

When I asked if she'd any ideas about who it was, she said they both reckoned it must be the Revenue, but what they weren't sure about was whether it was the English Revenue or the French. To start with they thought it must be the French, on account of Gabrielle having a lot of French clients that the Frog tax inspectors would probably like to get the goods on, but that doesn't square with it always happening at Daffodil meetings. The Daffodil setup's all geared to saving tax in the U.K., so on balance they think it's probably our lot.

I was a bit spectical at first, or whatever the word is for thinking your instructing solicitor's having you on about something, but Clemmie was dead serious about it. She says the U.K. Revenue play pretty rough nowadays—not as rough as the French, but much rougher than they used to. She reckons that these days they wouldn't turn a hair about bugging your telephone and searching your wastepaper basket and things like that, and she doesn't see why they should draw the line at putting a tail on someone if there was enough tax involved to make it worthwhile.

I asked her if all this had anything to do with whatever it was that happened in the Cayman Islands that everyone wanted not to talk about, but she pretended there wasn't anything and I'd just imagined it. You can't call your instructing solicitor a barefaced liar, even if she is an old mate, so I couldn't find out any more about that.

Anyway, I promised I'd stick to Gabrielle like a postage stamp for the rest of the weekend, which actually sounded like rather a jolly scheme, and if any sinister chaps in false beards started leaping out of the undergrowth, I'd be on hand to biff them.

I say, Larwood, is this tax-planning business really as exciting as these Daffodil characters seem to think or do they just make believe it is to make life more interesting? I mean, if I'd known it was all about codes and secret documents and biffing chaps in false beards, I wouldn't have minded going in for it myself—let's have some of it in our book.

Saturday turned out pretty quiet from the men-in-false-beards angle. Gabrielle picked me up at the Grand after breakfast, and we drove round Jersey looking at the historical bits—castles and Norman manor houses and things like that—with stops for the odd swim and the occasional cream tea. We talked about what a lot of fun the Normans must have had, riding round in armour and fighting tournaments and having seigneurial rights over peasant wenches. Gabrielle thinks I'm very sensitive to historical atmosphere—I think I am too, actually, but a lot of people don't notice it.

I'd been a bit worried at first that she might want to talk tax planning the whole time, so I'd explained straightaway I wasn't really a tax chap, just a sort of general knockabout Chancery chap. She seemed quite pleased, though—she said the kind of lawyer they needed in the Daffodil business wasn't the kind who looked things up in books but the kind who had an instinct for realpolitik, and that's what she thinks I've got. I suppose that's Krautspeak for having a bit of sense.

We met up with Clemmie and Malvoisin for dinner and found a place to go dancing, so all in all it was a pretty good sort of day, except for not spotting any sinister characters lurking in the undergrowth. I did spot old Wellieboots again, sitting in the bar of the place where we had lunch—I think he's jolly sinister, but I suppose he doesn't count.

Today was a bit different.

We'd fixed up to meet at St. Clement's Bay, which Gabrielle said was her favourite place in Jersey. The idea was to get there at low tide and walk out across the sand to something she calls the Sirens' Rock—that's her private name for it, it's called something different on the map. She says it's the one that the witches used to dance round and lure fishermen onto, like you were talking about last week.

There's another big rock in the garden of some-one's house that's called the Witches' Rock, but Gabrielle doesn't think it's the right one because it's on dry land. She says the proper one must be one of the ones that are covered up by the sea when the tide's in.

It's in the bottom right-hand corner of the island, quite near where her hotel is, so it seemed a bit silly for her to drive into St. Helier to pick me up. I told her I'd get there under my own steam and got up early and walked there.

When the tide's in it looks like you expect the seaside to look, with a sandy beach and lots of blue water next to it, all nice and neat like on a postcard. When the tide's out it looks quite different, like a desert with damp problems—acres and acres of squelchy brown sand covered with seaweed and spiky splodges of rock all over the place, with shiny bits where the water's got stuck between them.

I thought as soon as I saw her that Gabrielle was looking a bit under the weather, as if maybe she hadn't slept too well. I didn't say anything, though, in case it was just a hangover and it would be unsuave to show I'd noticed.

It takes about an hour to walk out to this rock of hers, and you couldn't exactly call it walking dryshod— you've got to take your shoes and socks off and roll your trousers up, and you still get fairly wet. Gabrielle didn't seem to mind, though—she seemed to quite like getting wet, and by the time we got there she'd perked up a good bit.

She'd brought a thermos of coffee and some rolls from her hotel, so we sat on the rock and had a picnic breakfast. We didn't talk much to begin with, just sat and drank coffee and listened to the sea gulls. I kept thinking what funny-coloured eyes she'd got, not green and not brown, like the bits of the sea that were stuck between the rocks and you couldn't tell what colour they were.

And then she started telling me she thought her room had been searched last night when we were out at dinner. She said it wasn't obvious, but she knew how she'd put her things away and she was sure that when she went up to bed some of them weren't in quite the right place.

I asked if there was anything missing, because after all she is a contessa and she does look like the sort of bird who might have some quite nice jewellery with her, so someone on the lookout for the odd diamond bracelet to snaffle might think she was a pretty likely prospect.

She said she didn't think there was anything missing, but if someone was looking for jewels, they wouldn't have found any—the only valuable thing she's got with her is a gold fountain pen with her initials on that was a birthday present from her husband, and she always keeps that in her handbag. She didn't think it was a diamond snaffler, though—she thought it was the chap who'd been following her at Daffodil meetings.

So then she told me all about it, and of course I didn't let on that I'd already heard about it from Clemmie. The thing I'm a bit surprised about is that she really is rattled, like Clemmie said she was. She's a tremendously sporting sort of bird and I'd have thought being shadowed by the Revenue was the kind of thing she'd get rather a kick out of—after all, even when the Revenue are playing rough, they're not actually going to get physical, are they?

I suppose what's really getting her down is not being a hundred percent sure about it. She says herself that it's mostly just a feeling she's got—if the person she's being followed by came and stood in front of her she wouldn't know it was them. So sometimes she thinks she might be going a bit loopy and imagining things.

I told her she was talking bilge, because even if she isn't being followed, it doesn't mean she's loopy. People do follow people, so if you think you're being followed by someone and you're not, that's not being loopy, it's just being wrong—being loopy is if you think you're being followed by purple elephants, unless you are of course.

Anyway, I pointed out I'd be around all the time she was in Jersey, so there wasn't anything to worry about—I mean, either the Revenue chaps were imaginary, in which case they couldn't do her any harm, or they weren't, in which case if they tried to, I'd jolly well make them wish they were. She seemed quite chuffed about that and said I'd made her feel a lot better.

And after all that, what do you think the silly grummet is going to do tomorrow?

The Daffodil Settlement owns shares in a company that's meant to be resident in Sark—I suppose you'd know what the point is, I'm blowed if I do—and that's where the directors have got to have their board meetings. The directors are the Daffodil gang plus Philip Alexandre—that's the chap who was supposed to have made the settlement but didn't. He lives in Sark and owns a hotel there, and the Edelweiss outfit always use him when they need a Sark resident to be a settlor or a director or anything like that. So we're going over there tomorrow for the directors to have a board meeting and me to give them my advice about what to do with the trust fund—flying over to Guernsey in the morning and going across to Sark on the ferry. Well, that's what the rest of us are doing—Gabrielle's going on her own and doing something different, and she won't tell me what it is.

I've pointed out to her that if I'm in one place and she's in another, I shan't be able to do much about sinister chaps from the Revenue leaping out of the bushes at her, but she just looks mysterious and says I'm not to worry about her. Which is a bit much, considering she's the one who made me start worrying about her in the first place. Honestly, Larwood, there are some birds you just can't reason with, and if you don't know them well enough to biff them there's not a lot you can do about it.

I didn't like to ask her about what happened in the

Cayman Islands, so I still don't know what it was. Is that
where you went last year or was it the Turks and Caicos? All I remember is that you got goofy about some
chap.

We're reckoning to be finished in Sark in time to
get the evening plane from Guernsey, so I should be
back in London sometime tomorrow night, worse luck.
If anything interesting happens, I'll tell you on Tuesday
morning.

Over and out—Cantrip

The arrival of Ragwort and Selena distracted Julia
from her Finance Bill and me from further reflection on
Cantrip's telex message. Not until Selena had purchased a
bottle of Nierstein and we were all comfortably settled
round the little candlelit table did it occur to me to ask Julia
whether it was in fact the Cayman Islands or the Turks and
Caicos that she had visited in the previous year.

She answered, with a dreamy and distant look, that it
was indeed the Cayman Islands.

CHAPTER  4

EXTRACT FROM *THE GUIDE TO COMFORTABLE TAX PLANNING*

Cayman Islands: A group of islands in the Western Caribbean consisting of Grand Cayman, Little Cayman, and Cayman Brac. A British Crown Colony settled in the seventeenth century by retired pirates, survivors of shipwrecks etc. Capital: Georgetown, Grand Cayman.

Pop.: 17,000. Total area: 100 square miles. Access: Approx. 1 hour by air from Jamaica or Miami. Principal industries: Tourism and financial services. Facilities include 400 banks and more telex machines per head of population than anywhere else in the world. Recommended season for meetings: October to March.

Note 1: An ample supply of English newspapers,

which are much prized by the inhabitants of Georgetown, will ensure a cordial welcome.

"Properly regarded," said Selena, gazing thoughtfully
into her glass, "your experiences last year in the Cayman
Islands could be incorporated very nicely, Julia, into this
book that you and Cantrip are writing. Have you considered at all why your heroine is so cold and aloof, so reluctant to admit to any of the gentler passions?"

"I confess," said Julia, "that I have assumed these quali-
ties to be natural to her."

"Oh no, surely not—I don't think that would be at all
sympathetic. No, as I see it, when Cecilia Mainwaring first
came to the Bar she was a warm, generous, open-hearted
girl whose clear, candid eyes gazed with trusting eagerness
on the world about her. What has happened to change her?
Why does that generous heart now wear the mask of cold
indifference? Why do those candid eyes now flash with icy
disdain? Ah, you may well ask."

"You suggest that it is because she went to the Cayman
Islands?"

"Because she went to the Cayman Islands, as you did,
Julia, for reasons connected with her practise as a tax barrister, and there, as you did, she met—a man." Selena invested the word with overtones of the monstrous. "A man
much older than herself, an urbane and sophisticated man,
experienced in the ways of the world. What could she know
of such men, poor Cecilia, whose life had been spent in the
chaste cloisters of Oxford and Lincoln's Inn? Accustomed
to the innocent banter and boyish camaraderie of her contemporaries, how could she resist his subtle and practised

charm? In the sensuous warmth of the Caribbean night, fragrant with the scent of a hundred exotic flowers, she gave him her heart. He trifled with it for a while as lightly as a child with a new toy, and as lightly afterwards cast it aside."

"Oh Selena, how sad," said Julia, deeply moved. "But whether it's an entirely fair account, so far as my own visit is concerned—"

"A most affecting tale," said Ragwort, "remarkable for bearing no resemblance whatever to what happened to Julia in the Cayman Islands. If I recall the story correctly, Julia, you behaved extremely badly, and took advantage of a harmless, good-natured man who had not deserved ill of you."

Julia, always willing to see both if not more sides of every question, seemed to find some difficulty in choosing between the versions of events proposed by her two friends. I suggested that she should tell me, quite simply and in her own words, precisely what had occurred.

In the previous November she had been appearing in a case before the Grand Court of the Cayman Islands—the details, though no doubt, as she claimed, of absorbing interest to any student of the law relating to bearer securities, are of no relevance to my present narrative. She had been accompanied by her instructing solicitor, who happened to be Clementine Derwent, and their visit had coincided with a meeting of those concerned with the Daffodil Settlement. The discretion customary among Swiss bankers and their advisers had precluded any mention of the actual name, but save that Clementine's firm was at that time represented by Oliver Grynne, the senior partner, the meeting had been attended by the same people as that which had just taken place in Jersey and could safely be presumed to relate to the same matter.

"You will no doubt tell me," I said, "that there is some perfectly good reason for those administering a Jersey settlement to meet in the Cayman Islands."

"Oh, certainly," said Julia. "It wouldn't do at all, you see, for the funds of the settlement to be directly invested in the shares of companies resident in a high-tax jurisdiction such as the United Kingdom or the United States. The sensible thing is for the trustee of the settlement—in this case Edelweiss (Channel Islands) Ltd. —to own shares in a private company resident in, let us say, the Cayman Islands and for that company to own shares in another private company resident in, let us say, Sark. The Sark company would be the one which owned the underlying investments—shares in ICI or General Motors or whatever it may be. The directors of the private companies, of course, would include one or two officials of the trust company and their professional advisers. And since a company is treated for tax purposes as resident in the country where its directors take their decisions, it's essential for the directors of each company to have at least one board meeting a year in the place where it's supposed to be resident."

"There is nothing remarkable, then, about your having encountered the same group of people in the Cayman Islands whom Cantrip has been advising in Jersey?"

"By no means," said Julia. "The world of tax planning is in some ways a fairly small one—one sees the same doorplates on the offices in Georgetown and St. Helier as one would in Bishopsgate or Lombard Street. I already knew most of the people involved in the Daffodil Settlement."

I asked if she had had any previous acquaintance with Cantrip's contessa.

"I'd met her once before—Clementine introduced me to her at a tax-planning seminar in Luxembourg about two years ago. Stingham's are the London solicitors for the Edelweiss group, so she and Clementine have a good deal to do with each other. We all played truant together from one of the official dinners and did our bit to reduce the problem of the champagne lake. I'd been hoping I'd run into her again sometime, but she doesn't seem to travel abroad very much. Most of what she does can be done from her office in Monte Carlo."

"What exactly does she do?"

"She invests other people's money for them—according to Clementine, with astonishing brilliance."

"The name," I said, "seems vaguely familiar. Wasn't her husband once noted for some kind of sporting activity? Riding horses or driving motorcars or something of that sort?"

"I think he was a tennis player," said Julia.

"Ah yes," I said, remembering now that it was indeed in that sport that the Count di Silvabianca had fifteen or twenty years before achieved celebrity. Though he had never been quite among the first rank of players, his title and his exceptional good looks had combined to make him interesting to the gossip columnists and a certain portion of the public. I concluded that the Contessa shared Julia's taste in profiles.

They also had in common, it seemed, an extreme distaste for the advances of Edward Malvoisin, which neither Julia's diplomatic deception nor the Contessa's devotion to her husband were ever quite sufficient to discourage. They had commiserated, on their first evening in the Cayman Islands, about the need to avoid doing or saying anything during their stay which Malvoisin might construe as encouragement.

"The trouble was," said Julia, "that we could think of very few things that he wouldn't construe as encouragement. We had no doubt, for example, that for either of us to appear on the beach in any form of bathing costume, however decorous, would seem to him the clearest possible invitation to seize upon us in the manner of a hungry schoolboy claiming the last cream bun. And it would have been difficult, of course, to avoid him altogether. Fortunately, however, it turned out that Clementine found him unobjectionable—it's curious, isn't it, how tastes differ in these matters?—and agreed, as it were, to draw his fire in exchange for Gabrielle and me each buying her a large piña colada."

"Gideon Darkside," I said, "also sounds like someone whom one might wish to avoid—did you know him as well?"

"Oh yes," said Julia with a weary sigh, "I knew Gideon Darkside. I once had the misfortune to call him as a witness before the Special Commissioners for the purpose of proving that certain accounts he had prepared were an accurate reflection of the events which had occurred. I had imagined, in my innocence, that this was a mere formality. I was therefore disconcerted when he was cross-examined on behalf of the Revenue for five hours, during which it became clear that any similarity between what had actually happened and what the accounts said had happened was purely accidental. And when he found that this was attracting unfavourable comment from the Commissioners, he became hurt and resentful—he seemed to think that preparing false accounts was a perfectly usual and accepted method of tax planning."

"I suppose," said Ragwort, "that he is simply one of those all too numerous people who have no idea of the difference between right and wrong."

"I suspect," said Julia, "that he thinks things are wrong only if one enjoys them, and is able on that basis to regard himself as a man of the highest moral character. But at least there was no difficulty about avoiding him—he makes a point of always being too busy for idle amusement. He likes it to be known, you see, that he works harder than anyone else—that is to say, that he spends more time giving bad advice to his clients than other people do giving good advice to theirs."

"So you knew everyone," I said, "except Oliver Grynne and Patrick Ardmore?"

"Oh," said Julia, "I'd met Oliver Grynne once or twice. As I may have mentioned, I'm quite often instructed by Stingham's. I rather liked him—he was slightly pedantic sometimes, and he had a morbid obsession about keeping fit, but he was a very good lawyer. No, the only one I hadn't met at all was Patrick Ardmore."

Julia lit a Gauloise and adopted what she intended, I believe, to be a very casual expression.

"On our first evening in Grand Cayman I was sitting with Clementine and Gabrielle in a little bar called the Cayman Arms, overlooking Georgetown Harbour, buying piña coladas in accordance with the bargain previously mentioned. Gabrielle had mentioned that her colleague from Jersey might be joining us, but it didn't at once occur to me, when Patrick Ardmore came into the bar, that he was the person she had referred to. He had—I don't quite know how to describe it—a slightly adventurous look, which one doesn't usually associate with bankers."

"I should hope not indeed," said Ragwort.

"All the same, he was not at all the kind of man I usually find attractive. He had unquestionably entered on his fifth decade, and it did not seem to me that his profile, even in youth, would have had the classic perfection of— say, yours, my dear Ragwort. He had not, it is true, let himself go, as men so often do when they have found someone to marry them and think they don't need to take any trouble with their appearance anymore—there was no blurring of the jawline or unsightly bulge over the waistband. Nonetheless, as he approached our table I was surprised to find myself thinking . . ." Julia paused and looked dreamily at the ceiling, drawing deeply on her Gauloise.

"Thinking," said Ragwort, "if that is indeed the appropriate word for what we take to have been a not wholly cerebral activity—thinking what, precisely?"

"Thinking," said Julia, "and I agree, of course, that it was not a process in which the intellect was predominant— thinking, as it were, 'Dear me, what a remarkably stylish bit of goods.' Or words to the like effect. What I chiefly experienced was a sudden shortness of breath and a peculiar queasiness in the pit of the stomach, similar to mild indigestion."

"At her first sight of him," said Selena firmly, "her pulse quickened, and she was stirred by a strange emotion which she could find no words to describe."

By a fortunate or unfortunate coincidence, it had happened that Julia and Ardmore were staying at the same hotel, close to the midpoint of West Bay Beach, while the rest of the party were accommodated at another establishment on the same long stretch of golden sand but a mile or two further north of Georgetown. It was accordingly natural that they should form the habit of concluding the evening in each other's company, drinking a last glass of wine together under the palm trees at the bar beside the swimming pool.

"And it was on these evenings," said Selena, "amid the exotic scents of the Caribbean night, while the air throbbed with the intoxicating rhythms of the calypso and the waves foamed sensuously across the sand, that this man without pity or scruple undertook his conquest of a trusting and innocent heart. Under the tropic moon he murmured to her of—what precisely did he murmur of, Julia?"

"Mostly," said Julia after some reflection, "of the effect of tax legislation on investment policies, that being a subject of mutual interest. And he always asked how my case was going and seemed to like hearing about it. The trouble was, you see, that quite apart from the feelings I have mentioned, I found him—I found him very amusing."

"You mean," said Selena, "that he laughed at your jokes."

"Yes," said Julia.

"I am afraid," said Selena, "that very few women can resist a man who laughs at their jokes, and a man such as Patrick Ardmore would all too easily have realized that you are not one of them. Oh, poor Julia, it's too heartless."

Ragwort, however, was unwilling to admit that laughing at Julia's jokes, in whatever climatic conditions, was sufficient to constitute a campaign of seduction and demanded further particulars in support of the charge.

"Did he pay you compliments? Did he say, for example, that you had nice eyes or pretty hair or anything of that kind?"

"Good heavens, no," said Julia, apparently slightly shocked by the suggestion.

"We are speaking," said Selena, "of an experienced and sophisticated man, well practised in the arts of persuasion. He is, after all, a banker—that is to say, he spends his life persuading people to pay for the privilege of lending him money and again for the privilege of borrowing some of it back. He would have realised at once, I daresay, that Julia likes being the one who says silly things about people's eyes and hair and would be rather resentful of someone stealing her lines."

"Did he deceive you," continued Ragwort, "as to his matrimonial standing or suggest that his present arrangements were in any way unsatisfactory?"

"Oh no," said Julia. "He spoke frequently of his wife, and always in terms of the highest regard and affection. So I was encouraged to think that he was well disposed towards women."

"As he no doubt intended that you should be," said Selena, "since everyone knows that a man who is ill-natured even towards his wife is hardly likely to behave well towards any other woman. But you must remember, Julia, that men are very deceitful about such things, and it's quite possible that he didn't really behave nearly as well towards his wife as he would have wished you to believe."

"Did he," said Ragwort, "attempt any form of physical familiarity, as by holding your hand, patting your shoulder, or anything of that sort?"

"No," said Julia, "nothing like that at all."

"It would not take much sophistication," said Selena, "to realize how much Julia dislikes men who are physically aggressive."

"In short," said Ragwort, "did this man do or say anything which he might not have done or said if you had been a young man introduced to him in similar circumstances and whose company he found agreeable?"

"No," said Julia pitifully, "absolutely nothing."

It was infamous: Casanova would have blushed; Don Juan would have raised an eyebrow and murmured "Cad." It was inconceivable (said Selena) that a man of mature years and wide experience of life should without design have adopted a course of conduct so precisely calculated to reduce Julia to a state of hopeless infatuation. He had done it all on purpose; and Julia, unversed in the ways of men and the world, had not suspected him of any ulterior motive.

"I don't think," said Julia, "that one can quite say that. My Aunt Regina has often warned me that when men make themselves agreeable they generally have some ulterior motive, and I was not so naive as to think Patrick an exception."

"You suspected him," said Ragwort, "of having designs on your person?"

"Oh no," said Julia. "I thought he wanted free tax advice."

Patrick Ardmore's tax problem—although he had expressed it in hypothetical terms and made no mention of names, Julia had no doubt of the identity of those concerned—related to the Daffodil Settlement. It arose from the fact that whenever Gabrielle recommended buying any shares in the United Kingdom the arrangements for the purchase were dealt with by Gideon Darkside.

"As I have mentioned," said Julia, "shares in United Kingdom companies were supposed to be registered in the name of the Sark company. But Darkside noticed one day that registering them in the name of a nonresident company tended to involve a certain amount of extra time and paperwork, adding perhaps as much as twenty-five pounds to the cost of each transaction. So in order to save, as he put it, 'a lot of unnecessary fuss and bother,' he decided to register them instead in the joint names of the two directors resident in this country—that is to say, of himself and Oliver Grynne."

Leaning back in her chair in the manner of a woman who has made a shocking and sensational disclosure, Julia was rewarded by Selena and Ragwort with the gasps and cries of horrified astonishment which she evidently considered appropriate. I gathered that the consequences of Darkside's action might not be altogether satisfactory from the point of view of taxation.

"They vary," said Julia, "as Oliver Grynne pointed out to Darkside when he found out what had happened, from the inconvenient to the catastrophic, depending on the precise circumstances. When Darkside was eventually persuaded of this he suggested what seemed to him a simple and obvious remedy: he and Grynne would transfer the investments into the name of the company which ought to have held them in the first place and there would be no harm done."

"Provided," said Selena, wrinkling her nose, "that the matter never came to the attention of the Revenue."

"Quite so," said Julia. "If, however, one of Her Majesty's Inspectors of Taxes happened to be looking through the register of shareholders of some major company or other and noticed a substantial holding in the joint names of a United Kingdom solicitor and accountant, he might begin to wonder in what capacity they held it and whether they'd included it in their tax returns. And if they hadn't, he might ask them why not."

"I suppose they would say," said Selena, "that they had been holding as bare nominees for a nonresident company not liable to file returns of income in this country."

"Yes," said Julia. "But if the man from the Revenue were in one of his suspicious moods, as men from the Revenue so often are, he might insist on verifying that statement by reference to their internal records. And since Darkside regarded the distinction between the trust and the company as a mere legal technicality and of no practical significance, his internal records clearly indicated that the shares were held by himself and Grynne on the trusts of the Daffodil Settlement."

"Dear me," said Selena, "how very embarrassing."

"It is not unknown," said Ragwort, "for embarrassing internal records to be by some sad mischance accidentally lost or destroyed and replaced by others nearer to the heart's desire."

"The same thought," said Julia, "had of course occurred to Gideon Darkside. He could do nothing, however, without the cooperation of Oliver Grynne, who naturally declined to assist in any course of action which might culminate in a fraud on the Revenue. So the shares remained in their joint names, and there was a stalemate."

"It is not entirely clear to me," I said, "why Patrick Ardmore should be in need of advice on the position. As I understand it, no action was required on his part—it was a matter for Darkside and Grynne."

"Theoretically, yes, but Darkside thought that if the other Daffodil directors could be persuaded to share his view, Oliver Grynne might be brought under sufficient pressure to concur in a transfer of the shares. By this time, you see, he had begun to realise that his little economy might prove to be rather expensive, and he was becoming concerned about his own position."

"As one does," said Selena, "when facing the prospect of a claim for professional negligence. The potential liability in damages would presumably be substantial?"

"In view," said Julia, "of the total value of the fund, one would certainly imagine so. Darkside, of course, didn't feel that he was in any way to blame for the problem. He thought that it was all the fault of the lawyers—lawyers in general, because they'd invented this silly technical distinction between trusts and companies, and Oliver Grynne in particular, because he unreasonably refused to cooperate in an innocent little deception of the Revenue. The fact that Grynne was being vigorously supported by Edward Malvoisin served only to confirm his feeling that he was the victim of a conspiracy on the part of the legal profession. He felt very bitter about the whole thing, and by the end of a week he and Grynne were barely on speaking terms."

"In these circumstances," said Selena, "the atmosphere at meetings of the Daffodil directors must have been . . . ?"

"Distinctly fraught. So Patrick was quite pleased to be able to discuss the problem with someone who knew something about the relevant tax law but wasn't otherwise involved. And he was kind enough to say," said Julia, blushing, "that he found my comments extremely helpful, and to express his gratitude by inviting me to dinner on my last evening in the Cayman Islands."

Over dinner at the Grand Old House, warmly recommended by *The Guide to Comfortable Tax Planning* for the excellence of its cuisine and the romantic charm of its surroundings, Patrick Ardmore had continued relentlessly with his strategy of paying no compliments, refraining from physical contact, and making frequent references to his devotion to his wife. Poor Julia, naturally finding this irresistible, had not known what to do.

"When afflicted by feelings of the sort I have described," said Julia, "one would normally adopt the forthright and vigorous approach recommended by Shakespeare in his celebrated poem 'Venus and Adonis.' I don't say that it's invariably successful—on the contrary, I have often known it to end in the most wounding of rebuffs—but at least one has the consolation of knowing one has done the right thing and acted in accordance with the best possible precedent. When, however, the object of one's desire is a man much older than oneself, who can't sensibly be complimented on the perfection of his profile or the smoothness of his complexion, that approach doesn't seem to be quite appropriate. I accordingly found myself at a loss. The trouble was, you see, that I didn't want to do anything which might make Patrick feel embarrassed and want to avoid me. It was absurdly sentimental of me, because there was no particular likelihood of our meeting again anyway, but I couldn't help it."

"She was at the mercy," said Selena, "of feelings beyond her control."

"Yes," said Julia. "And yet at the same time I thought

how sad it would be to discover in thirty years' time that after all he, too, would have liked to make an advance but had also refrained, perhaps for some motive similar to my own. So I felt confused and didn't know what to do."

"Her mind," said Selena, "was a whirl of conflicting emotions."

"Yes," said Julia. "So the impasse—which I take to be the correct expression for a situation in which no one makes a pass at anyone—continued throughout my stay and until after dinner on my last evening. And might indeed not have ended then, except that on the way back to our hotel I tripped over something, and Patrick took my arm to prevent me falling over. This had a very peculiar effect on me, even worse than the breathlessness and indigestion which I have previously mentioned—I felt as I suppose an ice cream might feel when hot chocolate sauce is poured over it."

"Her senses reeled at his touch," said Selena triumphantly, having evidently felt that without this phrase the story would be somehow incomplete.

"Yes," said Julia. "And it was at this point that I thought of Alcibiades. The distinguished general, as you may remember, found himself as a young man in a somewhat similar position with regard to the philosopher Socrates, and the tactics which he employed on that occasion are recorded in some detail in Plato's *Symposium*. Although in that particular case they were unsuccessful, one somehow has the impression that Alcibiades was a young man of considerable expertise in such matters—I felt I could do no better than follow his example."

"You mean," said Ragwort, looking puzzled, "that you

invited Patrick Ardmore to a friendly wrestling match in the nearest gymnasium?"

"No, no, Ragwort, of course not. I doubt very much if there is a gymnasium in Grand Cayman—there is certainly no mention of such a thing in *The Guide to Comfortable Tax Planning*—and even if there were, one could hardly expect it to be open at midnight. No, the essence of the Alcibiades strategy, as I understand it, is to make no advance oneself but to find ways to make it clear that one would be happy to receive one. So I invited Patrick to help me to finish off a bottle of wine which I had in my room and which would otherwise be wasted—and you will surely admit, Ragwort, that considering how late it was, he could without any incivility or embarrassment have said no."

"But," said Selena, "he didn't?"

"No," said Julia, looking pleased with herself. "No, he didn't. So we went up to my room and after pouring the wine I disposed myself on the bed in what I hoped was a seductive attitude—that is to say, one which I thought might indicate to a man of experience and sophistication that if he made an advance it would not be rebuffed."

"But," said Ragwort, "he didn't?"

"No, he didn't. He sat on a chair and talked about currency investment. I recalled, however, that Alcibiades had not allowed himself to be discouraged by Socrates continuing to talk about the nature of virtue and truth and so forth, but had decided, when all else failed, to express himself with perfect candour. So I said that I would not by any means wish him to feel obliged to make any advance to me if he were not inclined to do so, but that, if he were, then in view of the lateness of the hour, it would perhaps be a pity to delay further. Which left him quite free," said Julia defensively, "to say no if he wanted to."

"But again," said Selena, "he didn't?"

"No," said Julia, again with a dreamy and distant look. "No, he didn't—he asked me if I would like him to undress me." She declined to say more. It was not going, she said, to be that sort of book.

The question whether Patrick Ardmore was a heartless and cynical seducer or merely, as Ragwort still maintained, a good-natured man who had discovered too late that there is no such thing as free tax advice seemed still to be unresolved. Wondering what view the man himself might have taken of the matter, I enquired what his manner had been on the following morning.

It appeared, however, that from his demeanour on that day no significant conclusions could be drawn, for it had not been a day like other days—it had been the day on which Oliver Grynne had died in a drowning accident.

"And I suppose," said Julia, frowning slightly into her wineglass, "that that's what the Daffodil people don't want to talk about."

"It must have been very distressing for them all," said Ragwort. "It sounds from what you have said as if they would all have been old friends of his—apart from Darkside, of course."

"They were, and of course they were extremely upset —Gabrielle in particular, I think. Even so, it seems a little curious that six months later they still don't even like to mention it. I wonder if it's because . . ." She fell silent, still seeking enlightenment in her wineglass.

"Julia," I said, "what was there that was odd about it?"

The body had been found quite early in the morning.

The solicitor had been in the habit, while in the Cayman Islands, of rising early, drinking a large glass of orange juice on the terrace of his hotel, and taking a swim before breakfasting further. On the morning of his death he had evidently been swimming in an area of underwater rocks, had dived and struck his head, and thus been rendered unconscious. He had been taking his exercise in an area not much frequented at so early an hour, and there was no one at hand to assist him.

The burden had fallen on Clementine of telephoning her firm's office in London to tell them of the death of the senior partner. Her task had not been made easier by having also to tell them that a medical examination showed him to have consumed, shortly before his death, the equivalent of two double measures of vodka.

"I don't think I'd exactly call that odd," said Selena. "I can imagine that Stingham's wouldn't want it generally known that one of their senior partners was in the habit of drinking vodka before breakfast. But it would explain how he came to have an accident."

"Except," said Julia, "that he'd given up alcohol on health grounds several years before. He was a strict teetotaler."

The candlelit shadows of the Corkscrew seemed for a moment less companionable than usual, and I felt for the first time the curious sensation of coldness which I was afterwards to associate with the Daffodil affair.

"But so far as I know," continued Julia, "no one thought there was anything sinister about it. The obvious explanation was that someone else on the terrace had ordered a large vodka and orange juice—one does find people in the Cayman Islands who might think that a suitable breakfast beverage—and the waiter had confused the orders."

"But surely," said Ragwort, "there must have been some kind of investigation to establish whether that had happened?"

"Well no. As Selena has suggested, the chief concern of Stingham's was to see, if at all possible, that there was no reference in the newspapers to the fact that Oliver Grynne had been drinking—you can imagine what the *Scuttle* would have made of it, for example. Well, Patrick had one or two quite influential friends in Georgetown, and he thought he could probably arrange for that aspect of the accident to be kept quiet. But that depended on the authorities assuming that it was quite normal for Grynne to have been drinking vodka. If they'd known that it wasn't they'd have been bound to investigate, and it would have become public knowledge. So they all decided simply to say nothing about his being a teetotaller. Darkside, I need hardly say, was not involved in these discussions, but there didn't seem much risk that he would think of volunteering that particular item of information to the authorities."

Selena divided the remainder of the wine equitably among our glasses.

"It does occur to me," she said absentmindedly, "that if one were going to attack someone while they were swimming, it might be rather sensible to ensure that they had consumed a large quantity of alcohol, especially if they weren't used to it. No doubt I'm being fanciful."

"Extremely fanciful," said Ragwort. "But . . . how convenient for Gideon Darkside that Oliver Grynne should have died."

CHAPTER 5 ═══

EXTRACT FROM *THE GUIDE TO COMFORTABLE TAX PLANNING*

Sark: Smallest of the Channel Islands, lying between Guernsey and Jersey. Closer geographically to the former, and comprised in the same Bailiwick, but originally colonised (in 1585) by 40 Jerseymen under the patronage of Helier de Carteret, Seigneur of St. Ouen. Area: 1,348 acres. Population: 500. Capital: None to speak of—social and commercial activity centres on the Avenue, an unmade-up road running between the Bel Air tavern and the Post Office and containing several souvenir and jewellery shops. Tractors are the only permitted form of motor transport; bicycles and horse-drawn carriages can be hired. Principal industries: Tourism and financial services. More company directorships per head than anywhere else in the world. Access: Regular boat service from Guernsey;

for boat and hydrofoil services to Jersey and St. Malo, enquire locally.

Note 1: Avoid if prone to seasickness.

A slender, fair-haired girl stood hesitating in the doorway of the Corkscrew, as if in surroundings unfamiliar to her, looking from one to another of the groups of lawyers gossiping at candlelit tables. Upon seeing us, she approached our table, and I saw that it was Lilian.

She accepted with some demur the offer of a glass of wine. The purpose of her coming, it seemed, was to deliver to Julia a telex message received a few minutes earlier in 63 New Square. A colleague of Julia's, knowing something of her ways, had looked for her next door in 62; Lilian, knowing something more, had volunteered to look for her in the Corkscrew.

"It's extremely kind of you," said Julia, "to take so much trouble. Does it seem to be urgent?"

"It's not actually marked 'Urgent,' " said Lilian, blushing slightly. "But—I couldn't help reading the first couple of lines, and I thought you ought to see it right away. Because Mr. Cantrip's supposed to be in West London County Court tomorrow, and—and Henry's going to be terribly cross."

"Oh dear," said Selena.

THE SIRENS SANG OF MURDER

Telex M. Cantrip to J. Larwood transmitted
Sark 6:15 p.m. Monday 30th April

Yoo-hoo there, Larwood, guess who? Me again, un-
foreseenly Sark-stuck. Tell Henry hard cheese on West
London County Court, they'll have to make do with
Ragwort.

If Henry thinks I did it on purpose, you might point
out that Sark isn't exactly a major centre of exciting and
sophisticated entertainment—just a flat-topped lump
of rock in the middle of nowhere, with not much to do
unless you've got a big thing about sea gulls. Gabrielle
says it's like the Garden of Eden, but there wasn't much
to do there either, was there? Except for eating apples.

Anyway, the way I see it, it's all Darkside's fault.
The plane to Guernsey made him feel sick and the boat
to Sark made him feel sicker and the horse and carriage
made him feel sickest of the lot. If Henry thinks it can't
take long to get anywhere on an island three miles by
one, tell him to try doing it in a horse-drawn carriage
sitting next to a chartered accountant who looks like a
corpse with liver trouble and groans every time the
horse starts to trot a bit.

We had to amble along at about one mph, getting
plenty of time to look at the butterflies and wildflowers
and wave graciously at the passing peasantry. Passing,
in view of our speed, was something the peasantry did
pretty easily, including an old biddy wrapped up in
black shawls just like the one in the Grand Hotel the
other evening—don't suppose it was the same one,
though.

What with the sun shining and the birds singing
and so on, I wouldn't actually have minded much about
going slowly, except I was worried about Gabrielle be-

ing on her own somewhere with chaps from the Revenue lurking in the undergrowth.

Philip Alexandre hangs out on the part of the island called Little Sark—almost a separate island, just joined up to the rest by a long thin bit called the Coupee, like a kind of bridge about a hundred yards long, with a three-hundred-foot drop on both sides and railings to stop you falling over. It's just about wide enough for a carriage, though not with much room to spare, but they're not allowed to take passengers across it, so we had to get out and walk.

Even that took quite a lot longer than it might have done, because the chap driving the carriage thought this was the right time to fill us in on the local spookery and witchcraft statistics. He's a boozy-looking character called Albert, who works for Philip Alexandre as a sort of general handyman, and he seems to think he's got a patriotic duty to tell everyone there are more ghosts and witches per square foot on Little Sark than anywhere else in the Channel Islands, and more at the Hotel Alexandra than at the Sablonnerie down the road.

On Halloween and nights like that, he says, the Devil used to ride across the Coupee in a big black coffin, and the witches used to fly over from Guernsey on their broomsticks and dance on the beach with no clothes on. He's not sure if they still do it, but he thinks if they don't, it's because of television.

Edward Malvoisin and Clemmie started ragging each other about it, with him saying that witches were all rot and her saying they weren't and her betting him he wouldn't dare walk across the Coupee at midnight and him betting her he would.

Darkside came back from the dead enough to say

we hadn't come all this way at great trouble and expense, etc., to talk a lot of nonsense about witches. Ardmore said if we could get in touch with the ghost of the settlor and ask it what to do with the trust fund, that would solve all our problems. When Darkside worked out this was a joke he decided to feel sick again and not be well enough to go on for quite a long time.

So that's how we didn't get to Philip Alexandre's place until nearly midday. It's really just a farmhouse, but he's added a few extra bathrooms and a cocktail bar and calls it the Hotel Alexandra.

The bar was looking a good bit more stylish than it would normally have done on account of having Gabrielle in it, sitting on a high stool and drinking champagne—it's funny how seeing Gabrielle in a place makes it feel all sort of Parisian. The chap behind the bar, doing a lot less for the decor, was Philip Alexandre himself—he's a skinny old chap who looks as if he'd been pickled in walnut juice for about a hundred years, but quite genial when you get to know him. They were chatting away together in that funny kind of Frogspeak people talk here and didn't seem to have been missing us at all.

Plan A had been to have the board meeting and then a spot of lunch and be driven back in time to catch the 3:30 boat to Guernsey. I thought at first we might still manage it that way, as long as people didn't talk too much at the board meeting, but that was before they told me that they had to get through 126 other board meetings as well as the Daffodil one.

One two six, just in case you think I've mistyped it. That's because Patrick and Gabrielle have set up Sark resident companies for 126 different clients and they all have to prove that this is where the board of directors take their decisions.

Plan B was skipping lunch, proposed by Darkside and not finding a seconder.

Plan C was to have lunch first, then the board meetings, and then drive back in time for the 5:30 boat to Guernsey. It worked pretty well, up to a point—I mean, it was a jolly good lunch.

They didn't need me for the first 126 board meetings, so I went and sat in the garden and read a book. There's a stack of old novels in the dining room by a chap called John Oxenham, and I borrowed one called *Perilous Lovers.*

It's all about Sark in the old days, when there wasn't anyone living here—just the witches flying over from Guernsey for the occasional orgy. The heroine's called Clare of Belfontaine and she's married to a frightful rotter who's madly jealous about her and has her cast away on Sark without any clothes, absolutely not a stitch, but she makes herself a sort of skirt out of bracken. Bet you couldn't do that.

It's a pity our book's not about the old days when people did things like that—it would make it a lot easier to put in exciting bits. Anyway, I've been thinking about it, and what I think we need is some sort of extra interest for Carruthers on the romantic side. I mean, it's all right him fancying Eliane in a way, and marrying her after she turns out to be an heiress, because we want to have a happy ending. But the way I see it is that under all the suavity and daredevil charm, he's a tremendously sensitive sort of chap who thinks pretty deeply about things, and I don't see Eliane as the kind of bird who's going to appreciate that side of him.

So what I thought was that there ought to be some

other bird that he's got a tremendous thing about on a sort of spiritual level, and it can't ever come to anything because she's married or something, but deep down she's the only person who really understands him. She'd be quite a lot older than him, but sort of ageless and a bit mysterious, like the Moaning Lizzie—not miserable, though, a frightfully good sport, and laughing a lot at things.

Where was I? Oh yes, waiting to go on in my big scene as Counsel advising on the Daffodil problem. Which when it came didn't exactly go like a breeze, because what I told them was that if they couldn't exercise their discretion the way the settlor wanted them to, and they wouldn't exercise it any other way, the descendants of the Palgrave chap were going to scoop the jackpot, so they'd better start finding out who they were.

I knew they wouldn't like it and they didn't. They were still arguing the toss about it when someone noticed it was quarter to five and time we were on our way back to the harbour. So we looked round for Albert and the carriage and there they weren't. He'd taken someone to catch the 3:30 boat and not been seen since —it turned out he'd stopped for a swift one at the Bel Air Tavern and forgotten to start again. I suppose we might still have made it to the harbour on time if we'd run all the way, but it wasn't an idea that anyone seemed keen on.

So here we are for the night, and no way of getting a plane to London before tomorrow evening. Like I said, absolutely not my fault and hard luck on West London County Court.

Looking on the bright side, it means I can go on reading this book about Claire of Belfontaine. I've just got to the bit where the chap she really fancies gets cast away on Sark as well. Her husband's fixed it all on purpose so that they'll die in a state of sin—people had jolly funny ideas in the old days, didn't they?—but they've decided to scupper him by being all chaste and noble and not getting up to anything. So I don't really want to leave until I find out what happens.

If I don't make it back to London by tomorrow night, tell Henry the witches have got me. There's a cottage here that used to belong to a bird called Rachel Alexandre, who was burned as a witch in 1600 and something—Philip's frightfully proud of her. It's got three bedrooms, and of course Gabrielle and Clemmie bagged two of them as soon as they knew we were staying overnight, so I thought I'd better grab the third with a view to keeping an eye on them. No sign of any chaps from the Revenue lurking in the bushes, though.

Over and out—Cantrip

"Poor Mr. Cantrip," said Lilian, turning her wineglass between anxious fingers. "I hope he'll be all right."

"I can see," said Ragwort, "no reason why he should not be. From the point of view of his own pleasure and convenience, he seems to have arranged things admirably. It is not his plans for tomorrow, for example, which are to be disrupted by an unexpected excursion to West London County Court. Why should he not be all right?"

"I was in Miss Derwent's office this morning," said Lilian. "To arrange about collecting my books—you know, the ones my uncle left me that Mr. Cantrip was so kind about. The girls there think there's something—I don't know, something unlucky about this case that Mr. Cantrip's working on. It's the same one Mr. Grynne was dealing with last year when—when he died. They say it was awfully unexpected."

"No doubt it was," said Selena. "One could hardly expect his doctor to have diagnosed a tendency to accidental drowning."

"Of course," said Julia absentmindedly, "if it happened to be Halloween, we might have worried about Cantrip being carried off by witches. The more so since he has comprehensively disregarded my advice to avoid girls, women, and crones—these repeated encounters of his with elderly ladies in black shawls would have, at that season, a most sinister aspect. Fortunately, however, it is some months away."

"But surely," said Ragwort, with an expression of some surprise, "it is not only at Halloween that the powers of darkness are particularly to be feared? There is at least one other occasion in the year when the witches of Europe climb on their broomsticks and fly across the mountains to gather in their accustomed meeting places. Have you not observed the date and its significance?"

"It's the thirtieth of April," said Selena. "Which means that the courts begin sitting again tomorrow."

"It is indeed the thirtieth of April," said Ragwort. "Which means that tonight is Walpurgis Night."

Nurtured as I have been in a sceptical tradition, I am disinclined to believe in witchcraft. No other reason having occurred to me for Cantrip to remain longer in the Channel Islands, I was surprised, on encountering my friends in the coffeehouse on the following morning, to find Julia in possession of yet a further telex from him.

Sarah Caudwell

TELEX CANTRIP TO LARWOOD TRANSMITTED SARK
8:00 A.M. TUESDAY 1ST MAY

Phew—if Henry complains about being one suave
Chancery junior short of strength, tell him that after
last night he's jolly lucky it's not permanent.

Look here, Larwood, what I want to know is why
birds nowadays aren't like they used to be in the old
days. Yielding is what birds were in the old days, and
what I specially like about birds being yielding is that
they can't start being it till they've got something to
yield to, viz they jolly well wait to be asked.

You remember this book I told you about, the one
where this bird and this chap are stuck on Sark with no
clothes on being all chaste and noble? Well, there's a bit
where the chap feels tempted by his baser nature, and
he goes striding off into the storm until he conquers it,
and in some ways you can see it's pretty sickening for
him. On the other hand, when he isn't being tempted
by his baser nature, he doesn't have to worry about the
bird not bothering to conquer hers and dragging him
off into the bracken and telling him to get on with it.
That's because it's all happening in the old days, and
you can't help thinking that in some ways it must have
been jolly restful.

The thing that gets me, looking back on last night,
is that there was actually a stage when I was quite
looking forward to getting a solid eight hours of health-
giving zizz. Which just goes to show how right all those
chaps are who say what a waste of time it is expecting
things to turn out the way you expect them to, because
they never do.

We'd all adjourned to the bar for a swift one after
dinner, but Gabrielle drank hers quite fast and said she

felt like an early night. She'd been a bit edgy all evening, because on the way over from the cottage before
dinner she'd thought she'd spotted someone prowling
about at the far end of the garden. She wasn't sure—
she'd only seen him for a second or two and it was
getting dark—and she pretended it didn't worry her,
but I could see it did.

I wouldn't have let her walk back on her own, even
if there hadn't been anyone prowling. It's not far from
the farmhouse to the cottage, but it was pretty dark and
a bit spooky. The weather had changed while we were
having dinner and the moon kept getting covered up
with clouds and the wind was making a sort of wailing
noise in the telegraph wires.

So I said I'd quite like to turn in early as well, and
then Clemmie said she would, too, and we all walked
back to the cottage together. We left Patrick Ardmore
and Edward Malvoisin drinking whiskey and playing
darts, and Darkside drinking barley water and looking
disapproving.

Right then—at ten-thirty there I am respectably
tucked up in bed, just meaning to read another chapter
of this book before I go to sleep, when there's a knock
on the door and Clemmie waltzes in, wearing a pink
thing with a lot of frills and saying "Well, how about it?"
or words to the like effect.

I know what Ragwort says you ought to do when
your instructing solicitor makes a pass at you—adopt an
attitude of dignified remonstrance is what he says, viz
make a long speech about the traditions of the English
Bar and tell her there's nothing doing. Well, it's all very
well him saying that. If a bird makes a pass at you and
you turn it down, either she takes it personally and gets
miffed or she doesn't take it personally and thinks

83

you're a dead loss, and either way it doesn't do a lot for the chances of her sending you another brief.

Another thing that cramped my style for remonstering was that she kept shushing me, because Gabrielle was in the room next door and Clemmie didn't want her to hear us. It's jolly difficult to make a speech about the dignity of the English Bar if you've got to do it in a whisper.

And then all the lights went out. I suppose we were on course for putting the light out anyway, but it's one thing putting it out on purpose and knowing you can put it on again and another suddenly finding it's pitch dark and knowing you can't.

It looked as if all the lights in the cottage had gone, and I didn't think it would be much fun for Gabrielle to be all on her own in the dark, worrying about the Revenue chaps prowling round in the garden. So I whispered a few soothing things to Clemmie and pootled out onto the landing in my pyjamas to do the heroic and chivalrous bit, viz call out to Gabrielle to sit tight and not worry while I went and looked for the fuse box.

I don't actually know why I'm supposed to be any better at finding the fuse box than anyone else, but most birds seem to think nowadays that there are two things chaps are useful for and the other one's mending the electricity. Which just goes to show that Gabrielle isn't like most birds nowadays, because she said I mustn't bother about it and she'd be all right until morning, and I said was she sure and she said absolutely.

So I pootled back, bumping into a lot of furniture that hadn't been there when the lights were on, and by the time I got to my bed again Clemmie'd sort of settled down in it. After that she wouldn't let me say anything, not even in a whisper, and I couldn't remonster any more at all.

I think Clemmie's one of those birds that get more enthusiastic in bad weather, because the weather outside got worse and worse, with the wind howling round the chimney as if it was trying to get a part in a horror picture, and the worse it got, the more enthusiastic she was.

It was quite lucky really that she wouldn't let me say anything. She was wearing one of those rather nice kinds of scent that smell like cinnamon toast, and what with that and all the enthusiasm, I started feeling like saying things I'd have felt a frightful ass about afterwards, specially with a sensible sort of bird like Clemmie that I've been mates with for years.

When the racket started outside I didn't really feel much like going to investigate. It's a bit difficult to explain what kind of racket it was—it was like all the kinds of racket you can think of, all happening at the same time. There was a noise like horses galloping and a noise like roofs falling in and a noise like a lot of people yelling at each other, and the wind decided to put in an extra effort in the special effects department.

The first thing I thought was that the Third World War had broken out and there wasn't a lot I could do about it. The second thing I thought was that the Alexandra wasn't a terribly likely place for anyone to start a world war, but it was a jolly likely place for the Revenue to make a raid on—you know, the way they did on those Rossminster chaps a few years ago. I know they're not supposed to go around making raids on people outside the jurisdiction, but after what Clemmie and Gabrielle had been telling me I didn't think they'd worry about a little technicality like that.

85

I still didn't feel much like getting out of bed, but I couldn't help feeling that Clemmie and me were going to look pretty silly if we were just lying there being cosy while our clients were being rounded up and interrogated in their nightclothes and having their documents seized. I got this across to her as well as I could in whispers and got up and strode out into the night.

Well, I didn't stride exactly, because I couldn't find the bottom bit of my pyjamas and I'd had to wrap myself up in a blanket, and when you're trying to get down the stairs in the pitch dark with a blanket wrapped round you in a cottage you haven't been in before you don't exactly stride, but in the end I made it to the front door.

It wasn't as dark as it had been indoors—there was a light on in the farmhouse, and the moon came out just as I got outside. I still couldn't make out what was going on, though—just that there seemed to be a lot of it, with more horsey noises and people shouting at each other in English and local Frogspeak. So I stood on the doorstep and called out, "I say, what's going on here?" trying to sound sort of dignified and masterful.

Just after that there was the most ghastly scream I'd ever heard, partly a sort of shriek and partly a sort of groan, like someone waking up unexpectedly in a graveyard.

Then something hardish and heavyish went whizzing past my ear and smashed against the wall behind me, and the message seemed to be that someone was trying to kill me.

Well, what they said afterwards was that it was just a misunderstanding and they were frightfully sorry. What I said was that if Albert's aim had been an inch or two better, they'd have been in a pretty permanent minus-Cantrip situation and sorry would have buttered jolly few parsnips, so the explanation had better be good.

Albert's story was that he'd stayed a bit longer than he ought to at the Bel Air Tavern. Well, I knew that, because that's why we missed the 5:30 boat, but he seems to have thought that after that he might as well be hung for a sheep as a lamb and make an evening of it. So he'd stayed on there until nearly midnight, and by the time he started for home he wasn't what you'd call sober—more what you'd call sloshed as a newt.

The horse knew the way pretty well, though, and between the two of them they were getting on all right until they got to the Coupee. They'd just started across when Albert got a major attack of the heebie-jeebies— he can't describe it properly, he says, but he felt a sort of prickling at the back of his neck and remembered about all the ghosts and witches and decided that one way or another this was the place where he most didn't want to be.

Once you've started driving a carriage across the Coupee there's no way you can turn round, so he thought the best idea was just to get to the other side as fast as possible. He says the horse felt the same way about it. Silly of them really, because in the dark and with a gale-force wind blowing, they'd have done better to take it slow and steady. But they didn't see it that way at the time, and they hurtled across as if the Devil was after them, which actually Albert seems to have thought he was.

You could say they were lucky in a way. They'd just about made it back to Little Sark when one of the wheels hit a stone and the carriage went over on its side —if it had happened ten yards sooner, they'd have gone over the cliff on one side or the other and that would have been curtains for both of them.

Albert was thrown out into the road, but not badly hurt, and he managed to pick himself up and get the horse free of its harness without too much trouble. Then something made him look round, and he saw the woman in white standing there a few yards away from him.

It seems that women in white are pretty bad news in the Channel Islands. I can't make out exactly what they're meant to be, or what they're meant to do if they catch you, but the general idea is that you don't want to see them at all, and if you do you get out fast.

So Albert didn't stop to say "Good evening" or anything, he just scrambled up on the horse and headed full tilt for the Alexandra, not daring to look behind him in case he saw the woman again.

He was too scared to ride all the way round to the stables. He just headed straight for the wall and jumped it, landing on sundry potting sheds and hen coops, etc. —jolly lucky the horse didn't hurt itself. Philip Alexandre came out and started yelling at him, but he didn't much mind about that as long as he'd got away from the woman in white.

Then the moon came out and he saw her again, standing there in her white robes in the doorway of the Witch's Cottage and calling out to him in a hollow voice.

Well, what I said was that even if he didn't have the sense to tell the difference between a ghost and a Chancery junior wrapped in a blanket, he might at least have had the sense to know that if I was a ghost, chucking bricks at me wouldn't have done him any good, because they'd just have gone straight through.

THE SIRENS SANG OF MURDER

Albert said he knew that really, but he'd lived a sinful life and couldn't remember any prayers, so bricks were the best he could do. He's not going to be sinful any more, he says—he's going to give up booze and go to church every Sunday, so that the woman in white won't come after him again.

Serves him right, because the upshot of all these shenanigans is that the Coupee's blocked at this end. I went to have a look first thing this morning and there's no way you can get round the carriage or over it without risking breaking your neck. Philip Alexandre reckons it'll take a couple of hours to move it, and until then Little Sark's completely cut off from everywhere else.

Clemmie'd gone back to her room by the time I got to bed again, and I haven't seen her yet this morning. I haven't seen any of the rest of the gang either. There's no way we're going to get the first boat over to Guernsey, so I suppose they've all decided they might as well stay in bed.

We still ought to catch the evening plane all right, but life among the tax planners being what it is, don't let Henry count any chickens.

Over and out—Cantrip

The news that Cantrip had survived Walpurgis Night, gratifying as it was, caused us no great astonishment: we did not know how grave had been his danger, or that not all his companions had been so fortunate.

CHAPTER 6 ⸻

"Toadsbreath, my good man," said Cecilia Mainwaring, raising her superbly groomed eyebrows, "I have already told you that I know no more than you do of the present whereabouts of my learned friend Mr. Carruthers, and it becomes you very ill, Toadsbreath, to doubt my word on the matter. I go so far as to say that it is the height of impertinence."

"Beg pardon, Miss Mainwaring," mumbled Toadsbreath, respectfully tugging his forelock. "I didn't mean no harm."

Cantrip, on the following morning, was still absent from the customary gathering in the coffeehouse. He had not returned to Chambers, nor had any further communication been received from him. Suspecting Julia, as his coauthor and habitual confidante, of knowing more of the matter than she chose to admit, Henry had interrogated her (said Julia) in a manner somewhat less deferential than could properly have been adopted by an infant-school teacher towards a delinquent six-year-old.

Save in that respect, however, the boy's continued absence occasioned no anxiety among his friends. The Channel Islands are a delightful place to be during the first week in May, and a more conscientious young man than Cantrip might have yielded to the temptation to extend his visit.

It was judged imprudent, in view of the circumstances —that is to say, the uncertain state of Henry's temper—for Ragwort and Selena to linger over coffee. Arranging to meet again in the Corkscrew for lunch, we all walked together to New Square. I had already said my farewells and turned on my way towards the Public Record Office, eager to devote myself once more to the gentle service of Scholarship, when Lilian came running down the steps of 62, calling out to me to wait for a moment.

"Oh, Professor Tamar," she said, rather charmingly breathless, "Miss Derwent was on the telephone. She rang to ask if Mr. Cantrip was back in Chambers yet. And when I said he wasn't, she asked about you—if I happened to know if you were in London at the moment. So of course I said you were and you'd probably be looking into Chambers sometime this morning. And she said, if I saw you, would I please ask you to ring her as soon as possible."

The message perplexed me. I had no personal acquaintance with Clementine Derwent and could imagine no reason why she should wish to speak to me.

The telephone call which I made from Selena's room a few minutes later afforded but little enlightenment. The matter, it seemed, was of some complexity, and could not satisfactorily be explained at a distance. Clementine's office was in the Gray's Inn Road, no more than five minutes' walk away. If in the course of the day I could find time to visit her there, she would be most grateful.

Those who believe, as most members of Lincoln's Inn are inclined to do, that any serious study of the law requires an atmosphere of dust and antiquity would have been unfavourably impressed by the offices of Messrs. Stingham and Grynne. The thickness of the carpets, the subtlety of the lighting, the freshness of the flowers arranged in cutglass bowls—all these would have caused them grave doubts of the soundness of the advice provided there. On the other hand, these features did seem to indicate that a passable number of reasonably prosperous clients were not dissatisfied.

The room occupied by Clementine Derwent on the third floor of the building, though presumably not so large as those allotted to full partners in the firm, was nonetheless sufficiently spacious and well appointed, with a view eastwards to the domes and spires of the City, to be suggestive of rapid advancement. She rose to greet me, leaning across her desk to offer me her hand.

Her full-skirted cotton dress was drawn neatly in at the waist, and her glossy black hair was cut, I daresay at great expense, in a style of becoming softness. Neither of these measures could quite disguise her resemblance in face and figure—the former round, snub-nosed, good-humouredly pugnacious, the latter trim and muscular—to an engaging but undisciplined schoolboy. It would have seemed inapt to call her pretty—the epithets she brought to mind were those descriptive of a crisp eating apple.

A sensible, well-balanced young woman, one would have said at first sight, who would not readily allow any personal or professional difficulty to weigh so excessively on her mind as to interfere with sound sleep and healthy appetite. I was surprised, therefore, as she resumed her place at her desk, to observe in her unmistakable signs of tension and anxiety.

"Professor Tamar," she said, with a nervous abruptness which I could not think characteristic of her, "I hope you don't think it's awfully peculiar of me to ask you round here. I'm a friend of Michael Cantrip, you see, and he's talked a bit about you. I've got a problem that I hoped you might be willing to help with."

My perplexity deepened, and did not diminish when she began to tell me of the existence and provisions of the Daffodil Settlement. It seemed tactless to mention, since she repeatedly stressed the confidentiality of the matter, that I was already aware of them. I would not have wished her to form an unfavourable view of Cantrip's capacity for discretion.

"So you see," she concluded, "if the worst comes to the worst—I mean if we can't find the letter of wishes and can't find out who the real settlor was—then we're going to have to give the whole fund to the descendants of Sir Walter Palgrave. It's idiotic, of course, because no one ever meant them to get a penny of it, but it looks as if we'll have no choice. And we've been advised by Chancery Counsel— well, by Canters, actually—that we'd better try and find out who they are. So I wondered if you'd be interested. I mean, you are a legal historian."

I could scarcely forbear to smile, for the notion was of course absurd. The tracing of missing relatives, with all respect to the no doubt very estimable persons accustomed to undertake such enquiries, can hardly be regarded as a branch of Scholarship. Recalling, however, that Clementine, like Cantrip, had spent her formative years at Cambridge, where such distinctions are perhaps but imperfectly understood, I sought some way to explain without wounding her that such an investigation would be inappropriate to my academic standing and qualifications.

"I'm afraid," she continued, "that my clients will want the fee to be calculated on a time-costed basis. Would you consider doing it for sixty pounds an hour?" I suppose that my expression indicated surprise. It had not occurred to me, such is my innocence in these matters, that she would offer any pecuniary inducement. She looked apologetic. "Plus expenses, of course. I'm sorry, I know it's not terribly generous."

I found myself obliged to reconsider the matter. By the modest standards of the unworldly Scholar, the offer seemed not ungenerous; and yet, were I now to decline it, she could not but think that my reason was the inadequacy of the financial reward. I could not endure to be suspected of so grasping and sordid a motive: I indicated that I would undertake the investigation on the terms she had proposed.

"Tell me," I said, "is there anything you already know about the descendants of Sir Walter Palgrave, or am I to begin, as it were, with a clean slate?"

The question unaccountably caused her to blush.

"Well, Sir Walter Palgrave himself was a judge, of course—end of the nineteenth century. I expect you know lots more than I do about him." As a student chiefly of the mediaeval period, I could not truthfully claim any extensive knowledge of the Victorian judiciary, but I realised why the name had seemed faintly familiar. "I got a copy of his will from the Probate Registry. It looks from that as if he left six daughters, so the people we're looking for are probably their children or grandchildren. But the will only gives their Christian names, so I'm afraid it doesn't get us very far."

"No matter," I said, "it provides a starting point. You know nothing else that might be relevant?"

"Well"—she blushed again—"not officially. I mean, I haven't told anyone else about it." She hesitated. I adopted an expression, as I hoped, of sympathetic encouragement. "You see, a few months ago I got engaged. To a chap," she added helpfully, as if supposing me unaware that when a young woman becomes engaged it is customarily to a young man. "He's a solicitor as well—his name's Peter. Well, one evening we happened to start talking about the way the law seems to run in families. You know—the same names keeping on cropping up in the law reports over a couple of centuries. So I asked him if there were any other lawyers in his family. And he said there wasn't anyone close, but his grandmother had been a daughter of Sir Walter Palgrave."

I began to understand her embarrassment. For a solicitor to continue to advise in a matter in which her prospective husband had a financial interest would be, I readily perceived, of dubious propriety.

"I suppose the Law Society would say that I either ought to chuck Peter or chuck handling the Daffodil Settlement. But I'm jolly well not going to chuck Peter, because he's awfully nice. And Daffodil's the biggest thing I've ever dealt with on my own, so I don't want to chuck that either."

It was a sad dilemma. A Victorian novelist, I daresay, could have done something very remarkable with the story of such a conflict between love, duty, and ambition. It seemed to me, all the same, not quite sufficient to account for the signs of tension and anxiety which I had observed in her. I inquired if she had told her fiancé of the problem.

"Oh, absolutely not—that would make it all much worse. I did try to sound him out a bit about the state of the family, but I didn't get very far. He's an only child and so was his mother—Sir Walter Palgrave's granddaughter. But she died quite a long time ago, and she never seems to have talked to him about any aunts or cousins."

She opened a filing cabinet beside her desk and withdrew from it a long manila envelope.

"There's a copy of Sir Walter Palgrave's will in here and a short note of what Peter's told me. I'm afraid that's all the help I can give you." She handed me the envelope. "I don't suppose—I don't suppose you can tell me how long it's going to take to track these people down, but you will try and do it as soon as possible, won't you? I—my clients are anxious to know where they stand."

I assured her that I would begin my researches at once and proceed with such expedition as the nature of the task might permit. Our conversation seemed to be at an end. Clementine thanked me for my assistance with a bright smile and an undertone in her voice of some emotion which I did not immediately recognise. I was already rising from my chair when I identified it as disappointment.

One becomes accustomed in academic life to the unreasonableness of the young. They desire not merely to be understood, but to be understood by telepathy; not merely to be permitted to tell their troubles, but to be prevailed on to do so. The more care they take to conceal their feelings, the greater their disillusionment if one fails to discover them.

"My dear girl," I said, adopting the formula which I have found serviceable in such cases, "would it not be more sensible to tell me what is really the matter?"

"I don't know why you should think," said Clementine, looking down at her desk, "that there's anything else."

"We are dealing, as I understand it, with the sort of discretionary trust which could quite properly remain in existence for many years. The trust fund is safe, as I suppose, in the hands of the trustees and ex hypothesi no one is pressing for a distribution. No doubt it is desirable to identify the default beneficiaries, but most solicitors, if I may say so, would be content in those circumstances to proceed at a fairly leisurely pace. You are behaving, however, as if tracing the descendants of Sir Walter Palgrave were a matter of considerable urgency. Wouldn't it be better to tell me why?"

She continued for some moments to stare down silently at her desk, her head between her hands, as if uncertain how, if at all, to answer me.

"I suppose," she said at last, "because I think that one of them's probably a murderer."

It was plain that something serious had happened in the Channel Islands. Not without some effort of will, I listened patiently while she unfolded those parts of the story with which, unknown to her, I was already familiar: the odd circumstances surrounding the death in the Cayman Islands of Oliver Grynne; Gabrielle's suspicion that she was being followed; and the events which had led to the professional advisers to the Daffodil Settlement spending the previous Monday night on the island of Sark.

Had I thought that her narrative might culminate in any misadventure to poor Cantrip, I could not have refrained from interrupting to ask news of him; but I recalled that she had enquired for him earlier that morning in Chambers, apparently expecting him to have returned safely to London.

When she reached the events of Monday evening, I saw her hesitate, plainly deliberating what limits should be set to her candour. Discretion apparently prevailed—she left me to assume that after dinner she had retired to the respectable solitude of her own room.

On the following morning she had breakfasted in the hotel dining room in the company of Ardmore and Darkside. The waitress who served them gave them also a full account of the misadventures of Albert, as a result of which the road across the Coupee was blocked by the overturned carriage. They had remained in the dining room to await news of its removal, neither curious nor concerned as to the precise whereabouts of the rest of the party.

Soon after nine o'clock they were told that the Coupee was clear again, but the next boat for Guernsey did not sail until noon, and there seemed no merit in haste. The three of them, therefore, were still in the dining room when Philip Alexandre brought the bad news.

Two fishermen sailing along the eastern coast of the island had seen a body lying on the rocks below the Coupee. They had managed with some difficulty to take it on board their boat, conscientiously marking with an impromptu flag the place where it had lain. On reaching harbour, they had sent an urgent message to the Constable, the member of the Sark community responsible, under the authority of the Seneschal, for the maintenance of public order.

The Constable had recognised the dead man at once as a frequent visitor to the island, and had known that Philip Alexandre was the person with whom he most commonly had dealings. It was the Jersey advocate Edward Malvoisin.

"Of course," said Clementine, leaning back with a deep sigh, "it could have been an accident. So could Oliver Grynne getting drowned. But that means there've been two fatal accidents within six months to people connected with the Daffodil Settlement, and it struck me as a bit over the odds. I couldn't think what to do about it, though. I've nothing solid enough to go to the police with. And anyway, the clients would have fits—you know what Swiss bankers are like about secrecy. And then I thought of you, Professor Tamar. I remembered one or two things that Cantrip had said about you and about that problem Julia had in Venice and I thought—well, I thought that if you were involved in the case perhaps you might come across something."

"It is true," I said, "that I have had some little success in applying the methods of Scholarship to one or two somewhat similar matters." I was touched and rather surprised that the boy should have spoken to her of these achievements. They had not always seemed to me to receive in New Square the degree of recognition which an unprejudiced observer might think them to deserve. "I trust, however, that Cantrip has not given you an exaggerated notion of my abilities—there is nothing miraculous about them."

"Oh, I don't think so," said Clementine. "What he said was—well, what he actually said was that you were awfully good at picking up odds and ends of gossip and finding out things that weren't any of your business."

Making allowances for the Cambridge idiom, I supposed I must consider it a tribute. I enquired whether she had spoken of her fears to any of her colleagues.

"No—I didn't have a chance to talk to Patrick in private, and Gideon Darkside's the last person that I'd want to discuss it with. And I haven't seen Cantrip or Gabrielle at all since it happened. We didn't have time to look for them, you see—the Constable wanted us to go straight over to the harbour and confirm the identification, and anyway, Philip Alexandre seemed to think that they'd probably gone on ahead of us. So somehow or other we all missed each other —I think they must both have left Sark without hearing the news about Edward."

I knew that Cantrip had not yet returned to Chambers; the Contessa also, it seemed, was still absent from her office in Monte Carlo.

"I tried ringing her there this morning, and she wasn't back yet. But you see, Professor Tamar, I didn't really expect her to be. She'd been meaning to meet her husband somewhere near Paris and spend two or three days driving south with him. She says he gets fed up when she goes off on business trips, so she always tries to make up for it by having a short holiday on her own with him afterwards." Clementine smiled indulgently at this matrimonial bargaining. "If she left Sark without hearing about poor old Edward, then there's no reason for her to have changed her plans. I'm not really worried about her." I perceived, however, that this last was not entirely true.

"Your reasoning," I said, "is not as yet entirely clear to me. I quite appreciate that the descendants of Sir Walter

Palgrave, if of a mercenary disposition, would wish to ensure that the identity of the settlor was never discovered and that the trust company was therefore unable to exercise its discretion in accordance with his wishes. You tell me, however, that of all those concerned with the settlement, your late senior partner, Oliver Grynne, was the only one who knew the identity of the settlor. So far as his death is concerned, the Palgrave descendants have a motive—but what motive do they have for disposing of Edward Malvoisin?"

"I'm afraid," said Clementine apologetically, "that it's not quite as simple as that. You see, when I say that Oliver was the only one who knew who the settlor was, I don't exactly mean that the others didn't know. Well, not exactly. What I mean is—well, that they did sort of know, but they'd—well, sort of forgotten."

"Forgotten?" I said. Though I have no personal experience of such matters, I would have supposed that the establishment of a trust fund in excess of nine million pounds sterling would infallibly ensure that one's name lived, if not in history, at least in the memory of one's accountants and investment advisers. "Forgotten?"

"Well, Professor Tamar, what you've got to remember is that back in the early seventies the Edelweiss company in Jersey was setting up settlements like this by the barrel load. Patrick and Gabrielle were both there then, and between them they probably did several hundred a year— mostly in the couple of months before the Budget. You couldn't expect anyone to remember off the cuff which settlement was whose. And there wasn't anything special about Daffodil. It's a bit special now, of course, because Gabrielle did some rather brilliant things with the investments and the settlor never seems to have wanted much out of it, so it's built up into quite a tidy sum. But when it started it was quite an ordinary size of fund—a few hundred thousand quid."

I endeavoured to appear suitably contemptuous of so inconsiderable a sum.

"Each settlement would have been given a name—the year they did Daffodil they were all called after flowers— and the documents and correspondence relating to it would have been filed under that name. And they'd be awfully careful to see that the settlor's name was never mentioned anywhere on the file, because the whole idea was that if the file got into the wrong hands, there still wouldn't be anything to show who'd really made the settlement. But there'd be a code number on the file corresponding to a number on an index at the bank's office in Geneva, which would give you the name of the settlor. It's a tremendously sophisticated system."

"And completely foolproof, no doubt."

"Oh, absolutely. Well, it would be, except that the Daffodil file's somehow lost its code number. I suppose someone's secretary decided to replace the folder and didn't realise how important it was to copy the number on the cover."

"I see," I said. "But are you sure that Oliver Grynne had not also forgotten who the settlor was?"

"Oh yes, Professor Tamar, there's no doubt about that. The settlor was one of Oliver's personal clients, and it was Oliver who advised him to make the settlement and did all the arrangements. And naturally he went on being the contact man between the settlor and everyone else involved. It was through Oliver that they got the news that the settlor had died—he made an announcement about it on the first day of their meeting in the Cayman Islands."

"But in all the years since the settlement was made, did he never once mention the name of the settlor? And did it never once occur to any of the others to ask him what it was?"

"Well no. You see, Professor Tamar, in the tax-planning business one rather gets in the habit of not using the client's name, even in private, unless one absolutely has to—walls have ears, and all that. And none of the others would exactly have thought that they didn't know who the settlor was—they'd have thought they did know, but just couldn't remember offhand. Like a telephone number that one's got somewhere in one's address book. It wasn't until several weeks after Oliver died that we realised—"

"That you had, as it were, lost the address book?"

"Yes. I thought to begin with, when I found the name wasn't mentioned on Oliver's Daffodil file, that all I had to do was go through all his files for his personal clients and I'd be sure to spot the right person. Well, I've done that and not found anything. But of course that's all we've done so far—go through files in our various offices. I'm certainly not advising my clients to throw the sponge in at this stage. If everyone who was involved in Daffodil when it was set up really gets down to work on it—you know, going through their personal diaries and old letters so on, and working out exactly what they were doing and who they were meeting at the time—then I think that between them they're practically bound to remember something that leads us to the right answer." Her schoolboyish face, which had brightened with enthusiasm for this energetic enterprise, was clouded again by anxiety. "The trouble is, it looks to me as if someone else thinks the same thing."

"Were all those now professionally concerned with the settlement involved in its setting up?"

"Yes—except me of course. I didn't come into it until after Oliver died. It doesn't mean that they necessarily had any direct contact with the settlor. Edward Malvoisin would have been responsible for preparing the trust deed, because theoretically it was a Jersey settlement. But he'd have used a draft provided by Oliver, and probably drafted by Counsel in London, to make sure it did the right things from the point of view of U.K. tax law. And he'd have got his instructions through the trust company, so there wouldn't have been any need for him actually to meet the settlor."

"And how did Gideon Darkside come into the picture?"

"Well, I suppose Oliver thought there ought to be an accountant involved and he brought in Gideon. We used to have quite a close relationship with Gideon's firm in those days—they still had one or two people who actually knew something about tax, and Gideon was still relatively junior, so no one realised what a dead loss he was. I suppose it's quite lucky that Daffodil's the only case where we're still lumbered with him. I'd expect Oliver to have introduced him to the settlor, but Gideon claims he can't remember anything about it. And of course his idea of efficiency is to destroy all documents wholesale when they're more than six years old, so there's nothing at all on his files."

"The settlor, I suppose, would have wished at some stage to meet a senior representative of the company which was to be entrusted with his money—Patrick Ardmore or the Contessa?"

"Oh," said Clementine, with the expression of a schoolboy about to disclose some lively item of gossip about the headmaster, "Patrick may have dealt with some of the paperwork, but the meeting would quite definitely have been with Gabrielle. Poor old Oliver was absolutely potty about her, you see, so there's no way he'd have passed up an excuse to set up a meeting with her. I think that's why he hung on to the Daffodil case—he ought really to have handed it over to someone a bit more junior, but that would have meant not seeing her at Daffodil meetings." Her smile faded again. "So if anyone's going to remember anything about the settlor, Gabrielle's the most likely person. And that's why—I don't exactly mean I'm worried about her, Professor Tamar, but I'd be awfully pleased to know for certain that she really is safely on her way home with her husband."

Reflecting on what she had told me, I found myself suffering from a curious confusion of mind, of the kind which might be induced by some mild hallucinogen—the inevitable consequence, I suppose, of having anything to do with the world of international tax planning. Clementine's theories seemed at one moment entirely absurd and fanciful; at the next, utterly persuasive.

"I suppose," I said eventually, "that there will be an inquest on Edward Malvoisin?"

"The body's been sent over to Guernsey for an autopsy. The Guernsey CID will report back to the Seneschal of Sark and he'll hold an inquest. If there are no signs of violence, I suppose the verdict will be accidental death."

"Is it known from what point he fell? Was it from the

Coupee itself or could it have been from somewhere on Little Sark?"

"No, he must have fallen from somewhere near the middle of the Coupee. I saw the place on the way back—the fishermen had marked it with a flag."

"And they saw the body, as I understand it, while the entrance to the Coupee from Little Sark was still blocked by the overturned carriage. If that is right, then he must have left Little Sark sometime on the previous evening, before Albert's accident. But he was still in the bar, you say, when you retired for the night at about quarter past ten. It seems a rather eccentric hour to go out for a walk along the cliffs on a dark and windy night. Have you any idea why he went?"

"No—no idea at all," said Clementine. It seemed to me, however, that she had hesitated, as she had done before when deciding to be something less than candid.

"Is there any possibility that he might have committed suicide?"

"Oh no, Professor Tamar, not with Edward. Poor Edward, he may not have been popular with everyone, but he was always popular with himself."

"It could still have been an accident, however. Were it not for the previous death, you would suspect nothing more sinister."

"I suppose not," said Clementine. "But I don't actually see how it could have happened. Edward was quite heavily built, and the railings would have come up to his waist. If he'd simply stumbled, they'd have stopped him going over the edge. If he'd been leaning over them, I suppose he might have overbalanced, but why on earth *should* he lean over, specially in the pitch dark? I just don't see how it could have happened, unless . . ." She shivered and looked towards the window, as though seeing in the distance beyond not the sunlit thoroughfares of the City but the remote and desolate clifftop, which played, as I now recalled, so prominent and sinister a role in the folklore of Sark.

"Unless?"

"Unless there was something there he was so afraid of that he climbed over the railings to escape it."

I experienced again a sensation of coldness. I was seized at that moment, for no reason rationally explicable, by a curious conviction that the death of Edward Malvoisin had nothing at all to do with such modern and sophisticated things as settlements and companies but with something altogether darker and more ancient.

CHAPTER 7 ═══

Confidential as the interview had been, it would have been the height of pedantry to withhold its substance from those who were already familiar with the greater part of the story and on Cantrip's return would undoubtedly learn the rest. At lunch in the Corkscrew I accordingly did not hesitate to give my companions an account of it.

I observed as I approached the conclusion of my narrative that Selena was regarding me with a rather curious expression, such as in the genre of literature aspired to by Cantrip and Julia might have been described as quizzical. I invited her to explain its significance.

"I was only thinking," said Selena, "that Clementine's theory would require the person responsible for the two deaths to satisfy a number of rather unusual conditions. First, he or she must be one of the descendants of Sir Walter Palgrave, or so closely connected with one of them as to have an interest in their financial advancement. Secondly,

THE SIRENS SANG OF MURDER

he or she must also know a great deal about the Daffodil Settlement—not only that it exists, but enough about how it's run to foresee the problems that would be caused by the death of Oliver Grynne. That suggests someone, doesn't it, who has worked in one of the offices of the trust company or its professional advisers?"

"Moreover," said Ragwort, "it would have to be someone who could persuade Edward Malvoisin to go for a walk along the cliffs late on a dark and windy night. From what one has heard of his character, that surely suggests a young woman. A personable young woman, no doubt, but at the same time physically capable of pushing the unfortunate man over the cliff—a young woman, one might imagine, with a measure of training in some form of unarmed combat."

"So if Clementine's theory were right," said Selena, "which I don't for a moment say it is, then she herself would be the obvious suspect. One would have to assume that by asking for your assistance she was trying to make use of you in some devious kind of double bluff. We would not wish you, Hilary, to find yourself in a position of any embarrassment."

I pointed out that the capacity for rational thought was not confined, as Selena and Ragwort evidently believed, to the members of Lincoln's Inn, and that the possibility they mentioned had not escaped me. A little further reflection, however, had satisfied me that it could be excluded.

"I suppose you will agree," I said, "that Cantrip's account of the events of Monday evening may be accepted as truthful?"

"I fear that it must," said Ragwort sadly.

"Very well then. Cantrip left the bar of the hotel at

about a quarter past ten on Monday evening together with Clementine and the Contessa, and Edward Malvoisin was then alive and well. From then on, apart from the brief interval required to change into night attire, Clementine and Cantrip remained in each other's company until the moment when the drunken handyman came galloping into the garden—that is to say, until after the accident which blocked the entrance to the Coupee. We have no way of knowing whether Edward Malvoisin's death occurred before or after the accident, but in either case Clementine can have had no hand in it. If it was before, then it was while she was with Cantrip. If after, then at a place where it was physically impossible for her to have been at that time —unless you imagine, I suppose, that she could have scrambled down the cliffs and reached it by boat."

"No," said Selena, "I don't suggest that. I've done some sailing in the Channel Islands, and there's nowhere on Little Sark to land a boat. And the currents are some of the most dangerous in the world—it would be suicidal to try to swim across." She sipped her wine, evidently still doubting the soundness of the conclusion. "I wonder if Clementine's fiancé really is still in Hong Kong."

As it happened I was able to reassure her on this point. Clementine had telephoned her fiancé on the previous evening and had found him in his office. No means of transport, however jet-propelled, could have achieved his presence at that time in Hong Kong if he had been in Sark on Monday night. It was true, of course, that my source of information was Clementine herself, but she would hardly have deceived me on a matter so easily verified.

During this discussion Julia had been lost in thought— or so at least I supposed, since I could see nothing in the composition of her prawn salad to cause her to sit gazing at it with such bemused perplexity. When she roused herself from her reverie it was to invite me to attend a seminar on international tax planning which she was to address on the following morning; she believed that the chairman, in view of my academic standing, would think it proper to waive the attendance fee.

"My dear Julia," I said kindly, "I am sure that it will be a most interesting and instructive occasion. I fear, however, that there is little hope of my acquiring an instant expertise in so recondite an area."

"I was not proposing," said Julia, "that you should attempt to do so. I have been provided with a list of those expected to attend, and it includes Gideon Darkside. I thought you might welcome an opportunity to meet him."

"From all I have heard of him," I said, "that seems most improbable. You mean, I take it, that you think I ought to meet him. Have you any reason to think that he knows anything about the descendants of Sir Walter Palgrave?"

"None at all," said Julia. "But your enquiry, as I understand it, is not merely genealogical—you are hoping to discover who, if anyone, is responsible for the alarmingly high mortality rate among the advisers to the Daffodil Settlement. It would be rather premature, don't you think, to exempt from suspicion all those who do not happen to be descended from Sir Walter Palgrave? You haven't forgotten, I suppose, that Oliver Grynne's death occurred at a most convenient moment from the point of view of Gideon Darkside."

We were all at least agreed that Cantrip could be in no danger—his acquaintance with the Daffodil Settlement was plainly too recent and too slight to present a threat. We must nonetheless, I fancy, have begun to feel a faint stirring of uneasiness about him. In the hope of now finding him safely at his desk, we rose from lunch rather earlier than usual and walked back to 62 New Square with uncustomary briskness.

On ascending the bare stone staircase to the first floor, we were encouraged to think these hopes well founded, for the door to the room occupied by Cantrip and Ragwort was standing slightly ajar.

"Oh, he must be back," said Ragwort. "I left the door shut when I went to lunch." In his eagerness to greet his friend's return, he entered the room with perhaps uncircumspect haste.

It was the opinion of the philosopher Parmenides that change is impossible: the state of affairs which exists at any given moment must be identical with that which existed at the immediately preceding moment, there being ex hypothesi no intervening moment in which any alteration could take place. What now occurred was a striking demonstration that this view is in practise mistaken. There existed at one moment a serene and elegant Ragwort, immaculate in pinstripes—above all, a perfectly dry Ragwort, his person free from any drop of extraneous moisture; at the next succeeding moment, with no intermediate process of development, there existed an entirely different Ragwort, with water cascading in abundance from every stitch and seam and an orange plastic bucket over his head.

From the interior of the room came a triumphant cry of "Gotcher," seeming at first to confirm that Cantrip had returned.

We soon perceived, however, that the only occupant

was one who should, to judge by appearances, have reached the years of restraint—a well-preserved septuagenarian, one would have guessed, probably of military antecedents, with neatly trimmed white hair and moustache and the clear suntanned complexion which ought to be the reward of healthy living and an easy conscience. This reassuring first impression was contradicted only by a certain black demonic brightness, which we could not fail to recognise, in the eyes beneath the snow-white eyebrows. It appeared that Cantrip's Uncle Hereward had arrived in London.

It was perhaps fortunate, though it seemed at the time regrettable, that Ragwort was for some minutes unable to remove the bucket from his head. This was due, as we afterwards discovered, to its having once contained some kind of glutinous substance, the adhesive properties of which were revived by contact with water. Though it is inconceivable that any words of a blasphemous or indecorous nature would in any circumstances pass Ragwort's chaste and beautiful lips, yet it is possible that in the first few moments of outrage he expressed himself with greater frankness than would have been seemly towards a man so much his senior. In the circumstances I have mentioned, however, his words were inaudible.

His feelings cannot have been soothed, I suppose, by the fact that Colonel Cantrip, plainly still under the impression that it was his nephew who stood dripping and indignant in the doorway—one young Chancery junior with a plastic bucket over his head is not easily distinguished from another—continued to dance gleefully round him with whoops and cries of triumph.

When at last apprised of his error, the old soldier apolo-

Sarah Caudwell

gised with every proper sign of penitence. He had been subjected, it seemed, to overwhelming temptation. Sitting waiting quietly for his nephew, he had happened to observe that the ledge over the door was of a kind peculiarly suitable for balancing a bucket of water; upon visiting the cloakroom a few minutes later, he had chanced to find there just such a bucket as he had had in mind.

"And you naturally felt," said Ragwort, "that the door and the bucket were in some manner predestined for each other?"

"That's it," said the Colonel, impressed by Ragwort's ready grasp of the position. "Thought I'd give young Michael a bit of a surprise, you see—liven him up a bit. Never thought of it being anyone else who came in. I say, lucky it was only you, isn't it, not one of the top brass?"

"That is indeed," said Ragwort, "one of the happiest aspects of the whole episode. If you will be good enough to excuse me, sir, I shall now go and see if I can find any clothes which drip rather less water on the carpet. Though, of course, another pleasing aspect of the matter is that I can drip almost any amount of water on the carpet without making it significantly wetter."

Detecting perhaps that Ragwort's manner towards him was courteous rather than cordial, Colonel Cantrip observed his departure with what seemed to be relief. "Bit peeved with me, do you think? Well, he's got a point, I suppose. Never thought of it being anyone but young Michael coming through that door—knew this was his room, you see, didn't realise he shared it with anyone. Where's the young blighter got to?"

It was beginning to be an interesting question.

* * *

In obedience to my promise to Clementine, I spent the afternoon at St. Catherine's House, searching the registers of marriage for entries relating to the daughters of Sir Walter Palgrave.

I approached my task in optimistic mood, thinking that the rarity of the name would make it a relatively easy one. Half way through the afternoon, however, my spirits were somewhat dashed by the discovery that one of the ladies in question had inconsiderately allied herself in marriage to a man by the name of Smith. The prospect of attempting to identify the offspring of their union among the births registered in the subsequent three decades made me almost regret the quixotic impulse which had moved me to accept Clementine's proposal. Moreover, I could not but reflect that if my whole investigation were to be conducted in St. Catherine's House, barely five minutes walk away from Middle Temple Lane, the payment of my expenses would do little to enhance the attractiveness of the arrangement.

I began to wonder whether my approach to the task entrusted to me had not been unduly literal. While Clementine's ostensible object in retaining my services was to trace the existing members of the Palgrave family, her real purpose, as I well knew, was to discover the truth concerning the deaths of Oliver Grynne and Edward Malvoisin. Could I, if I neglected the latter, properly claim credit, and indeed payment, for having pursued the former? It would be contemptible.

By now there might well be in existence as many as a hundred descendants of the late Sir Walter Palgrave. Even if I were eventually able, by my present methods, to identify them all, it would almost certainly be too late to investigate their whereabouts at the time of the two deaths. Nor could I disregard the possibility, already suggested by Julia, that if these deaths were not accidental, they had nonetheless been brought about for some other motive than that which Clementine supposed. A fund so substantial that a hundred thousand pounds or so could be abstracted from it almost unnoticed might offer enticing opportunities to those responsible for its administration—if any of these happened to have been taken, the threat of exposure might seem a more than adequate reason for murder.

By the time I returned to the Corkscrew that evening I had resolved on an entirely different approach to the matter. I had been at fault, I now saw, in indulging the natural preference of the Scholar for quiet, solitary research among the dusty documents of a bygone era. My attention should be concentrated not on a shadowy and hypothetical class of suspects of whom I knew nothing, but on those persons whom I already knew to exist and to be connected with the Daffodil settlement. I must not be deterred by the possibility that this might oblige me to travel to the Channel Islands, Monaco, or even, if necessary, the Cayman Islands.

Selena and Ragwort, sitting alone together at one of the round oak tables, shook their heads when I asked if there were any news of Cantrip.

"And now we know why not," said Ragwort, suppressing a sneeze. "He must have known perfectly well that his uncle was arriving sometime this week, and he's hoping to stay away until the coast's clear, leaving the rest of us to cope with the old ruffian. I suggest that when he comes back we sue him for enormous damages."

"Do you think," said Selena, "that we have any cause of action?"

"Certainly—there is quite clearly a liability under the rule in *Rylands v. Fletcher.* Having in one's possession a dangerous and mischievous thing, namely a lunatic uncle, and allowing him to escape and do damage." Ragwort failed to suppress a sneeze.

I enquired why Julia was absent from our company.

"She should be joining us shortly," said Selena, "but she's gone home to change—she's taking the Colonel to the theatre this evening. He seemed rather disappointed, you see, that he wouldn't be spending the evening with Cantrip—he'd been thinking, he said, that they might do a show and then have a bite of supper at one of the night spots. But of course, he said, it wouldn't be any fun on his own, so he'd just go back to his club and have an early night. He gave a rather convincing impression of being a lonely old soldier whose friends and contemporaries have long since fallen on distant battlefields."

"Whereupon Julia," said Ragwort, "who is in some ways a very impressionable girl and can be reduced to tears by two stanzas of Siegfried Sassoon, proposed herself as his companion. At this the old scoundrel brightened up amazingly."

"Well," said Selena, "at least she's taking him to something she actually wants to see—she's managed to get tickets for *All's Well That Ends Well,* with Roland Devereux in the lead. I'm not sure that it's exactly what the Colonel means by 'a show,' but then I'm not sure anything is that's currently appearing on the London stage."

Roland Devereux, I remembered, was a young Shakespearean actor who had recently become known to a wider audience by appearing in a television series. Recalling the now celebrated perfection of his profile, I was not surprised to learn that Julia was among his admirers.

"I fear," said Ragwort, "that there is rather more to it than that. There was once an acquaintance between them —of which it is perhaps not proper to speak further."

"Roland Devereux," said Selena, "unless I'm forgetting someone, was the last slender young man but three to be the object of Julia's hopeless and undying passion. I don't count you, of course, Ragwort, since the attachment is of a continuing nature. And I'm not counting Patrick Ardmore, who isn't a slender young man and has no business behaving as if he were. She spent a great deal of time admiring Roland Devereux's profile, with many allusions to Praxiteles and Michelangelo and so forth, and her admiration did not go wholly unrewarded. It was all quite a long time ago, but she still takes a sentimental interest in his progress."

It was at this point that Julia herself arrived. The rather exuberant décolletage which she had judged suitable for the evening's entertainment, though it attracted favourable comment from two members of the Building Bar at the next table, was regarded by Ragwort with some disapproval.

"My dear Julia," he said, as he poured her a glass of Nierstein, "your dress, if I may say so, seems to have been designed for a young woman somewhat—as it were, somewhat smaller than yourself."

"It's the size I always take," said Julia rather defensively.

"Or possibly for a young woman of the same size, but of somewhat different shape. A young woman—dear me, how can one express it with delicacy?—let us say, with rather more fully developed shoulder blades."

"There's nothing wrong with Julia's shoulder blades," said Selena. "And anyway, they're completely covered. Take no notice, Julia—it's a very attractive dress."

"I should not have liked the Colonel to think," said Julia, "that I regarded the evening as less than festive. As it is, I feel rather conscience-stricken about my choice of entertainment—I suppose what he'd really like is something with girls taking their clothes off."

"Oh well," said Ragwort, "you have certainly done your best to compensate for any disappointment he may feel on that score. I do hope you won't catch cold—I assure you, it's most disagreeable at this time of year."

The auspices for the evening seemed not altogether propitious. I could think of few subjects of conversation in which Julia and the Colonel might share an interest, and none upon which they might be in sympathy. I suspected that on almost any social, political, or ethical question the old soldier would be scandalised by Julia's opinions, she outraged by his. Moreover, as she herself had previously acknowledged, the Colonel was the sort of man who has an incorrigible propensity for getting into trouble, and Julia was not the sort of woman who would know how to keep him out of it.

"There's nothing to worry about," said Julia, with an excess of confidence which I found in itself alarming. "I have worked out a strategy for dealing with him. I intend to model my behaviour in all respects on that of my Aunt Regina. My Aunt Regina, so far as I can discover, doesn't believe that men progress much morally or intellectually after the age of six, and she treats them accordingly. She always gets on splendidly with men like the Colonel—two of her husbands were of just the same type."

"My dear Julia," said Ragwort, "your ambition to deal with men in the same manner as your Aunt Regina is very laudable. From the point of view of realism, however, it is somewhat similar to your deciding to play tennis in the style of Miss Martina Navratilova."

"The trouble is," said Selena, with a certain wistfulness, "that you and I, Julia, have been brought up in an era of emancipation and enlightenment, and we have got into the habit of treating men as if they were normal, responsible, grown-up people. We engage them in discussion; we treat their opinions as worthy of quite serious consideration; we seek to influence their behaviour by rational argument rather than by some simple system of rewards and punishments. It's all a great mistake, of course, and only makes them confused and miserable—especially men like the Colonel, who have grown up with the idea that women will tell them what they ought to do without their having to think about it for themselves. But I'm afraid it's too late to put the clock back."

"I don't claim," said Julia, "that I could maintain the impersonation of my Aunt Regina indefinitely. But I only have to do it for one evening, and most of the time we shall be watching the play."

"What about afterwards?" said Ragwort. "Where are you taking the appalling old menace for dinner?"

"Guido's. I suppose it's not quite what he means by a night spot, but I wanted to take him somewhere where he couldn't get into any trouble. And I don't think, Ragwort, that you ought to refer to him as an appalling old menace. He fought with great distinction in the Second World War."

"Fought in it? He probably started it—it would be his idea of a joke."

"He got the DSO," said Julia.

"He's a dangerous lunatic," said Ragwort.

"I am not sure," said Selena, "that being a dangerous lunatic is inconsistent with having the DSO. One almost suspects that it may be a prerequisite."

My readers, having no doubt perceived that Julia is a woman by temperament and conviction inclined towards pacifism, will be, I daresay, as perplexed as we were by the tenderness of her regard for a man who had devoted his life, with evident enthusiasm, to the profession of arms. The truth is, I suppose, that being herself of a timorous nature, she has a romantic and disproportionate admiration for physical courage: of that, if of no other virtue, possession of the Distinguished Service Order is indisputable evidence. She attempted, however, to lend a veneer of rationality to her position, referring with passion and dubious relevance to the doctrine of equitable estoppel and the maxim *qui commodum sentit et onus sentire debet.*

Life in England in the second half of the twentieth century, it seemed to Julia, admittedly on the basis of a somewhat haphazard knowledge of modern history, had so far proved to be a good deal more comfortable than it would have been if we had lost the Second World War. The Colonel had done the fighting and Julia was enjoying the benefit. Would it not, in these circumstances, become her very ill to reproach him for his belligerence or to grudge as unduly troublesome an evening spent keeping him innocently amused?

"My dear Julia," said Ragwort with a sigh, "your sentiments do you credit. We must hope that you do not have cause to regret them. Where are you meeting the frightful old—the gallant and charming old gentleman?"

"At his club in Piccadilly, at seven o'clock. I'd better go —I wouldn't like to be late. Shall I see you at the seminar tomorrow, Hilary? I've told the chairman that you may be coming, and he is suitably enchanted by the prospect. Nine-thirty at the Godolphin Hotel—nine o'clock if you want coffee."

I assured her that I would be there, and she took her leave of us. We observed her departure with misgiving, and exchanged, I fear, some rather severe comments on Cantrip's wanton abandonment of his responsibilities. Poor boy, had we known what had by then befallen him, we could not have spoken with such harshness.

CHAPTER 8 ══════

For such a woman as Cecilia Mainwaring the public rooms of the Godolphin Hotel would have provided an admirable background. The sparkle of the magnificent chandeliers would have been appropriately reflected in the subtle gleam of her jewellery; the thick carpets would have yielded voluptuously to her elegantly shod feet; she would have swept imperiously down the wide staircase and reclined with regal seductiveness on the richly upholstered sofas.

All this, I need hardly say, was altogether wasted on Julia, whom I found there on the following morning bearing all the signs of a woman who has woken late and risen in haste, with insufficient time to comb her hair or find an unladdered pair of tights. She was sitting in an attitude of weariness in one of the deep armchairs, drinking coffee as if it were essential to her survival, and apparently engrossed in the most recent edition of the *Daily Scuttle*. Conscious, as I supposed, that this was unsuitable reading for a person of cultivated taste, she attempted on observing my approach to conceal it behind a cushion.

I enquired if she had spent an agreeable evening with the Colonel.

"I cannot say," said Julia, "that 'agreeable' is quite the mot juste."

"I suppose," I said, "that he was rather bored by *All's Well That End's Well*?"

"On the contrary, he enjoyed it enormously, suspending disbelief to an extent that the producer can hardly have dreamt of. He took in particular a great fancy to Helena, whom he described as 'a damned fine girl,' and a corresponding dislike to the Count of Roussillon, whom he judged to be unworthy of her affections. So strongly, indeed, did he feel on the subject that in the middle of the fifth act he rose from his seat and shouted, 'Shame, sir, shame, you're a scoundrel,' and I had some difficulty in persuading him to sit down and be quiet."

"My poor Julia," I said, "it must have been a most difficult evening. No wonder you are looking a trifle worn."

"You wrong me, Hilary. Deficient as I may be in moral fortitude, I venture to say that the trifling embarrassment of being almost thrown out of a London theatre would not alone have reduced me to the shattered wreck of humanity which you now see before you."

"Oh dear," I said. "What else?"

"We went to Guido's for dinner, and the Colonel remained preoccupied with the events of the play. He was anxious to believe that in spite of having been perfectly beastly to Helena throughout five acts Roussillon was really deeply in love with her, and would thereafter make her an ardent and devoted husband."

There seemed to me to be little in the text to justify so sentimental a reading. Roussillon's attitude to Helena at the beginning of the play is one at best of indifference. By the end of it, when she has forced him virtually on pain of death into an unwanted marriage, and tricked him under cover of darkness into an unintended consummation, is it probable that he will be more kindly disposed towards her? She has demonstrated, no doubt, the intensity of her feelings; but outside the conventions of the romantic novel, intensity of passion affords no guarantee of reciprocity.

"I'm afraid," said Julia sadly, "that I am of the same opinion. I have always supposed the title of the play to be ironic. Roussillon will continue to be beastly to her and they will live miserably ever after. Moreover, it is clear that he has only his looks to commend him, and in a few years' time he will no doubt be losing them. Helena will realise too late that she has tied herself down to a bad-tempered and illiterate oaf who doesn't laugh at her jokes, and she'll wish she'd stayed in Paris and pursued her medical studies."

It seemed all too probable.

"But the Colonel, as I say, was anxious to believe otherwise, and I endeavoured, so far as my critical conscience would allow, to agree that he might be right. We were still debating the subject when some of the cast came in— Guido's, as you know, is rather popular with the theatrical profession—including Roland Devereux, who plays the Count of Roussillon." Julia paused and lit a Gauloise. "The Colonel plainly felt that this presented him with an ideal opportunity to ascertain the truth of the matter. Before I could do anything to prevent him, he was leaning over Roland, shaking his fist and shouting, 'Look here, you young blackguard, she's a damned fine girl and she loves you—are you going to treat her decently or aren't you?"

"Disconcerting, no doubt, though a remarkable tribute to the quality of the young man's performance."

"I am sure that if Roland had understood the position, he would have felt deeply flattered. He did not appreciate, however, that the Colonel's reproaches were addressed to him in the character of the Count of Roussillon rather than *in propria persona*. And unfortunately"—she paused again and drew deeply on her Gauloise—"unfortunately, you see, I did once happen to have some acquaintance with Roland Devereux. A very passing and distant acquaintance."

"I have been given the impression," I said, "that it was passing but not entirely distant."

"Well, in terms of time it's extremely distant. Buried, one might almost say, in the mists of antiquity. In spite of which, Roland leapt instantly to the conclusion that I was the girl to whom the Colonel was referring. So instead of simply telling the Colonel that he didn't know what he was talking about, he engaged in a spirited defence, pointing out that it was I who had been, as it were, the pursuer, and that whatever my feelings might be, his own were not engaged. This confirmed, of course, the Colonel's worst fears about Roussillon's attitude to Helena, and his gallant old heart was moved to indignation on her behalf."

"Dear me," I said, "what a very unfortunate combination of circumstances."

"Yes indeed," said Julia. "Not made less so by the fact that the gossip columnist of the *Scuttle* was sitting two tables away, together with his photographer." With a heavy sigh she extracted the newspaper from its hiding

place under the cushion. "I suppose you might as well see it
—everyone else will have done."

> Popular stage and TV star Roland Devereux didn't say
> "I'll be talking to my lawyer" when he got an unwanted
> extra helping in fashionable Guido's restaurant in Cov-
> ent Garden last night. Also dining there was nubile tax
> barrister Julia Larwood, apparently an old flame of Ro-
> land's. He says the romance is definitely over, and these
> days the curvaceous lawyer certainly seems to be going
> for the older man—her companion for the evening was
> well into the senior citizen bracket. But he didn't seem
> to think much of the way young Roland had treated her
> —our picture shows how he made his feelings known.

The accompanying photograph, it is fair to say, showed
Julia to some advantage, though emphasising, to an extent
that Ragwort would have frowned on, the décolletage previously mentioned. It showed Roland Devereux, on the
other hand, at one of those moments when even the most
photogenic of actors can hardly appear at his best, that is to
say when a military gentleman of advanced years is empty-
ing a plate of spaghetti over him.

"Do you think I can sue them," said Julia, "for calling
me nubile?"

"I fear not," I said. "As you know, it means merely that
you are of marriageable age, though no doubt the readers
of the *Scuttle* believe it to have some more stimulating
significance. Never mind, Julia, there can be few such people among your acquaintance—one never meets anyone
who actually reads the *Scuttle*."

"I know," said Julia despondently, "but everyone always knows what's in it. Extraordinary, isn't it?"

There was nothing I could say to persuade the poor creature that she would ever again be able to show her face in Guido's, or in any other restaurant in London, or in any place frequented by the theatrical profession, or indeed anywhere within fifty miles of any newsagent selling copies of the *Scuttle*. She began to reflect on the possibility of emigrating to the British Virgin Islands.

I had been glancing from time to time towards the increasing throng of men in pinstriped suits gathered round the registration desk, where pretty girls in uniforms were issuing identity badges and bound copies of the lecture notes. I could discern no one, however, who seemed to correspond to the impression I had formed of Gideon Darkside.

The only one who at all attracted my notice was a man who looked to be of a very different sort from the uncharismatic accountant. Though no less soberly dressed than the others, he was somehow of a more carefree and light-hearted demeanour than was generally characteristic of the participants in the seminar. He had twice seemed to be disposed to move in our direction, but then to think better of it and turn away. Finally, however, he appeared to make up his mind to approach.

On observing him, Julia blushed and spilt her coffee over her lecture notes.

I had not at first glance supposed him the sort of man to whom Julia would be susceptible. Tawny-haired and amber-eyed, like a slightly dilapidated pet lion, he had passed by some twenty years the perfection—as Julia esteems it—of the quarter century, and was of a build rather muscular than slender; but he had not had the carelessness to lose his figure or the misfortune to lose his hair, and his manner of dress, though at first sight suggesting the casual, revealed to a more attentive gaze the fastidious elegance which Julia always finds so attractive in others. He looked, moreover, like a man who would laugh at her jokes.

He greeted her with the slight apprehensiveness often to be observed in men when they meet after some lapse of time a woman last encountered in conditions of erotic intimacy; but his voice was singularly pleasing, echoing the charming cadences of Dublin.

"Hello, Patrick," said Julia, making a vague and entirely useless gesture towards her inadequately combed hair, "what a nice surprise. I didn't see your name on the list."

"Surely to God, Julia," said the Irishman, "you don't think I'd come to a thing like this under my own name, do you, with spies from the Revenue lurking in every corner? I have colleagues who'd go to much greater lengths than simply travelling under a false name. They'd think it was insanely reckless of me to come to the U.K. without even putting on a false beard."

It was clear—though Julia, having evidently forgotten my presence and perhaps also my name, was plainly incapable of performing an introduction—that the Irishman was Patrick Ardmore. There was no prospect, however, of her leading the conversation into channels useful to my enquiry: I judged it discreet to melt, as it were, into the background, leaving her to her blushings and burblings until the announcement of the first lecture.

* * *

To the actual or prospective owner of any considerable fortune, the morning's proceedings would doubtless have been of absorbing interest. Such a person would have listened spellbound, I daresay, while Julia and her fellow speakers debated the schemes and stratagems by which income or capital may be protected from the grasping fingers of the Inland Revenue, comparing the merits of Panamanian private companies, Liechtenstein anstalts, and Cayman Island trusts, and earnestly drawing attention to the fascinating opportunities offered by the double taxation treaty with Ireland.

The rewards of Scholarship, however, are not of a material nature, and I fear that my attention wandered. Still, the management of the Godolphin Hotel had provided me with a comfortable chair, an abundance of iced water, and a handsomely bound notepad to scribble on. If I was wasting my time, it was at least in conditions of greater luxury than are to be found in the lecture halls of Oxford.

The time came for questions. From a few rows behind me a voice originating in that part of the Midlands where everyone seems to suffer permanently from a slight cold in the head addressed the platform in a tone of some resentment. We had heard a lot, said the voice, about domicile and residence and suchlike technicalities, and the lady lawyer had talked as if there was a big difference between tax that wasn't payable and tax that the Revenue couldn't recover. These technical distinctions might be very interesting, said the voice, to highly paid lawyers sitting in Lincoln's Inn, but quite frankly they weren't much help to a simple hardworking accountant trying to give practical advice to real-life clients. What the voice had to tell its clients was whether they'd have to pay tax or not, and if they didn't, then the voice quite frankly didn't give a row of beans whether that was because it wasn't payable or because it wasn't recoverable.

With the composure of a young man not easily shocked, the chairman invited Julia to reply.

"It really rather depends," said Julia, "on how much one minds about going to prison. Let us suppose, for example, that you advise a client to remove all his assets from this country in order to avoid tax on his death. If your client is domiciled outside the United Kingdom, then the result of his taking your advice will be that there is no tax liability. So your advice is perfectly proper, and if you failed to give it you would probably be liable for professional negligence. On the other hand, if your client were domiciled in the United Kingdom, the result would be that there was still a liability but the Revenue couldn't enforce it. In these circumstances you would probably be guilty of criminal conspiracy, and you could be sent to prison for it. But I agree, of course, that if you don't mind about that, then the distinction's of very trifling importance."

"In steering the difficult course between the Scylla of negligence and the Charybdis of conspiracy," said the chairman, "it is always prudent to obtain the advice of Counsel. I think we'd all agree about that." The speakers, all members of the Revenue Bar, nodded their approval of this satisfactory conclusion. "I hope that answers your question, Mr.—Mr. Darkside, isn't it?"

I looked round in time to identify the questioner, who was shaking his head in manifest dissatisfaction. Cantrip had not wronged Gideon Darkside in suggesting that he was of cadaverous aspect, for the paucity of the flesh covering his long bones had little in common with the muscular leanness of health; his thinning black hair lay lank across his skull, and his skin had the pallor of a fish which has been dead too long to make wholesome eating.

Lunch was preceded by what were termed cocktails. I contrived when these were served to be within a few paces of the accountant and to receive my glass of sherry at the same time that he accepted a grapefruit juice. I had thought that some trifling accident with my glass, not involving the sacrifice of an excessive amount of sherry, would provide a natural pretext to engage him in conversation; but before I could execute such a manoeuvre he moved briskly away, with the object, as it proved, of talking to Patrick Ardmore. The Irishman greeted him with what looked more like resignation than enthusiasm.

"Glad you're here," said the accountant. "Wanted a word with you."

"Of course, Gideon, by all means," said the Irishman rather wearily.

The two men found seats at a small occasional table some distance removed from the general throng. Though they somewhat lowered their voices, I was able, by appearing engrossed in my lecture notes, to remain within earshot of their conversation.

"Look, Patrick, I want you to tell me what's been going on."

"Certainly, Gideon, by all means. In what connection, precisely?"

"This business of Edward Malvoisin of course. What's happening about the inquest?"

"The inquest is on Saturday, but I understand that the Guernsey CID have already made their report to the Seneschal. They see no reason to doubt that his death was accidental."

"And doesn't anyone want to know what he was doing wandering about on the Coupee in the middle of the night?"

"The notion seems to have got about," said Ardmore with pellucid innocence, "that he probably had a business appointment of some kind—something he didn't want the rest of us to know about."

"A business meeting? At midnight? How did anyone get a damn-fool idea like that?"

"Advisers on financial planning are in a fiercely competitive business these days, as of course you know, Gideon. If a high-net-worth individual wants advice on his tax affairs in the middle of a rainy night on Sark, then you have to be there, don't you, or risk losing the client?"

"I never heard such a load of poppycock."

"Or her tax affairs," added Ardmore, with a sidelong glance and a world of innuendo.

"Oh, I see, they think he was off to see some woman. Well, that makes more sense, I suppose, specially in Malvoisin's case. And how do they think he came to go over the edge?"

"The CID don't think there's any great mystery about that after all. At about midnight on Monday poor old Albert was driving his horse and carriage along the Coupee, drunk as a lord and with some idea that the Devil was after him, and you've seen for yourself that there's not much leeway. If Edward was there and trying to get out of the way . . ." The Irishman spread his hands in a gesture designed to convey the sequel.

"Is that what the authorities think?"

"It's the obvious explanation. There's no question of Albert being charged with anything, of course—he's a Sark man and very well liked, and he didn't mean to do any harm to anyone. Well, Gideon, I think that's all I can tell you."

Ardmore looked at his watch, drained his glass, and began to rise, but the accountant stretched out a hand as if to restrain him.

"Just a minute, Patrick—what have you done about the pen?"

"The pen?" said Patrick Ardmore, with almost convincing perplexity, and then, at an exclamation of impatience from Darkside, "Oh—that pen. I'll be returning it, of course, as soon as I've got someone going over to Monte Carlo—I wouldn't like to trust it to the post. My dear man, you weren't thinking I was going to steal it, were you?"

"Of course not—stop pretending to misunderstand me. I think you ought to have told someone about it—someone in authority."

"You mean the Seneschal? My dear Gideon, the Seneschal's a busy man with many responsibilities—why would I go troubling him about a little item of lost property that I can return to the owner myself without any difficulty?"

"I'd like to know how she came to drop it there," said Darkside, with a sort of sullen malice.

"Would you? What a thirst you must have, to be sure, for useless information."

"And when."

"On the way across or on the way back, if she went back before us. I don't understand you, Gideon. What is it you want? To make people think there's something to investigate when they're satisfied there isn't? Policemen seconded from London and crime reporters from the national press, all wanting the exact details of why we were on Sark and what we were talking about? I'd have thought you'd be the last person to want that, in view of what we were discussing the other evening."

"Well," said the accountant sulkily, "if you're not going to say anything, then I won't either. But it's your decision, and I accept no responsibility for it."

"Oh, I quite understand that," said the Irishman. "You really must excuse me, Gideon. There are some people I've promised to see at lunch."

I had been invited to lunch with the chairman and speakers, at a table where both wine and conversation were expected to flow more freely than among the paying participants. I fear, however, that I repaid the courtesy but poorly, for my mind was too much preoccupied with the conversation I had just heard to allow me to contribute much by way of gossip or argument.

Julia, I noticed, seemed now in more cheerful spirits. Either the pleasure of the encounter with Ardmore or the satisfaction of having safely delivered her lecture had evidently erased from her mind the possible necessity of emigrating to the British Virgin Islands. As we were finishing our main course, however, one of the waiters approached her and murmured something which seemed to cause her anxiety. With a rather confused apology to the chairman, she rose and left us.

A few minutes later, while we were still eating a most excellent pudding, I observed the entry to the dining room of a uniformed page boy. He approached the table where Patrick Ardmore was sitting and handed him a note. Ardmore, having read it, also rose and left. The page boy continued on his way to Darkside's table, and a similar procedure followed, though Darkside's response seemed somewhat more hesitant. Seeing that the page boy was now moving in my direction, I made haste to finish my pudding.

CHAPTER 9 ══════

Amateurs of military anecdote will no doubt be better versed than I in the history of the Remnant Club, founded in the early nineteenth century by a group of officers, survivors of the Peninsular campaign, whose conduct had to their astonishment proved insufficiently sedate for other gentlemen's clubs in the neighbourhood of St. James's. Occupying as its premises an agreeable Regency town house just off Piccadilly, it has a relatively small membership, distinguished rather for gallantry than prudence, and is not much used for the entertainment of outside guests. Curiosity, if nothing else, would have compelled me to accept Colonel Cantrip's invitation to join him there after lunch.

It was no more than five minutes' walk from the Godolphin Hotel. A club servant of extreme antiquity, whose hobbling progress seemed to bear witness to ancient and honourable wounds, conducted me to the library—a long, oak-panelled room, smelling of leather and tobacco smoke, with shelves full of military histories and little-known memoirs.

The Colonel was sitting in a deep leather armchair looking rather pleased with himself, the demonic brightness of the eyes beneath the snow-white eyebrows undimmed by any remorse for the events of the previous evening. Facing him, at opposite ends of a long low sofa, sat Patrick Ardmore and Gideon Darkside—the former, brandy glass in hand, giving every sign of ease and contentment, the latter with his legs stretched stiffly out in front of him in an attitude which looked to be as lacking in comfort as it was in aesthetic charm. The Colonel effected introductions and asked me what I would drink.

Although Julia was absent from the gathering, presumably detained by paramount obligations with regard to the seminar, it had plainly been contrived with her assistance, possibly even her encouragement. Quite what she had said of me to persuade the Colonel that I ought to be there, and what role he expected me to play, I could only speculate, but he evidently believed my presence indispensable to his purpose—which was, it appeared, to find out what had happened to Cantrip.

"Thing is," said the Colonel, "I'm getting a bit worried about the lad. Been AWOL more than forty-eight hours now. Twenty-four I wouldn't worry about, but forty-eight starts looking like trouble. Well, he's a bit of a po-faced young blighter at times, but I wouldn't like anything to happen to him. The girls wouldn't like it either—I'd never hear the last of it from the girls." His look of sudden apprehension conjured up a regiment of female Cantrip relatives bitterly reproaching him for the loss of their cherished kinsman.

THE SIRENS SANG OF MURDER

"Well," said the accountant, "I've always known instructing Counsel meant a lot of fuss and bother, but this is the first time I've been told I ought to hire a nursemaid to see him home."

"Are we to understand," said Ardmore, seeming at least in some measure to share the old soldier's anxiety, "that Michael has not yet returned to London? And that you've had no news of him for the past two days?"

"That's right," said the Colonel. "Tried ringing him at home this morning—no answer. Went round to what he calls his Chambers—not a sign of him. Then I got talking to the secretary there—nice little thing—what's her name? Lily? Eileen? Something like that."

"I believe," I said, "that her name is Lilian."

"That's right. Well, I got talking to her, and it came out she was damned worried about the boy. She's got a soft spot for him, apparently, and I can tell you, Professor, she was nearly in tears, poor little thing. She's heard that some pretty rum things happen to people who get mixed up with this Daffodil business, and on Monday night some chap got himself killed. She didn't know the details, though, and there was no one else down there who knew a damn thing about anything. I knew young Julie Larwood was lunching at the Godolphin, so I thought I'd pop round there and see if she'd heard the same story. And she told me that these two gentlemen had been with Mike in the Channel Islands, so if we had a word with them, we could get the whole story straight from the horse's mouth. So here we are."

The degree of responsibility for the Colonel's conduct implied by the pronoun *we* in his penultimate sentence was sufficient to make my blood run cold, but I could think of no way of disclaiming it.

"I might have known," said Darkside. "I might have known that Larwood woman was at the bottom of all this nonsense. No offence, Colonel, but I'm a busy man, and quite frankly I think I've been brought here under false pretences. I came because you implied in your note that you could tell us something relevant to the Daffodil settlement, not to hear about a lot of silly rumours put about by a lot of silly women."

"Colonel Cantrip," said the Irishman, ignoring his colleague, "if I thought there was any cause for you to be worried about Michael, then I would be as concerned as you are, but I'm quite sure there is not. It's true, I'm very sorry to say, that one of our colleagues met his death in an accident on Monday night. But if you'll allow me to tell you about it, you'll see that it has nothing to do with your nephew in any way at all."

He gave the same account of Edward Malvoisin's death that he had earlier recommended to Darkside, attributing it to an unlucky encounter with the drunken Albert in his career across the Coupee, but he delivered it now with a more unqualified conviction and the fluency of a man long practised in reassuring nervous clients of the safety of their investments. It had been, he concluded, a very tragic accident, but Cantrip had been in no way involved.

"Forgive me," I said, "but is that entirely certain? Has either of you actually seen him since?" Had any members of Lincoln's Inn been present they would probably have thought it helpful at this point to remind me that Cantrip had been alive and well and sending telex messages several hours after the time of the accident to the carriage, but fortunately there were none.

The Irishman seemed slightly disconcerted.

"I suppose—now that you mention it, Professor Tamar, I suppose not. The last time I saw him was on Monday evening in the bar of our hotel. He left us rather early, I remember. My colleague, the Contessa di Silvabianca, and our English solicitor, Miss Derwent, had been given rooms in an annex a little distance away from the main building and so had Michael. They both wanted an early night, and I think Michael felt that he ought to escort them back there. That must have been—sometime between quarter and half past ten, I suppose."

"You see," I said, "I was wondering whether Cantrip—whether Michael might conceivably have accompanied Edward Malvoisin on his nocturnal excursion."

"Oh, I hardly think so, Professor Tamar. If Edward had an appointment at that hour of night, it must surely have been of a very confidential nature—I can't believe he'd have wanted company. And they certainly didn't leave at the same time. Edward stayed in the bar with us until—oh, about half past eleven, I should think. Do you remember, Gideon?"

"I remember him saying he wanted to get to bed," said the accountant. "He didn't say anything about going out."

"The world is full of duplicity, Gideon. Since we know that in fact he did go out, we must infer that it was for some purpose he chose not to tell us of. And that's the last time we saw the poor fellow alive. Gideon and I stayed on until midnight, when Philip Alexandre closed the bar. We were on our way up to our rooms when we heard all the noise of Albert coming back. We looked out of the landing window to see what was going on, and there he was up on his horse and shouting out about the woman in white, with Philip swearing back at him in Sercquais. Then he climbed down and started hurling bricks about. It was plain enough that he was as tight as a lord, and it didn't occur to us that there was anything seriously wrong."

The accountant had been looking with increasing frequency at his watch and giving other indications of impatience to be gone. The Irishman, however, took no notice of them, evidently intending to finish his brandy at leisure. It occurred to me that he felt a genuine reluctance to leave the Colonel with his anxiety unallayed.

"I do assure you," he said, "that there is nothing sinister about the Daffodil Settlement, and I don't doubt that at the time of the accident your nephew was safe in his bed. And if he was up bright and early in the morning and across the Coupee as soon as it was clear, he'd have been away on the boat to Jersey without ever hearing a word about poor Edward Malvoisin. After that you couldn't blame him if he decided to stay on for a day or two. He's enjoying himself on the beach at St. Brelade's at this very moment, I daresay, with no idea of anyone being worried about him."

"He could be in Timbuctoo," said Darkside, "for all we can do about it. Well, Patrick, I don't know about you, but I've paid good money to attend this seminar, even if it is just a lot of fancy lawyers talking a lot of hot air, and we've already missed twenty minutes of the afternoon session. So if you don't mind, Colonel, I'll be getting back to it."

"Stay where you are," said the Colonel, with a brisk authority which I could imagine to have been of notable effect on the battlefields of his youth.

Darkside, already in the process of rising, now sank back, as if almost physically incapable of continuing his upward movement. I at first supposed him merely to have succumbed to the old soldier's forceful personality and commanding tone of voice; but he had more probably been influenced, I perceived after a moment, by the fact that the Colonel was pointing a pistol at him.

The Irishman gave no sign of being disconcerted by this turn of events. On the contrary, his amber-coloured eyes became bright with what seemed to be amusement, as if at the charming whimsicality of some eccentric but highly valued client. Darkside, though his lips moved in silent protest, appeared to have lost the power of speech: he gazed as if mesmerised at the pistol, and his pallor had taken on a greenish, putrescent tinge.

"You say there's nothing sinister about this Daffodil business," said the Colonel. "But one man's dead and another's gone missing. And the one who's gone missing is my nephew. In my book you've still got a lot of explaining to do. Right, they're all yours, Professor—you're the expert. Fire away."

Whatever Julia had said to recommend to him my skills in investigation, she had evidently failed to mention my extreme distaste for all forms of physical coercion. It would have seemed unkind to disappoint him, however, by declining to proceed with the questioning of the two witnesses whom he had presented to me at gunpoint with such innocent satisfaction. Moreover, though I did not quite believe that he would actually shoot anyone, I did not so entirely disbelieve it as to feel disposed to vex him.

Searching in vain, in the agitation of the moment, for any useful or appropriate question, I finally enquired, for want of anything better, whether those concerned with the Daffodil Settlement had had, on the previous Monday evening, any particular cause for celebration.

143

"No," said Patrick Ardmore, with the tentative care of a man just learning the rules of an interesting new game. "No, I don't think so, Professor. Why should you suppose we had?"

"To stay in the bar until midnight suggests conviviality."

"There was nothing convivial about it," said Darkside, outraged into croaking audibility. "We had important business to discuss."

"Indeed?" I said. "I am surprised that the bar of your hotel afforded sufficient privacy for the discussion of confidential matters."

"We had it to ourselves," said Ardmore. "There was Philip Alexandre behind the bar, of course—the owner of the hotel—but he hardly counts as a stranger. Do please acquit us of conviviality, Professor Tamar—it's very hard on Gideon to be suspected of such a thing."

Perceiving that this brief exchange would hardly be sufficient to satisfy the Colonel's expectations, I cast about rather desperately in my mind for some further line of questioning.

"I wonder if you would care," I said, "to tell us about the pen?"

The effect was gratifying—the two men stared at me with as much astonishment as if I had put my hand in my pocket and extracted a large white rabbit. I noticed with some relief that the Colonel looked deeply impressed.

"The pen?" said Ardmore, raising an eyebrow. Too late, however, for credibility, even if his companion had not at the same instant exclaimed, "How the hell do you know about that?"

"The fountain pen belonging to the Contessa di

Silvabianca, which you found on the Coupee near the place where Edward Malvoisin fell to his death. If you happen to have it with you, Mr. Ardmore, I should be most interested to see it."

The Irishman hesitated—he was evidently a good deal more troubled by my knowing about the pen than by being held up at gunpoint in a gentlemen's club in the West End of London. He must have decided, however, that since I knew so much there could be no further harm in compliance. After an enquiring glance at the Colonel, who gave a brisk nod of assent, he opened his briefcase and produced something which gleamed prettily in the dusty sunlight from the library window. He handed it across to me—a fountain pen made, as I judged, of solid gold, engraved with a graceful and intricate design which incorporated the initials of Gabrielle di Silvabianca.

"Would you care," I said, "to tell me how you came to find it?"

"I understood," said the Irishman, "that you were already informed on the subject."

"It would interest me," I said, "to know the precise details."

"Very well," said Ardmore, "if they interest you, then by all means—but I can't think why they should. It was on Monday morning, when we were on our way back across the Coupee—Miss Derwent, Gideon, and myself. Miss Derwent had run on ahead—I think she rather had the jitters about the place, not surprisingly in the circumstances, and wanted to be across as quickly as possible. I didn't much care for it myself, but I stopped about half way across to look down at the place where the fishermen had found poor Edward's body—they'd marked it with some kind of flag. I looked to see if there was any sign of how he'd come to fall—whether the railings were damaged or anything of that kind. There was something shining in the grass at the edge of the road and I bent down and picked it up. Then Gideon came up and wanted to know what it was. As you see, Professor Tamar, a very trivial incident, though I admit I'm a little puzzled about how you happen to know about it—I rather thought Gideon agreed with me that there was no point in mentioning it to anyone else."

"I haven't told anyone," said the accountant. "I said you ought to tell someone, but it's not my responsibility."

"Have you any idea," I said, "how the Contessa happened to drop her pen in that particular place?"

"I doubt very much," said Ardmore, "that it was she who dropped it. Edward had been having trouble with his fountain pen all afternoon, I remember—making blots on all sorts of vital documents. I suppose the Contessa must have lent him hers, and he still had it, poor fellow, when he went out that night."

"I didn't notice him having trouble with his pen," said Darkside.

"Indeed, why should you, Gideon?" said the Irishman generously. "I'm sure you had more important things to think of. Is there anything further, Professor Tamar, on which we can assist you?"

Glancing at the Colonel, I perceived a slight discontentedness in his expression, as if he did not yet consider that he had quite had his money's worth.

"There is just one further point," I said. "I believe that the Contessa has some family connection with Sark. Could you tell me—what precisely is her relationship to Philip Alexandre?" The bow, I admit, was drawn somewhat at a venture; but Cantrip had mentioned her talking in Sercquais, a language not generally studied in the lycées or universities of France.

"Oh, she's his niece," said the Irishman casually, evidently not thinking this an important or troublesome question. "Her mother was Rachel Alexandre—she married a businessman from Brittany. Colonel Cantrip, it is a great privilege to have been entertained in a manner, if I may say so, so much in accordance with the traditions of this very distinguished club, but we really ought to go back to the seminar. Oh, come along, Gideon, you don't suppose that thing's loaded, do you?"

A loud report and a shattering of plaster established that it was.

"Something further, sir?" enquired the ancient servant, appearing in the doorway of the library.

Problems insoluble to the Junior Bar require the advice of leading Counsel. At the hour when tea is customarily taken I found Selena, Ragwort, and Julia gathered in Basil Ptarmigan's room, intending to direct his mind on his return from court to the problems created by Cantrip's continued absence. These were, in ascending order of gravity: the inconvenience of undertaking those of Cantrip's professional obligations which were of an urgent nature; the lowering effect on morale of Henry's disaffection and Lilian's tearfulness—after hearing the latest gossip from the offices of Stingham and Grynne she was now referring to the boy as "poor Mr. Cantrip" and in the past tense; and the impossibility of any longer remaining responsible for the Colonel. Something must be done—Basil was to consider what.

Accepting with gratitude the offer of tea, I described what had taken place at the Remnant Club. My account was punctuated by pitiful cries from Julia, who in a brief reencounter with Patrick Ardmore at the seminar had been given no hint of any unconventionality in the Colonel's entertainment of his guests.

"This cannot go on," said Ragwort with magisterial sternness. "Buckets of water and plates of spaghetti are one thing, but pointing guns at people is a serious matter—and I don't suppose that he even has a licence for it. Heaven alone knows what the appalling old—I do beg your pardon, Julia—what the delightful old gentleman will do next."

I confessed myself unable to prophesy on that subject. Following the departure from the Remnant Club of Ardmore and Darkside, I had spent the afternoon in attempting to persuade the Colonel of the need to reflect a little on what we had learnt. Though he had eventually promised, with some reluctance, to take no action until he heard from me again, I could not be confident that his patience would survive the evening nor predict what he would do when it was exhausted.

"I suppose it would be too much to hope," said Selena, "that all this eavesdropping and pointing guns and so forth has actually produced any useful information."

"I have made a little progress," I said, "in my investigation of the death of Edward Malvoisin. It begins to look as if Ardmore and Darkside can be excluded from suspicion. They both say—or Ardmore says and Darkside does not dispute it—that they were together in the bar of the Alexandra from the time Edward Malvoisin left until the time of the accident. I did not feel able, in the rather trying circumstances of our conversation, to question them as closely as I would have wished on this point, and it may be that they were not in each other's company for literally every minute of that period, but the absence of either for a sufficient length of time to follow Malvoisin half way across the Coupee would surely have excited comment from the other. Like Clementine, they have what I believe is technically termed an alibi. That is on the assumption, of course, that they are not accomplices."

"If I say," said Julia, "that Patrick is not the sort of man who pushes people over cliffs, you will no doubt accuse me of sentimental prejudice. You surely can't imagine, however, that he would choose Gideon Darkside as an accomplice."

"I agree," I said, "that it seems unlikely, though the quest for profit, my dear Julia, makes strange bedfellows. Ardmore and Darkside together would have been in an admirable position to extract money from the trust fund for their personal benefit, and if Malvoisin had found out about it . . . Still, the conversation which I overheard at the Godolphin did not sound to me like one between co-conspirators. Moreover, Philip Alexandre is also said to have been with them at the material time, and one must assume, I think, that, if asked, he would confirm that—a conspiracy of all three seems decidedly improbable."

Selena refilled my teacup.

"It looks," she said, "as if all the people we know about are excluded. Unless you count the person the Contessa saw lurking in the garden, there seem to be no suspects left. Perhaps Edward Malvoisin's death really was an accident—Patrick Ardmore's explanation sounds quite convincing. What a shame, Hilary—you'll have to go back to the birth and marriage certificates."

I was obliged to remind her that thus far there was no evidence to exclude the Contessa di Silvabianca.

"She was in the Witch's Cottage," said Julia. "With Cantrip and Clementine."

"My dear Julia, you surely don't believe that Cantrip and Clementine, occupied as they were, would have noticed if the Contessa left her room and went out again. There would have been ample time for her to do so and to reach the place where Malvoisin met his death long before the accident to the carriage. Moreover, she would have had no difficulty in finding her way, even in pitch darkness— now that we know she is Alexandre's niece, we may assume her to be entirely familiar with the cottage and its environs. Apart from which, there is the matter of the pen."

On the subject of the pen Julia became indignant. She had never heard of such a thing—or at any rate she had never read of such a thing—or at any rate not in any piece of respectable crime fiction published since the beginning of the Second World War. A physical object, forsooth, with the initials of a suspect engraved on it—why, it was worse than a fingerprint. If we must have a clue of a physical nature—and in Julia's experience the best authors nowadays wholly eschewed such vulgarities—then let it at least be one invisible to the naked eye and identifiable only by the most sophisticated techniques of modern pathology. If the progress of the past half century was to count for nothing, then one might as well go back, said Julia scathingly, to murders committed by means of arsenic or for motives of matrimonial jealousy.

"I do not doubt," I said, "that in a crime novel having any pretensions to modernity, the pen would be quite inadmissible. As a mere historian, however, there is nothing I can do about it. Nature, as we know, does imitate Art, but I fear that she all too often falls short of the highest standards. Were you to turn your attention from fictional crimes to those reported in the newspapers, you would find that people are still leaving fingerprints and murdering unfaithful spouses for all the world as if they were living in the 1920s. In the more backward parts of the country they may even still be poisoning one another with arsenic. We cannot ignore the pen for the sake of literary fashion."

Apparently pleased with the role of hostess, Selena poured further cups of tea.

"You seem unconvinced," she said, "by the suggestion that it had been borrowed by Edward Malvoisin."

"It did not look to me," I said, "like the sort of thing which one would readily lend or forget to ask to be returned. I suspect that the story of Malvoisin having trouble with his pen was an extempore invention by Patrick Ardmore."

"We know, of course," said Ragwort, "that he and the Contessa are colleagues of long standing and evidently friends. And we have reason to believe," he added, looking severely at Julia, "that he is a man who might too easily allow good nature to prevail over principle. But would he go to the length of telling lies to protect her if he thought her responsible for Malvoisin's death?"

"He may merely believe," I said, "that she had an assignation with Malvoisin and would be embarrassed by its disclosure. That is, I suppose, a possibility—perhaps she resented Malvoisin's advances less than she appeared to."

"I'm afraid," said Julia sadly, "that Edward Malvoisin's advances were of the kind which a well-bred and good-natured woman usually resents a great deal more than she appears to. I wonder if it really was Gabrielle's pen that Patrick found on the Coupee. Would it be very difficult to have a duplicate made? One sees advertisements, in gift catalogues and so forth, for goods to be supplied with initials on them, and they don't require the initials to be one's own."

"My dear Julia," said Ragwort kindly, for he knows she is not well versed in such matters, "if I have followed Hilary's description of it, that is not at all the sort of thing we are talking about. We are talking in effect of an item of jewellery, designed and made to order for a particular customer and intended to be entirely exclusive. No jeweller who valued his reputation would dream of duplicating the design without the consent of the original customer."

I had begun to feel a certain uneasiness. The longer I reflected on the matter, the more suspicion seemed to direct itself towards the interesting and attractive figure of the Contessa: whose mother, it seemed—I was conscious of the absurdity of attaching any sinister significance to such a thing—was the namesake and descendant of Rachel Alexandre, burnt as a witch in the intolerant seventeenth century.

It had occurred to me that none of those with whom I had spoken had actually seen the Contessa or heard any news of her since the night of Malvoisin's death. My anxiety was perhaps irrational; for I knew of no reason for her to wish Cantrip any harm, but when two persons simultaneously disappear, of whom one may be reasonably suspected of murderous propensities, it is difficult to feel no concern for the safety of the other.

This dismal train of thought was happily interrupted by the entry of Lilian, in possession of a new telex message.

CHAPTER **10** ═══

TELEX M. CANTRIP TO J. LARWOOD TRANSMITTED
HOTEL CLAIR DE LUNE MONTE CARLO 4:00 P.M.
THURSDAY 3RD MAY

Yoo-hoo there, Larwood, it's me here—ace investigator Catseyes Cantrip reporting back to base. Bet you'll never guess what I'm doing in Monte Carlo. Well you won't, not in a million years, so I'll tell you.

Things started happening just after I'd bunged off my last telex. I was on my own in the office at the back of the Alexandra and I suddenly saw this awful face at the window—sort of inhuman-looking, with glaring eyes and lots of teeth. First thing I thought was that it was a werewolf or something from outer space. Second thing I thought was that it looked just like old Wellieboots when someone tries to cite the Duke of Westminster's case. Third thing I thought was that it actually was old Wellieboots, and I was right.

I went sort of cold all over, same as you'd have done if you'd seen him without warning like that in a place you'd never expect him, but luckily we hadn't made what the Yanks call eye contact, so he didn't know I'd spotted him.

Well, you don't find High Court judges prowling round Sark glaring through office windows just for the fun of the thing, do you? The way I saw it was he must be up to something pretty sinister, and it didn't take long to work out what it was. I mean, we all know how steamed up he gets about people dodging tax and people like you telling them how to do it and the Revenue not being tough enough with them, and when you think about it, it must get a bit frustrating for him not being able to do anything worse than sit in court and wriggle his eyebrows at them. So one fine day he decides to breeze over to the nearest tax haven and rootle about in person, with a view to getting the goods on a few hardened tax planners and slinging them in jug until they're too old to be a danger to the public.

It was obviously my clients he was out to get the goods on, so I'd got to do something pretty fast—I mean, that's what Counsel's for, isn't it, to stop judges slinging his clients in jug?—but I wasn't too sure what. I suppose I could have gone straight out and confronted him, but I didn't know exactly what to confront him with. Anyway, I wasn't too keen on coming up against the eyebrows alone and unarmed and stone-cold sober, and I don't honestly think Carruthers would have been either, or Cecilia Mainwaring if it comes to that.

So I decided what I'd better do was follow him, discreetly and at a longish distance, and find out what he was up to. I gave him a minute or so to get ahead of me and then I slid out of the office and started after him

—he was about fifty yards away, making for the Coupee.

The way he behaved when he got there was pretty suspicious, if you ask me. There were two chaps with a tractor trying to unblock the entrance, and someone with nothing to be shifty about would have gone straight up and asked how long it would take or something like that. Wellieboots just stood looking at them from a distance for a bit, and then went and sat on a bench by the edge of the cliff and did an imitation of an innocent tourist admiring the view. So I went and sat on the bench on the opposite side and did an imitation of another innocent tourist.

Bit of a waste of talent really, because there wasn't much of an audience—just the two chaps trying to haul the carriage away and an old biddy in black nattering away with them like bosom pals. Same one I saw the day before, I suppose, unless there are lots of them in Sark. She must have been chatting them up with a view to hitching a lift—as soon as the entrance was cleared she nipped up on the tractor beside the driver and got driven straight across, riding shotgun.

Wellieboots stopped pretending to look at the view and made off along the Coupee, with me following and being careful not to get too close. I don't suppose he'd have recognised me, specially without a wig and gown —I've only been in front of him a couple of times in the Companies Court, asking for the usual compulsory order, and he didn't give me the feeling I'd made a lasting impression—but I thought I'd better be on the safe side. Actually I needn't have worried, because he never looked round once—just kept going all the way to the Avenue and down the hill to the harbour.

There was a boat at the quayside with a long queue

of people waiting to go on board. When Wellieboots
joined on the end of it I was a bit baffled—I hadn't
exactly been thinking of leaving right away, without
saying good-bye to Gabrielle or anything. Still, it
seemed pretty wet to give up at that stage, and I'd got
my briefcase with my pyjamas and toothbrush in it, and
this jolly good book that I told you about and I was still
in the middle of, so in the end I decided to go on board
as well.

It didn't make much odds as far as I was concerned
whether the boat was going to Jersey or Guernsey, and
I thought I'd feel a bit of an ass if I asked the chap
selling tickets, so I just kept quiet and gave him as much
as he wanted. I got a seat a good bit away from old
Wellieboots, next to a couple of characters talking
about corpses. They started with one who'd been
brought in that morning on a fishing boat and went on
to all the drownings and shipwrecks off Sark in the past
four hundred years or so—cheerful sort of subject when
you're putting out to sea.

After two or three hours we got near to some land
again, but it didn't look much like Jersey. It didn't look
much like Guernsey either. There was a huge great
wall, tremendously historic-looking, with long black
roofs like witches' hats sticking up at the back of it, and
I hadn't the faintest idea where it was.

If you're an ace investigator hot on the trail of a
villainous High Court judge it's a good thing to know
what town you're in, so I nipped off the boat as fast as I
could to find out where we were. The first thing I spotted was that everyone was talking Frogspeak, so putting two and two together I deduced we were probably
in France.

I felt a bit miffed at first. I've nothing against

France, except for it being full of foreigners, but it wasn't where I'd have expected old Wellieboots to go if he wanted to get the goods on my clients. I started thinking poor old Catseyes Cantrip might be on a wild-goose chase. Still, having got this far I was blowed if I was giving up right away, so when he got ashore I started tailing him again.

He went through a big gate in the historic-looking wall into a square with four or five cafés in it—you know the kind they have in France, tables on the pavement with sort of conservatories over them. He went and sat down in one of them, skulking in a corner pretending to read a newspaper, and I went and skulked in a corner in the one opposite. I was getting jolly hungry by this time, so I ordered a few ham pancakes and hoped he wouldn't move on before I got a chance to eat them.

He kept squinting at the café next door to the one I was in, as if he was watching for someone to come out of it. So I kept an eye on it as well, to see if I could spot who he was watching out for. When I saw who it was I simply couldn't believe it. You won't either, because it was Gabrielle.

Which absolutely just wasn't possible. Wellieboots and I had been across the Coupee as soon as it was open and gone straight down to the harbour and got the first boat going, so there was no way anyone could have got to France any faster than we did. But there she was.

"How very extraordinary," said Julia, pausing in bewilderment from her reading of the telex. "How on earth can she have done it?"

Sarah Caudwell

"Who knows?" I said. "Perhaps she flew over on her broomstick."

In truth, however, the reappearance at this juncture of the Contessa in the Place Chateaubriand in St. Malo was a matter of no greater astonishment to me than I can suppose it will be, dear reader, to yourself.

She didn't look as if she was doing anything frightfully secret or mysterious—she just went into the bank next door for a minute or two and then came back and sat down and started ordering lunch.

I couldn't go over and say hallo and ask how she'd got there, because of not wanting to be spotted by Wellieboots. It was obvious by this time that she was the one he was out to get the goods on, and of course I jolly well wasn't going to let him, but the way I saw it was that my best chance of foiling him was to let him go on thinking she was all alone and at his mercy, little knowing he'd got Catseyes Cantrip to reckon with.

That meant I couldn't let Gabrielle spot me either, in case she waved at me or something and blew my cover. It seemed a pity to be sitting eating lunch in the same square and not being able to talk to her, but looking on the bright side it was still a lot better than doing a possession action in West London County Court. Hope that turned out all right, by the way.

To get to the bank I'd have had to walk straight past her, so I had to get the waiter to change me some money into francs. He gave me about half the going rate of exchange and looked at me as if I was loopy. He thought I was even loopier when I asked for my bill before I'd finished eating, but I didn't want to get caught on the hop if anything happened suddenly.

I nearly did, all the same. I was taking more notice of Gabrielle than old Wellieboots, like anyone would with any sense, and she'd only just started making signals for her bill when I looked round and saw him heading for the gateway. So quick as a flash I was up and after him.

What happened next was pretty sinister. He pootled along to a car park a few hundred yards from the gate, went over to an oldish blue Renault, and climbed into the driving seat, cool as a cucumber. Then he just sat there, obviously waiting for Gabrielle to come along and drive off in one of the other cars.

Which to the razor-sharp intellect of the ace investigator meant just one thing—viz that he hadn't only known where she was going to be and what she was going to be doing, but he'd known it enough in advance to fix up to have a car waiting for him in the same place as hers. Well, have a think about ways he could have found all that out, and if you can think of one that isn't jolly sinister I'll buy the next three bottles of wine in the Corkscrew.

Did I ever tell you about an old mate of mine at Cambridge who was an absolute whiz with locks? He wasn't all that hot on land law, though, and he gave me some quite useful tips in exchange for helping with his essays. One of the things I used to practise on was the boot of a Renault—in top form I could do it in ninety seconds flat, just with an ordinary penknife like one's always got in one's pocket. And the car Wellieboots was sitting in was exactly the same model.

It seemed sort of meant, somehow. I walked on a bit, so as not to be coming from the same direction he was expecting Gabrielle from, and then I looped back, doing an imitation of a suave young English milord strolling casually through a car park. When I got to the Renault I ducked down at the back of it and got to work —there was a wall behind me, and not a lot of people about, so I'd have been unlucky to get spotted.

It took me just under two minutes, which wasn't bad considering I was out of practise. I'd just finished when I saw Gabrielle walking across the car park towards a rather snazzy Mercedes. Wellieboots must have seen her, too, because he started his engine. So I opened the boot and nipped in.

It was one of those things that seem like a good idea at the time and a slightly less good idea about a minute later, but by that time we were moving quite fast.

Don't let's have a bit in our book where Carruthers gets stuck in the boot of a car for five hours. I suppose there are some chaps who write books who could go on for pages about it and make it sound jolly exciting, but I just don't see how they do it. You can forget describing the scenery for a start, because there isn't any.

It was the most boring five hours I've ever spent, even counting that time you got me to see three Shakespeare plays one after another in the same day. It was a lot more uncomfortable as well, because the only way there was room for me was with my knees scrunched up against my chin and my head at right angles to my spine, and not able to move anything more than about an inch. I couldn't even risk dropping off to sleep, because I'd got my handkerchief looped round the door handle and I had to keep hold of both ends of it to keep the door sort of shut but not shut at the same time—I'd never tried opening the boot of a Renault from the inside, and I thought it would be a bad time to find out I couldn't.

It felt as if we were driving mostly on motorway, and by the time we stopped I suppose we must have gone about two hundred and fifty miles. I was practically past caring whether anyone spotted me climbing out, but I made myself count to sixty to give Wellieboots time to get clear. Then I opened the door a bit and had a squint round.

It was beginning to get dark, and I was in a big garden with walls round it at the back of a largish house. There didn't seem to be anyone around, so I crawled out. I thought for a bit that I was never going to be able to stand up straight again, but I managed it in the end. Then I looked round and there was the Mercedes, parked a few yards away.

When I got outside into the street I could see the town we were in was the kind of place Gabrielle would be keen on—tremendously historic-looking, with a big castle and lots of cobblestones, and a covered market like you see in old towns in the country. The place we were parked at the back of looked like a rather grand sort of hunting lodge, but when I got round to the front it turned out to be a hotel, called after some bird called Blanche.

It seemed like a pretty fair bet that Gabrielle and Wellieboots would both be having dinner there, so I pootled in and asked for a table.

The headwaiter gave me a slightly cross-eyed sort of look, as if I wasn't quite as swanny as he'd have liked me to be—that's Frogspeak for having a clean shirt on and a crease in your trousers and generally not looking as if you'd spent the past five hours in the boot of a Renault. Still, he gave me a table all right—tucked

away in a corner where no one would notice me, which
was fine as far as I was concerned.

He can't have thought Wellieboots was all that
swanny either—he was at a table in another darkish
corner, with a boar's head with big tusks mounted on
the wall behind him. There wasn't a lot of difference
between them, but the boar was friendlier-looking.

It was quite a while before Gabrielle came in, and
when she did she was with a tall dark chap who I suppose you'd say was frightfully good-looking—not all
that young, though, and probably putting on weight a
bit if he hadn't had his clothes cut so as to hide it. I
couldn't think to begin with how he came into the
picture, but then I remembered her saying she was
going to meet her husband somewhere on the way
back from the Channel Islands. So obviously that's who
it was.

The headwaiter perked up like anything, because
Gabrielle was looking tremendously swanny, and took
them to a table outside on the terrace, with lots of
flowers and candles and things. Her husband must have
fixed it up in advance to make it all sort of romantic.
You'd have thought he hadn't seen her for months—he
kept kissing her hand and looking into her eyes and
generally being pretty soppy—but I suppose foreigners
always carry on like that, specially Italians.

I could see that Gabrielle was in a bit of a tizz,
though. She kept taking things out of her handbag and
putting them down all over the place, as if there was
something that ought to be there and wasn't—the sort
of thing you're always doing but she usually isn't—with
a lot of hand-waving, and all the waiters gathering
round trying to look helpful and sympathetic. I thought
she must have lost her chequebook or her credit cards

or something, but one of the waiters eventually got round to serving me and, according to him, it was her pen. I still didn't think it was like her to make such a fuss, but I suppose it was the one she told me about that was a present from her husband, and she was in a flap in case he was miffed about it.

"Or do you suggest," said Selena, regarding me with an expression not wholly sceptical and again refilling my teacup, "that it was because she remembered where she might have lost it?"

"But if she lost it," said Julia, "in such dramatic circumstances as that would seem to imply, then surely she would have noticed long before she reached—where do we think all this happened?"

"It sounds to me," said Ragwort, evidently making an unsuccessful effort to resist the sin of envy, "remarkably like Dourdan. It's a charming little town between Paris and Chartres and during the Middle Ages was a favourite residence of the French royal family. There is an admirable hotel there named after Blanche of Castile, the mother, as of course you know, of the sainted Louis IX."

I don't say there's any meal that I'd willingly go five hours in the boot of a Renault for, because actually there isn't, but if there was, the one I had on Tuesday evening would probably be it. They gave me pancakes with bits of lobster in them and a sort of rabbit stew cooked with wine, and I started thinking that being an ace investigator wasn't too bad after all.

There didn't seem much risk of anyone going any

further that night, so I nipped out to the reception desk and booked a room and got them to fix up a hired car for the next morning. I had to wave a lot of plastic of course—you can say what you like about credit cards leading people into debt, but they're jolly useful when you haven't got any money.

I wondered if I ought to leave a note for Gabrielle to warn her what was going on, but I thought there was too much risk of Wellieboots intercepting it. So I lurked around long enough to make sure she and her husband went upstairs before he did, in case he'd got any ideas about searching their room, and then I went to bed.

I couldn't manage to get my paws on a telex machine, and if Henry says I ought to have rung Chambers first thing in the morning to say where I was, tell him that's exactly the sort of fatheaded suggestion I'd expect him to make. Henry's idea of first thing in the morning is nine-thirty, which is ten-thirty in France, and by then we'd all been on the road for more than an hour, heading for the south.

I was in a rather nifty little Peugeot, with the Mercedes ahead of me and Wellieboots tagging along behind in the Renault. I'd had this tremendously subtle idea of staying in front of him, so that he wouldn't be suspicious about always seeing me in his rearview mirror. It meant he kept seeing me ahead of him of course, but you wouldn't think of someone following you from the front, would you?

We were driving through one of those bits of France where the hills have vines growing all over them and the names on the signposts make you feel as if you're driving through the wine list in a rather high-class restaurant. It makes you start thinking about lunch a lot sooner than you normally would—by twelve

I was pretty peckish and by one I was simply ravenous. The signposts started featuring a town called Beaune, which somehow sounded as if it might have some nice restaurants, and I hoped we might be going there, but the Mercedes went straight past the turning. It stopped a bit further on, though, at a place with vineyards all round it and a roof made of pink tiles, which called itself the *auberge de* something or other.

It would have been a chance to have a quick word with Gabrielle before Wellieboots turned up, and afterwards I wished I'd taken it, but her husband still looked as if he was being a bit soppy, and I felt as if I'd sort of be barging in on a two's-company situation. So I kept out of sight until they'd gone into the courtyard at the back, where the restaurant was. Then I went and sat in the bar, which looked out on the road, to watch for old Wellieboots.

The barman brought me the menu and a glass of blackcurrant juice—he was a youngish chap, slightly depressed-looking, as if he'd got problems or toothache or something—and reading the menu made me even hungrier. There was still no sign of old Wellieboots, and I couldn't think what had happened to him—the Mercedes was parked in full view of the road, and not exactly what you'd call inconspicuous, so he'd have had to be pretty dim to miss it.

After a bit an oldish chap came along who seemed to be the owner and gave me some more blackcurrant juice and asked me what I'd like to eat. He was a red-faced, twinkly sort of chap, the kind you'd get to dress up in a red cloak and white whiskers for a Christmas party. Which would be a mistake, because if ever there was a chap who'd take any chance he got to chisel a starving two-year-old out of its last lollipop, it was this twinkly chap.

What gets me is that the two-faced old skuldug-gerer was so tremendously hospitable, saying what a privilege it was to have an English visitor and being sympathetic about my problems with lunch—viz whether to have the duck or the cassoulet with goose and how to make sure I'd got room for *marrons glacé* at the end.

When we started talking about what kind of wine I was going to drink, he twinkled like anything and said he'd got one or two things that were rather special and weren't on the wine list. He wouldn't offer them to everyone, he said, because there were some people a really fine vintage burgundy would simply be wasted on, but he could see I wasn't one of them. So how about coming down to the cellar and tasting them, to see which I liked best?

It meant I had to stop watching out for old Wel-lieboots of course, but I'd more or less decided by then that he must have got lost somehow and wasn't going to show up. I think the blackcurrant juice must have had something in it, because I'd started feeling slightly squiffy and trailing High Court judges didn't seem as important as it had before.

So I followed him, absolutely like a lamb, along a passageway and through a trapdoor and down into the cellar.

There were a lot of bottles on racks with grilles over them and a cupboard with some glasses and a couple more bottles. He opened them both and poured me a glass from each of them, and I went on thinking how tremendously hospitable he was. Then he twin-kled again and told me to take my time about tasting them while he want upstairs to see how things were going in the kitchen.

There was something about his last twinkle that reminded me of someone, but I couldn't remember who. I was still trying to think who it was and why it somehow made me feel a bit nervous when the light went out and I heard the bolt being drawn across the trapdoor.

I yelled out, "What's going on?" and all I got was, "Rest tranquil, my brave, rest tranquil." I'll make him rest tranquil all right if ever I get my hands on him, the double-crossing son of a six-headed rattlesnake.

And then someone else gave a fiendish sort of laugh, like an armadillo choking on a pineapple. I'd have recognised it anywhere, specially as the last time I heard it was when I was in the Companies Court and couldn't remember the terms of the usual compulsory order. You're probably not going to believe it, but I absolutely swear it was old Wellieboots.

And what I want to know is, are High Court judges allowed to lock Counsel up in cellars and, if not, what's one supposed to do about it?

CHAPTER **II** ═══

This being a question preeminently suitable for consideration by leading Counsel, it was a happy coincidence that Basil Ptarmigan should at this moment return to his room. While he removed his wig and black silk gown, accepted a cup of tea, found the papers for his next consultation, and expressed in flattering terms his pleasure at my presence, the news was conveyed to him of Cantrip's incarceration by a member of the senior judiciary.

That Sir Arthur Welladay had power, in certain circumstances, to send Cantrip to prison seemed to Basil to be beyond dispute. If Cantrip in proceedings before him were to commit some flagrant contempt of court, as by throwing a heavy volume of the law reports at his head, the judge could quite properly instruct the tipstaff to commit him to the Tower—of that there was no doubt.

On the other hand, to encourage a French innkeeper to lock him up in a cellar, when Cantrip had done no worse than stow inoffensively away in a motorcar—a motorcar, moreover, being driven by the judge, so far as one could tell, in his private rather than his judicial capacity—was not, in Basil's opinion, at all the same thing. He would not say that the judge had no jurisdiction to do it—it might be overaudacious, in the absence of clear authority, to go so far as that; but if he had jurisdiction then he had exceeded it; or, if he had jurisdiction and had not exceeded it, then at the very least he had exercised it in a most improper manner.

It would not do—something would have to be done. One should have a quiet word, perhaps, with someone at the Lord Chancellor's office, where they would know the procedure for dealing with cases of this kind. It was true, of course, that many very eminent judges had continued to exercise their judicial functions with perfect competence while suffering from more or less serious forms of derangement. One had only to think of—

"Basil," said Selena, interrupting what would undoubtedly have been a most interesting account of judicial insanity since the beginning of the nineteenth century, "are you suggesting that Mr. Justice Welladay has simply gone mad?"

"Oh, certainly," said Basil, with that perfect equanimity in the face of the unexpected which is so vital to a successful practice at the Bar. "What other explanation can there be? It's very sad, of course, but one should certainly have foreseen it—poor Arthur, he's been giving some very odd judgments lately, as Julia and I both know to our cost."

"I know," said Selena rather doubtfully, "that you both had cases in front of him last term and that he decided against you."

"But apart from that," said Ragwort, "there have surely been no overt signs of instability?"

"Ah, my dear Desmond, you have not known him as long as I have. On the subject of tax avoidance he has never, I think I may say, been entirely rational."

"It seems very hard on Cantrip," said Julia, "to be locked up as an expert in tax planning."

"I suppose that Arthur regards him as guilty by association—it shows how far his affliction has gone. By the way, I should not have imagined that the cellars of French country inns were normally equipped with telex facilities—do we happen to know if Arthur let Michael out of the cellar, or did he escape?"

Julia, thus prompted, resumed her reading of the telex. A quite deplorable possibility began, as she read, to present itself to my mind.

Another thing that let's not have in our book is a bit where Carruthers gets locked up in a wine cellar. It's almost as boring as being stuck in the boot of a Renault —not so uncomfortable, because you can move about a bit, but just as dark and a lot more nervous-making, because at least with a Renault you know you'll get out in the end.

Mind you, it wouldn't be so bad for Carruthers, because he'd have us on his side. We could put in a window wide enough to squeeze out of, with bars he could loosen with his penknife. I didn't have anything like that—just solid stone walls without an opening anywhere except for the trapdoor. Or we could have some incredibly attractive bird about the place who's fascinated by his suave sophistication and comes and lets him out. The only people I'd had any chance to fascinate were the twinkly chap and the depressed-looking barman, and it didn't look as if I'd done frightfully well. And we could make him a smoker, so he'd have a lighter or some matches to brighten things up a bit. And while we're about it we might let him have a packet of nice sandwiches in his pocket.

The trouble with real life is that you don't know whether you're the hero or just some nice chap who gets bumped off in chapter five to show what a rotter the villain is without anyone minding too much. I hadn't a clue why they'd locked me in the cellar in the first place, and as far as I could see it was just as likely as not that they meant to leave me there until I died of starvation—which actually felt like being in the next half hour or so. I didn't even have the choice of drinking myself to death on vintage burgundy, because apart from the two that the twinkly chap had opened the bottles were all behind burglarproof grilles.

I drank one glass of the wine he'd poured and tried to look on the bright side. Actually there wasn't one, but one thing that struck me was that if you're running a restaurant, sooner or later you have to send someone down to the wine cellar. So I decided that if anyone did come down I was jolly well going to make him let me out, whether he wanted to or not.

I took my tie off and fastened it across the steps to the trapdoor, hoping the twinkly chap would be the first person down and break his beastly neck, or at any rate be in a good position for being biffed on the head with a bottle. Then I drank another glass of burgundy to try to keep my strength up and settled down at the bottom of the steps to see what happened, with the bottles beside me ready for biffing. After a bit I fell asleep, which actually is about all you can do when you're locked up in a cellar in the dark.

The next thing I knew the light had come on and someone was looking through the trapdoor saying, "Monsieur, come quickly please."

It sounded like a good offer, so I got up and started up the steps. I forgot about the tie and scraped my shins and swore a bit, and the chap at the top started shushing me. It was the depressed-looking barman, and I couldn't get a word out of him except "Shush" until we were out-of-doors and well away from the restaurant.

It was dark outside, though not as dark as in the cellar, and according to my watch it was nearly eleven —which meant I'd missed dinner as well as lunch. I wasn't too sure where the barman chap was taking me, so I kept hold of the bottle just in case he tried to push me down a well or anything—he didn't look like the sort of chap who pushes people down wells, but after what had happened already I didn't feel like going by appearances.

In the end it turned out he was just taking me back to the Peugeot—they'd put it round the back, out of sight of the road. He sort of waved me towards it and said, "Monsieur, no trouble, please?"

Well, no one can say I'm the sort of chap who makes scenes about the steak not being rare enough or having to wait twenty minutes for coffee, but when I go into a restaurant for lunch and they leave me to starve in the wine cellar for nine hours I think I'm entitled to feel pretty miffed. So I told the barman chap that personally I didn't see why there shouldn't be trouble, lots and lots and lots of it, and if I didn't get a jolly good explanation I was going to tell the whole story to the local fuzz, not to speak of Interpol and the British ambassador and the chaps who publish the Michelin Guide.

Actually, of course, the last thing I was going to do was pop round to the local fuzzery, because in the first place it would have taken hours and in the second place it wouldn't have done any good and in the third place I'd have had to tell them about Wellieboots, and you can't go setting the foreign fuzz on a fellow member of Lincoln's Inn, can you, even if he is pretty villainous? But I didn't see why I should tell the barman chap that.

His English wasn't all that hot, so he may have missed some of the finer points of what I was saying, but I could see he was getting the gist. When I got to the bit about the Michelin Guide, he definitely looked stricken and started trying to plead with me. He said, "My uncle is an old man, monsieur," and tapped the side of his head to indicate loopiness. "The war, monsieur."

I was just going to tell him pretty sternly that other people had uncles who'd been in the war as well, and it hadn't made them loopy enough to go locking people in cellars, when I realised who it was that the twinkly chap had reminded me of with his final twinkle. He'd looked just like my Uncle Hereward does when he's going to do something frightful, and if I'd tried to tell the barman character that my Uncle Hereward wasn't loopy enough to lock people in cellars, I couldn't have looked him in the eye when I said it. So I gave up and said I comprehended absolutely.

I did point out though that being on the verge of starvation makes people a bit edgy, and he nipped off to the restaurant and came back with a loaf of bread and a chicken leg and some pâté and some cheese and things. He stayed with me while I was eating them and we shared the bottle of wine I'd brought up from the cellar and talked about uncles and got quite matey.

He said it hadn't been his uncle's idea to lock me up—he'd been egged on to do it by an Englishman, a big man with thick eyebrows and lots of teeth who was a friend of his from the old days. That was all the barman chap knew about it, but at least it showed that hearing old Wellieboots laugh hadn't been a hallucination.

I was getting a bit worried about Gabrielle by this time, because now I knew Wellieboots wouldn't stick at putting people in cellars I didn't know what he would stick at, and I felt pretty miffed with myself for not warning her about him when I had the chance. I decided the only thing for it was to go on heading south to Monte Carlo and hope he didn't manage to do anything too serious before I could get in touch with her again. I thought if I kept going and she and her husband had stopped overnight somewhere, we'd probably get to Monte Carlo at about the same time.

I had the roads pretty much to myself and there was a big river going the same way as I was, so I made quite good going and didn't get lost much. I suppose I ought to have been worrying about not getting back to Chambers and Henry being frightfully miffed, but actually I wasn't. There's something about the stars all shining and the air being warm and smelling of oranges that makes you not think much about Henry and more about how nice it would be to write poetry and read it to someone.

The sun was just coming up when I got to a town called Avignon. I think I've got a sort of intuition about the kind of places that Gabrielle might fancy—it was another of these historic-looking places with a wall all the way round it, and it struck me as soon as I saw it that she'd have wanted to stay there. I drove in through one of the gateways and half a minute later there was the Mercedes, parked in a side street next to a tremendously elegant-looking hotel.

I did a bit of cautious pootling about, and there in the next street was the Renault, so I knew that Wellieboots was still on the trail. I didn't think anyone would be on the move for at least a couple of hours, so I found a strategic spot to leave the Peugeot and went off to look for breakfast.

There was a big square with a clock tower on one side of it and lots of cafés. The one at the top already had an awning up over the terrace and looked as if it was open, so I sat down there and asked for coffee and croissants.

One thing I'd made up my mind about was not passing up another chance to warn Gabrielle what was going on, so I borrowed some paper from the café owner and wrote her a note explaining everything.

Life being what it is, I thought if I took it myself the first person I'd run into in the lobby of the hotel would be old Wellieboots, wriggling his eyebrows and wanting to know why I wasn't still locked in the cellar. So I asked the café owner if there was anyone who'd deliver it, and he offered to send his son, viz a quite bright-looking lad by the name of Gaston.

I told Gaston to make sure it wasn't just left in a pigeonhole but taken straight up to Gabrielle in her room, and to hang about a bit in case there was an answer, and to scarper prontissimo if he saw a big man with thick eyebrows and a lot of teeth. After he'd gone I started worrying in case he gave it to the wrong person, and then I started worrying even more in case it got to

Gabrielle and she simply thought I'd gone loopy, but there wasn't much I could do about it except eat another croissant.

The café owner thought it was all fantastically romantic. He'd got the idea that I was trying to make an assignation with a beautiful married woman and the chap with eyebrows was her husband, and explaining it wasn't like that seemed just too difficult to be worth it. He said it was like the troubadours—he said there used to be a lot of these troubadour chaps in that part of the world and they went in for having hopeless passions for beautiful married women who were tremendously virtuous. So they never got anywhere and had to spend all their time writing poetry and going off on the occasional Crusade. He said there was some Italian chap as well, who'd fallen for a bird called Laura, and Avignon was where he'd first met her.

Gaston was away for ages and I started to think he must have got kidnapped or something. By the time I saw him coming back I'd got so pessimistic I thought the letter he was holding was probably the same one I'd sent him with. It wasn't, though, it was from Gabrielle.

It didn't sound as if she thought I was loopy after all —actually it sounded as if she was pretty impressed, because it started, "Dear Michael, you are quite wonderful," so I felt rather chuffed.

Anyway, the gist of it was that if I carried on to Monte Carlo and booked in at the Clair de Lune, she'd get in touch with me there and we could work out a strategy for dealing with old Wellieboots. So here I am, and I'm jolly well not leaving Monte Carlo until I've found out what Wellieboots is up to and put a stop to him persecuting Gabrielle. Just tell Henry hard cheese and sucks boo.

Over and out—Cantrip

There was much indignation. Cantrip by his absence had imposed, it was felt, quite sufficient inconvenience on his fellow juniors without the additional burden of conveying to Henry the unconciliatory message suggested in his final paragraph. Ragwort was especially severe. His sense of the world's unfairness, assuaged in respect of St. Malo and Dourdan by the thought of Cantrip starving in a wine cellar, had been rekindled by the image of him breakfasting in the ancient city of the Popes, oblivious and undeserving of its architectural and artistic glories.

My own attention remained preoccupied by the deplorable possibility which had presented itself and was beginning, the more I reflected on it, to seem increasingly probable.

"Basil," I said, when at last I had a chance to be heard, "there is a question, if you would be so kind, which I should like to ask you. When you spoke a day or two ago of teasing Sir Arthur Welladay—"

I was interrupted, however, by the reappearance of Lilian, announcing the arrival of Colonel Cantrip. Knowing his concern for the safety of his nephew, she had telephoned him at his club to tell him of the telex message, and the old soldier had lost no time in coming round to New Square to see it for himself.

Expressing in graceful phrases his delight at the Colonel's visit, Basil gave no sign that he had or could have any claim on his time more pressing than the entertainment of this new and honoured guest. The Colonel was settled in a comfortable armchair and provided with a cup of tea. Julia, after a moment's hesitation—she no doubt wondered, but sensibly not for long, if his feelings might be wounded by the reference to himself—handed him the telex.

"My dear Hilary," said Basil, extending his long hands in a gesture which seemed to promise a cornucopia of enlightenment, "there was some matter on which you thought that I might be of assistance?"

"It is concerned," I said, "with the provisions of a discretionary settlement, of the kind which I understand to have been in vogue in the early part of the 1970s. Julia was telling me a few days ago that at that time the Revenue regarded the persons entitled in default of appointment, even if they never actually received anything from the settled fund, as liable for tax on gains realised by the trustees. A practice developed, I gather—Julia called it 'teasing the Revenue'—of naming as the default beneficiary some person professionally committed, as it were, to upholding and defending their opinion—the Chancellor of the Exchequer, for example, or the chairman of the Board of Inland Revenue. Have I understood the matter correctly?"

"Perfectly correctly," said Basil. "I cannot attempt to improve on Julia's account of it. You must understand, of course, that it was not generally intended that the Revenue should ever become aware of the existence of the settlement, but it was thought that if they did, the inclusion of such a provision would embarrass them sufficiently to afford us all a little innocent amusement. Dear me, I'm afraid you will think us disgracefully frivolous."

"And may I ask," I continued, "whether you ever happened—"

Henry entered, his brow dark with displeasure, to apologise with heavy sarcasm for interrupting the tea party and to inform Basil of the arrival of those attending his next consultation: "Mr. Netherspoon, sir, of Netherspoon and Co. With his client, sir—and you know what His Grace is like if he's kept waiting. I did remind you this morning, sir, I didn't think you'd have forgotten again already."

"I hadn't forgotten, Henry," said Basil. "I simply didn't expect them quite so soon. If punctuality is the politeness of princes, then it seems rather presumptuous of a mere duke to be so ostentatiously on time. Dear me, how extremely tiresome. Colonel Cantrip—Hilary—I'm afraid, as you see, that you'll have to excuse me."

Selena had already begun to collect teacups, Ragwort to plump up cushions, and Julia to shepherd the Colonel towards the door.

"Basil, forgive me," I said, "but I must ask you one further question. Did you ever happen, by any chance, to combine your teasing of the Revenue with your teasing of Sir Arthur Welladay by making him the default beneficiary under such a settlement?"

"Why yes," said Basil, his attention already almost entirely engrossed by the papers for his consultation. "Yes, Hilary, now that you mention it, I believe I sometimes did. I don't think I ever mentioned him by name—that would somehow have seemed rather crude. It seemed more elegant to bring him in by way of a class gift."

"To the descendants of a named individual?"

"Exactly."

"You would have had to know the name, then, of one of his parents or grandparents."

"Yes, obviously." He smiled gently at the notion of this presenting any difficulty. "But everyone knows, of course, that Arthur is a grandson of that very eminent judge, the late Sir Walter Palgrave."

CHAPTER 12

"I cannot imagine," I said with some asperity, "how any of you can hope to attain eminence in your profession when you are so shamefully ignorant of matters regarded as common knowledge by those whom you seek to emulate. If someone had told me yesterday that Mr. Justice Welladay was a descendant of Sir Walter Palgrave . . ." I was obliged to pause, for I could not immediately think what use it would have been to me to have learnt this a day earlier.

"You would have wasted a great deal of time," said Selena, taking rather unfair advantage of my involuntary aposiopesis, "trying to arrange to meet him, when as it turns out he was busy chasing countesses across France and locking people up in cellars."

We had adjourned by common consent to the first floor, where the Colonel, installed as by right of kinship at the desk usually occupied by his nephew, was continuing his perusal of the telex, chortling from time to time at those passages which evidently gave him particular satisfaction. It appeared, however, that he was not wholly inattentive to our discussion, for he now looked up from his reading.

"I say," he said, "this Welladay you're talking about—is he the chap that Mike calls Wellieboots?" We confirmed that he was. "I used to know an Arthur Welladay during the war—bit of a pompous young ass—wouldn't be the same one, would it?"

Ragwort extracted from the bookshelf behind him the latest edition of *Who's Who*. The particulars given there of the judge's military career established beyond question his identity with the Colonel's wartime acquaintance.

"Well, I'm damned," said the Colonel. "What's young Arthur Welladay doing locking Mike up in cellars?"

"That is indeed, sir, a most interesting question," said Ragwort. "We had at first assumed that Sir Arthur had simply gone—was merely suffering from the heavy strain of his judicial duties. But in view of the information which we have just elicited from Basil, it may perhaps be suggested that his conduct has more rational and at the same time more sinister motives."

"I say," said the Colonel, "you don't mean Arthur's the one who's going round bumping off people who get mixed up with this Daffodil business?"

Thus simply and directly stated, the proposition was at once perceived by the young barristers to be patently absurd. Sir Arthur Welladay was one of Her Majesty's judges and a member of Lincoln's Inn. Whatever one might say to his discredit—and Julia at least would have been willing to say a good deal—one could not suppose him capable of killing anyone.

The Colonel looked slightly surprised.

"Well," he said cheerfully, "you can't say that exactly, can you? I mean, he did the combined ops training at Achnacarry, so he damned well ought to know how to kill people. And you can't say he's never actually done it, because of course he has. Funnily enough, I think the first time must have been on Sark—I was there, in a manner of speaking."

They stared at him, reduced to uncustomary silence.

"Colonel Cantrip," I said, "I think that you had better tell us the whole story."

The events which the Colonel now recounted to us had taken place towards the end of February in the year 1944. Though recently wounded in action in North Africa, he had been considered sufficiently fit to return with his unit to England, where expectation was general of the imminent invasion of Normandy. To his evident dismay and indignation, he had found himself incarcerated (as he regarded the matter) in a military hospital in Portsmouth.

"Pretty grim sort of hellhole it was too," said the Colonel. "The matron had X-ray eyes and could smell alcohol at five hundred yards and the medical officer was a pigheaded Scotchman who wouldn't pass me as fit until I could dance a Highland fling three times round Ben Nevis.

"So there I was, sitting around with nothing to do except try to make enough nuisance of myself to get chucked out of the beastly place, when Squiffy Bodgem rolled in, with two bars of chocolate and a bottle of whiskey. Old mate of mine—we'd been on the same training course at Achnacarry in '41. We'd lost touch a bit since then —turned out he'd been Portsmouth-based for quite a while, running his own commando unit. Well, I didn't think hospital visiting was much in Squiffy's line, specially with armfuls of whiskey and chocolates, so I asked him what he was after.

"The gist of the story was that he'd got everything lined up for a raid on Sark in ten days' time—him and another officer and four men. He'd been quite surprised to get the go-ahead for it, because we'd pretty much shut up shop for raiding by that time—saving everything for Normandy. But he'd managed to persuade the powers that be that Sark was a likely place for picking up a few odds and ends that might be useful to the intelligence chaps—or even a prisoner or two, which would be even better of course. Well, Squiffy thought he'd persuaded them—most probably they just reckoned it would be worth making a bit of noise in the Channel Islands and maybe bluffing the Germans into moving a few more men over there from Normandy. Whichever it was, they'd told old Squiffy he could have a go, and of course he'd been as pleased as Punch about it.

"Then he hit a snag. The idea was, you see, to hitch a lift down there on a naval submarine, get as close in as the sub could take them, and finish the journey in a collapsible landing craft. In some places that would leave you with not much to worry about from the point of view of inshore navigation—just get the Navy to point you towards land and Bob's your uncle. Sark's a bit different—dodgy currents and a lot of nasty rocks where you wouldn't expect them, so if you're landing a boat there in the dark, it's better to know your way about a bit. No problem for Squiffy, though, because he'd got a Guernsey lad in his unit who'd been a fisherman before the war—got out the month before the Germans landed—and knew the Sark coast like the back of his hand. Then the Guernsey lad goes and makes a nonsense of a parachute jump in some training exercise and puts himself out of action, and there's Squiffy with no navigator.

"He was just wondering if he was going to have to call the whole thing off when someone told him about me being in Portsmouth locked up in the hellhole. He remembered me telling him I'd once spent my school holidays on Sark and done a bit of sailing there, and he thought I sounded like the answer to a maiden's prayer. He was a bit downhearted at first when he found I still had a leg in plaster, but I pointed out that if I was only navigating I wouldn't need to do any climbing, so it didn't make any odds."

"You hadn't mentioned," said Selena, "that your leg was still in plaster. That may perhaps explain the reluctance of the medical officer to pass you as fit."

"If he hadn't been so blasted pigheaded, he'd have taken it out of plaster," said the Colonel. "Anyway, apart from that I was as fit as a flea, so I told Squiffy to count me in on the party. He wanted to make it all official to start with —you know, have me seconded to his unit for the purposes of the operation—but I talked him out of that. 'Squiffy,' I said, 'once we start putting things in writing and signing them in triplicate, what's going to happen? You know what's going to happen,' I said. 'It's all going to end up on some chap's desk in War House. And what are the chaps in War House there for? They're there to find out if any of us have got a bit of fun lined up and put the kybosh on it. If you try to make it official, you can kiss good-bye to me as a navigator, and probably the whole operation. Squiffy,' I said, 'don't do it.' He saw the sense of it in the end, so I

stayed unofficial. Never stir up trouble when you don't
have to, that's my motto," said the Colonel virtuously.

Ragwort blinked.

"I managed to sneak out for a couple of training ses-
sions, and that's when I met young Welladay—he was the
other officer in the party. Nice enough lad, just coming up
to nineteen and still pretty wet behind the ears—Squiffy
was taking him along on this raid to give him a chance to
see a bit of life. Terribly keen and serious he was—would
keep on about freedom and justice and all that and saying
that was why we'd all volunteered for combined ops. I told
him I'd done it for the extra thirteen bob a day and the
chance of getting eggs for breakfast, but he went all pink
round the edges and wouldn't believe me. So in the end I
had to biff him, and after that we got on all right."

"Oh dear, Colonel," said Julia, in despairing protest.

Touched by this womanly remonstrance, the Colonel
patted her hand.

"The trip down on the submarine was a bit dreary of
course—stuffy and smelly and no room to move, you know
what submarines are like—and I can't say young Arthur did
much to brighten things up. I was telling Squiffy about my
getaway from the hellhole—you know, dodging Matron
and the M.O. and giving the chap in the next bed a yarn to
spin them when they noticed I was missing—and blow me
if Arthur didn't get in a flap about it. He'd known I was
unofficial, of course, but he hadn't known I was as unofficial
as all that, and he started worrying about whether going
AWOL from the hellhole made me a deserter within the
meaning of subparagraph something or other of paragraph
whatever-it-was of *King's Regulations.* That's the kind of

chap he was, you see—knew *King's Regulations* backwards and took it all seriously.

"I told him if we got back all right they probably wouldn't shoot me for it, and if we didn't, getting shot for desertion was going to be the least of my worries, but it didn't do any good. We were in the blasted sub for the best part of eighteen hours, and he went on about it the whole time, except when we were asleep—I daresay he dreamed about it as well. Nice enough lad, you see, but not a lot of sense.

"The sub came up about a mile off Sark around two in the morning. We got our gear together, blacked up with boot polish, and transferred to the landing craft. The skipper made a few dirty cracks about my chances of finding the right beach—the Navy never think anyone else knows how to navigate—and I told him we'd be back by six and expecting a decent breakfast.

"We got through the rocks all right and made a landing on the western side of the Coupee. There'd been two or three earlier raids on Sark and they'd all landed on the eastern side, up by Derrible Bay, but the latest word was that the beaches there were mined—the last lot had found out the hard way about two months before. So the western side looked like a better bet.

"There's a path at the northern end of the beach that takes you right up to the top—steepish, but not what you'd call a climb—and I got the landing craft in within a few yards of it. I told Squiffy I was making life a damned sight too easy for him, and off he went with the rest of the chaps.

"The next couple of hours were pretty quiet. We'd picked a night with no moon, of course, so I couldn't see my hand in front of my face, to say nothing of anything else. I couldn't hear anything either, which was a pretty good sign —if the chaps had run into trouble, there'd have been some noise. So I just sat in the landing craft with nothing to do except wonder what was going on and curse the M.O. for keeping me in plaster. The only thing I was worried about was getting back to the sub on time. It had been pretty decent of the skipper to give us until six—he had to get the sub underwater again by dawn, of course, and it didn't leave much leeway—so we couldn't expect him to cut it any finer.

"Then I heard firing—only two or three shots, but it sounded loud enough to wake up every German on the island—and it looked as if things might be going to liven up a bit.

"I made sure we were ready for a quick getaway, and a few minutes later I heard someone slithering down the path, making a good deal more noise than they ought to. It turned out to be Welladay and another chap—tough little Glaswegian called McCormack, straight from the Gorbals —he'd been shot in the shoulder and was bleeding quite a bit. Welladay wasn't hurt, but he was looking pretty shaken. I helped him haul McCormack aboard the landing craft and asked what the blazes had happened and where the others had got to.

"He said things had gone pretty well to begin with. They'd spotted a German sentry patrolling the Coupee and followed him back to base. That turned out to be a guard hut at the southern end, just inside Little Sark. He was on his own there and not expecting any trouble, so taking the hut was money for old rope. They had him tied up and gagged before he knew what was happening and just shoved him into a corner, meaning to bring him back with them when they were finished. Welladay and McCormack stayed to search the hut and keep an eye on the prisoner while the other three went off to scout round Little Sark.

"You probably think searching a guard hut would be pretty easy, but it wasn't as simple as it sounds. There was a desk and a cupboard, both full of all sorts of papers—too much to bring the whole lot back—so they had some sorting to do. Trouble was, it was damned difficult to know what was going to be useful from the point of view of intelligence. You couldn't expect to find something marked 'Hitler to Goering—Top Secret'; it was local newspapers and letters from girlfriends and things like that that the intelligence geezers got excited about. Toffee papers even —I once knew a chap in intelligence who claimed he could predict the whole German strategy for the next six months if he knew what they were wrapping their toffees in.

"So Welladay and McCormack were kept pretty busy trying to work out what was worth taking and what wasn't, with just an oil lamp to see by, and it's not too surprising that they weren't taking much notice of the prisoner. Pity they didn't, though—he must have had a gun stashed away quite near to where they'd left him, and whoever tied him up didn't seem to have made much of a job of it—so all of a sudden they were under fire.

"McCormack was hit and Welladay fired back— couldn't do anything else—and the German was killed. After that amount of noise, of course, they had to expect trouble pretty quickly. No more sorting papers—Welladay just stuffed what he could into a sack while McCormack checked the man was dead and took his gun, and then they got out fast.

"I was still telling young Welladay it was hard luck

about losing the prisoner but not his fault, and a damned good thing he'd reacted as fast as he did, when the rest of the chaps came scrambling down the path and into the landing craft. We didn't hang about to swap yarns, and we must have been about a hundred yards from shore and still rowing hard when McCormack said the thing that got us worried.

"I don't remember it exactly—something about the German having been 'a braw wee fighter' and what a fine trick it was to have fired the gun when his hands were still tied behind his back. Welladay said something like 'Oh, nonsense, McCormack, he must have got free before he starting firing,' and McCormack said, 'Oh no, sir, I noticed when I took his gun—his hands were still tied.' Welladay said, 'Are you sure?' and McCormack said, 'Oh yes, sir,' as if it was nothing to worry about—if McCormack had ever heard of the Geneva Convention he probably thought it was something to do with football. Welladay said, 'I see,' and sounded fairly sick.

"I felt a bit sick myself, because however you added it up, it came out not looking too good. When the Germans found the body it was going to look as if we'd shot an unarmed prisoner with his hands tied, and apart from what they'd make of it on the propaganda side, they were liable to take it out pretty roughly on our chaps in their POW camps.

"Not really young Welladay's fault—if a chap's firing at you, you assume he's got his hands free—but he ought to have checked all the same. I suppose he must have thought so himself—the next thing he said was 'I'm going back' and he was over the side and swimming for the shore before anyone could stop him.

"Everyone stopped rowing for a second or two—then Squiffy just shook his head and said carry on. We all knew the lad would be shot if the Germans got him—they didn't treat commando raiders as prisoners of war—but there wasn't a damn thing we could do about it. We were cutting it pretty fine already for getting back to the sub, and we just couldn't spare the time to hang around on the off chance of picking him up again. So we went on, and that looked like being the end of my acquaintance with young Arthur Welladay."

The Colonel sat looking out of the window across the sunlit lawns of New Square, his gaze perhaps drawn by the War Memorial, apparently oblivious of his immediate surroundings. The rest of us also remained silent, as if forgetting for a moment that the young man he spoke of had not after all died on the cliff tops of Sark on that bleak and moonless night in 1944 but had lived to enjoy success and age and high honours.

"But in fact," said Selena gently, after some moments, "it was not?"

"Not a bit of it," said the Colonel, his attention recalled to the present. "I ran into him in Normandy six months later. It seemed he'd got ashore all right and fallen in with some girl—she'd kept him hidden until the summer. When the news got through that the Allies had taken St. Malo, they'd escaped to Brittany together in a fishing boat. It was quite a romantic story, but I don't remember the details."

"You don't happen," I said, "to recall the girl's name?"

" 'fraid not, Professor," said the Colonel apologetically. "It's a long time ago."

"Julia," I said, "how old, in your estimation, is the Contessa di Silvabianca?"

"I've no idea," said Julia, looking bewildered. "Her looks have a degree of individuality which makes it difficult to judge, and she is not a woman of whom I should care to ask so personal a question. Since one knows that she is not precisely in her first youth, I suppose one might describe her as being in the full bloom of her second."

"Would you think it possible," I said, "that she was born at the end of 1944 or the beginning of 1945?"

"Oh, quite possible," said Julia. "Hilary, what on earth are you suggesting?"

"I am suggesting that the Contessa is Welladay's daughter. That would perhaps explain his evident interest in her movements. It would also mean, of course, that she, too, is a descendant of Sir Walter Palgrave."

"Hilary," said Selena, "you do realize, don't you, that you haven't a scrap of proper evidence for this idea?"

"And even if you're right," said Ragwort, "I would have thought that the settlement would probably be drawn in such a way as to exclude illegitimate issue."

"It does not necessarily follow," I said, "that it excludes the Contessa—if there was a child, there may well have been a marriage. I think it is time—if you will be so kind, my dear Ragwort, as to permit me to use your telephone— that I spoke again to Clementine Derwent."

Clementine's view of the urgency of my investigation had not altered in the day that had passed since our last meeting. When I told her that my enquiries had revealed one, perhaps two, of the descendants of Sir Walter Palgrave to be at present in Monte Carlo—I thought it premature and possibly indiscreet to disclose their identity—she at once undertook the arrangements necessary to enable me to travel there that night.

CHAPTER 13 ══

EXTRACT FROM *THE GUIDE TO COMFORTABLE TAX PLANNING*

Monaco: The principality of Monaco on the south coast of France, formerly a possession of the Republic of Genoa, has since 1308 been an independent state ruled by the Grimaldi family. In the mid-nineteenth century Prince Charles III averted national bankruptcy by building the Casino, the revenues from which rapidly eliminated any need for taxation.

The principality consists of three areas: On the spur of rock to the right of the harbour is the old town of Monaco, a not unpicturesque little township surrounding the Palace and now chiefly devoted to the sale of tourist souvenirs; on the hillside to the left is the modern town of Monte Carlo, consisting of the Casino, a number of shops selling jewellery and other luxuries, and an agglomeration of hotels and apartment blocks;

immediately behind the harbour, bounded by the Rue Grimaldi, is the Condamine, the business and commercial centre, where one finds the fruit and vegetable market and occasional vistas briefly reminiscent of Genoa.

Area: 375 acres. Population: 23,000. Access: By train, car, or helicopter from Nice. Principal industries: Gambling, tourism, and financial services.

Note 1: Monte Carlo is a town of steep gradients and few taxis, but exhaustion may be avoided by a perceptive use of the public lifts and escalators. If meeting a client at the Hotel de Paris, for example, after lunching with colleagues in the Condamine, on no account attempt the walk up the Avenue Monte Carlo. Take the *ascenseur* from the corner of the harbour to the Exotic Gardens and walk down. With care it is possible to reach almost any point in Monte Carlo from almost any other without ascending any significant gradient.

It will be, I fear, with some surprise, perhaps even with irritation, that you remark, dear reader, how many pages yet remain before my narrative reaches its conclusion, wondering, when the truth concerning the deaths of Grynne and Malvoisin is already plain, with what maundering irrelevancies I can have contrived to fill them. It would little become the Scholar, however, to sacrifice candour to vanity: whatever derision I may incur for my slow-wittedness, I am obliged to admit that to me, despite all I had learnt that day, the truth concerning these matters was still by no means clear.

To say that the evidence was as yet circumstantial

rather than conclusive, or that I had had no sufficient opportunity to reflect on it, would be but paltry excuses. If I
say anything in extenuation of my failure to perceive its
true significance, it must be, I suppose, that the truth was of
such a nature as to be, to a person of my temperament and
upbringing, almost literally unthinkable.

Though I continued, as I flew southwards over France,
to search for some thread of meaning in the tangled mass of
information which had presented itself, all remained dark
and obscure. I felt only a curious sense of foreboding—a
conviction, which I could not rationally explain, that Monaco was a dangerous place for Cantrip to be and that I
ought to persuade him, as a matter of urgency, to return to
London.

Although Clementine had made the most admirable
arrangements for my journey, including the hire of a motorcar to transport me from Nice airport to Monte Carlo, it
was after midnight, by local time, before I finally arrived at
the Hotel Clair de Lune. When I mentioned at the reception desk that I believed my friend Mr. Cantrip was also
staying there, I had little expectation of seeing him that
night. I was told, however, that I would find him in the bar.

It was a long room, furnished in devoted imitation of
the Belle Epoque with crimson velvet and gilt-framed
looking glasses. There were when I entered only three
people in it, but if there had been thirty I daresay the
woman sitting curled up on the sofa would still have been
the first to attract my notice. Dressed in grey-green chiffon
interwoven with silver, with some ornament also of silver
shining in her auburn hair, she looked like a nymph in
Ovid's *Metamorphoses* in the process of transformation
into a fountain, and there was about her movements a

corresponding fluidity and charm which would have se-
duced the eye from women with better claims to be
thought beautiful. She was holding a glass of champagne,
and the pleasant sound of her laughter reached me as I
entered. Sitting in a chair on her right was a tall dark man,
evidently in his middle forties, and still with enough good
looks to suggest that in his youth they must have been
spectacular. On her left was Cantrip, who appeared to be
the cause of her amusement.

Having been in some uncertainty whether Cantrip
would welcome my unexpected arrival, I was touched to
receive a greeting which seemed to express no less pleasure than astonishment. He introduced me to the Count
and Contessa di Silvabianca as a person whose presence
would be of inestimable value, and having demanded to
know what on earth I was doing in Monte Carlo cheerfully
cut off my reply after a scant three words: whatever it was,
I was to stop doing it and devote my entire attention to
what he termed "the Wellieboots problem."

I had arrived, it seemed, at a council of war—in consequence of a long-standing dinner engagement, this was the
first opportunity the Contessa and her husband had had
since returning to Monte Carlo for any discussion with
Cantrip of the events of the past three days. He had been
relating to them the story of his journey through France,
and resumed his narrative with such enthusiasm that there
was neither time nor need for me to wonder if I should
admit to any previous knowledge of it.

The Contessa's laughter was soon accounted for. Poor
Cantrip was still mystified, it seemed, by the fact of her
arriving in St. Malo no later than the judge and himself, and

she was too delighted by his perplexity to be in much haste to dispel it.

"Oh, look here, Gabrielle," said Cantrip, with the beginnings of indignation. "I've said I can't guess. Come on, be a sport and say how you did it."

"But, Michel," said the Contessa, "perhaps I do not want to be a sport. Perhaps I want to be very romantic and mysterious and to make you think I can cross the sea by magic. But I do not think I can make Hilary think so— professors at Oxford do not believe in magic." She looked at me, still laughing.

"My dear Gabrielle," I said, for she had invited me to address her by her first name, "I do not doubt that you have all the powers appropriate to an enchantress. I understand, however, that it is not unknown for those engaged in the profession of tax planning to make some alteration to their appearance when they cross international frontiers. I rather suspect that you left Sark in some disguise which Cantrip failed to penetrate and that you travelled on the same boat."

"Ah, you see," cried Gabrielle, clapping her hands, and apparently as pleased to be detected as she had been to deceive, "I knew one could not hide anything from an Oxford professor. Of course, Hilary, you are quite right. As you say, I do not like the French authorities to know my travelling arrangements. I do not like the idea that just when I am getting on a plane a gentleman may tap me on the shoulder and say 'One moment, Madame la Comtesse, there is a little problem with your passport, please answer a few questions,' and that somehow this little problem cannot be solved until I have told this gentleman the names of my French clients who have accounts in Geneva or Monte

Carlo. No, no, no, no, I do not like this at all." She wagged her forefinger, reproving some imaginary representative of the French fisc.

"Oh, I say," said Cantrip, "they wouldn't."

"But I assure you, Michel, I have friends to whom it has happened. So when I am going to Jersey, for example, I slip into the cloakroom in my favourite café in St. Malo and I put on—oh, some extra clothing, you know, in case it is cold in the Channel Islands. I put on a thick black dress over my other clothes, and some thick black stockings and some good solid shoes, and a head scarf and one or two shawls. And a big pair of glasses, of course, to keep the wind out of my eyes. And somehow when I come out I do not look so much like the vice president of a wicked Swiss bank with clients who do not want to pay their taxes, but more like a respectable Breton peasant lady who has buried two husbands and has some shopping to do in St. Helier."

"Oh, look here," said Cantrip, "you don't mean you were the old biddy in black? Oh, come off it, Gabrielle, you can't have been. What about your luggage? What about your passport?"

"But of course I was, Michel—did you really never recognize me? My luggage? I keep a suitcase with some clothes in it at the hotels where I usually stay—for travel I take just a little overnight case, inside the shopping basket. And my passport? Well, I still have my French passport, which does not say that I am the Contessa di Silvabianca but that I am Gabrielle Leclerc, who is a good French-woman born in Brittany in—oh, but you will not expect me to tell you in which year."

She smiled, almost as if she guessed how much the information would have interested me. Seeing her, I had begun to sympathise with Julia's inability to offer any useful estimate of her age. Her figure betrayed nothing—she was as slender as Clementine Derwent, though without giving the same impression of boyishness; the rich auburn of her hair might have owed much or little to art, and her face, dominated by large eyes of the ambivalent aquatic colour that Cantrip had remarked upon, was of the structure that changes little between the ages of thirty and fifty. There were some signs, it is true, of recent strain—faint shadows and hollows which suggested a loss of sleep and appetite, but this evening, at any rate, she seemed in the highest spirits. She rang for more champagne, saying that we must celebrate.

"Carissima," said her husband, regarding her with slightly mournful dark eyes, "I am happy that you are happy, but I do not quite understand what it is that we are celebrating. When I hear that you—my wife—the Contessa di Silvabianca—have been hunted across France like a wanted criminal, I do not see that it is something to celebrate." His voice grew warm with indignation at the affront to his aristocratic name.

"Because I know who is hunting me," said Gabrielle, reaching out to press his hand. "Giovanni, you know how worried I have been this past year."

"Of course, carissima, how should I not? You go away to these meetings about this Daffodil business and afterwards you are pale and nervous and frightened and not at all like my happy, beautiful wife." He spread his hands in a gesture of hopelessness. "What can I do? I have begged you to give up the Daffodil case and leave it to Patrick to look after and you will not."

"Ah, Giovanni," said his wife, "I know why you do not

like my beautiful Daffodil Settlement. It takes me away from home and you have no one to look after you. But I cannot give it up—it is my favourite portfolio and we have done wonderful things together. But it is true that I have been frightened. You see, Hilary, I have thought for more than a year now that someone was following me, spying on me, always when I was away, and always when I was working on this particular case—I must ask you to be discreet, we do not usually mention names. But I could not be certain, you see—I could not say 'There is the same man with the big nose and black beard that I saw yesterday.' It was a matter of instinct, of impression."

"Had you any idea," I asked, "who might be doing such a thing?"

"At first, of course, I thought that it was someone from the French Revenue authorities. But—there was something about it somehow that was not quite their style. I began to think that it was someone more sinister, more dangerous, and I was afraid, as Giovanni says. And at other times I wondered if I was imagining things and becoming a little bit mad perhaps. But now—now Michel has discovered that it is only Mr. Justice Wellieboots, who sits in court all day and wriggles his eyebrows at my friend Julia, and who does not frighten me in the least. I do not give that for Mr. Wellieboots." She snapped her fingers. "Yes, Giovanni, of course it is something to celebrate."

It was no doubt a sufficient explanation for her present high spirits; but I wondered if she might not have some further, undisclosed reason to be confident that Mr. Justice Welladay would intend no ill towards her.

"If we could be sure that this man could do you no harm," said her husband, "then it would be something to celebrate. But I do not see how we can be sure of it. I suppose that a judge is a very powerful person, and it is not safe for you to click your fingers at him. Why has he been following you? What does he want? What does he mean to do next? For myself, I cannot be happy until we know these things."

"It is evident what he wants, chéri. Michel has told us that he does not like people to avoid tax—he has heard something somehow about my Daffodil settlement, which has made such beautiful capital gains, and he thinks that if he can find out who the beneficiaries are he can make them pay tax, millions of pounds of tax. Poor Mr. Wellieboots, he doesn't know that he could follow me for a hundred years and read all my letters and listen to all my telephone calls and still not discover who the beneficiaries are, because I do not know it myself." She evidently found this thought irresistibly entertaining.

Cantrip, however, made haste to concur in her husband's opinion—he is not a young man to be easily persuaded, once launched on a career of knight errantry, that the damsel can deal with the dragon by herself. It would be a nightmare, he said, for Gabrielle to spend her life thinking that at any moment Mr. Justice Welladay might pop out of the bushes at her; something must be done to put a stop to it once and for all.

"Besides," he continued, "the more I think about it, the more I don't think the way he's acting is the way English judges are supposed to act. I mean, we've got things in England like the Bill of Rights and habeas corpus and things, and what they say is that judges can't go locking people up without giving them a chance to defend themselves. Well, I haven't done any constitutional law for a couple of years, so I can't swear that's exactly what they say, but that's the gist of it. So what I think is that Wellieboots has gone round the twist."

"Forgive me," said the Count, "I do not quite understand."

"Off his onion," said Cantrip helpfully. "Loopy. Nutty as a fruitcake. And the problem about people going nutty is that it's jolly difficult to tell whether they're harmlessly nutty or dangerously nutty. Anyway, that's why it's going to be so frightfully useful having Hilary here—I mean, Oxford dons are always going nutty, so if you can manage to chat to him for a couple of minutes, you'll be able to tell how serious it is, won't you, Hilary?"

"Michel," said Gabrielle, "I expect that Hilary has come to Monte Carlo to do something quite serious and important and will not at all wish to be involved in this matter of Mr. Justice Wellieboots."

Though perfect candour would have been injudicious, I wished so far as possible to avoid deception. I accordingly took the opportunity to explain that I myself was in Monte Carlo for reasons connected with the Daffodil settlement, that I had been commissioned by Clementine to investigate the genealogy of the Palgrave family, and that by a curious coincidence my researches had led me to the South of France. There were, I added, one or two points on which I would be grateful for Gabrielle's assistance, if she were able to spare the time to discuss them.

She seemed delighted to learn that we were all, in a manner of speaking, colleagues—that evening indeed she seemed delighted by everything—and promised me any help that she had power to give. She and Cantrip had had it in mind to meet again for lunch next day, and she suggested that I should join them. Perceiving, however, that he supported the invitation with something less than enthusiasm, I invented a pretext for refusal and arranged instead to lunch with her on the following Monday.

"I wonder," said Gabrielle as we were finishing our champagne, "how Mr. Wellieboots managed to steal my pen, and why he wanted it."

"Carissima," said her husband, "please do not start worrying again about this pen. I do not believe that anyone has stolen it—you have put it down somewhere and forgotten it. Such things happen."

"No, Giovanni, I have told you—I am always very careful with it, and I am sure that I could not have done that." She turned towards Cantrip and myself. "You see, I had a rather pretty gold fountain pen, with my initials on it, which Giovanni gave me for a present—I think you have seen it, Michel. And the other evening, when we were dining in Dourdan, I found that it was missing."

"Look," said Cantrip, "have you tried to remember when you last used it?"

"Of course I have, Michel, but I simply cannot. I know I must have been using it on Monday afternoon, when we were signing the company documents—I have grown up in an old-fashioned Swiss bank, you know, I would not have used a ballpoint for that. But I can't be sure that was the last time."

"Try looking in your handbag again," said Cantrip, no doubt recalling occasions when a fifth or sixth excavation of the multitudinous contents of Julia's handbag had at last brought to light some object long lamented as lost. When Gabrielle opened hers, however, we saw at once that it contained only an elegant minimum of necessary items—

diary, chequebook, comb, scent spray, and so forth. There were two ballpoint pens and a pencil, but no gold fountain pen was lurking in its depths.

"Is it possible," I said, "that you lent it to someone? To one of your colleagues, perhaps?"

"Oh, no, I would not dream of it, Hilary—it would ruin the nib, you know, if someone else used it."

So much then for Patrick Ardmore's explanation. I could of course have reassured her that the pen was safe; but I had no wish to disclose my knowledge of the matter, nor did I think that it would ease her mind to learn of the circumstances in which it had been found. No doubt she would be hearing soon enough from Ardmore.

"I was sure it had been stolen. And I was sure it had been taken by the person who was following me—not because it was pretty and quite valuable, but for some different reason—perhaps to compromise me in some way, because my initials were on it. But I do not see what chance Mr. Wellieboots would have had to take it, so perhaps after all I am mistaken." The thought seemed to cause her disproportionate uneasiness.

"Carissima," said her husband, "you have worried too much about this pen. Am I the kind of husband who is angry with you, and says you do not love me because you have lost my present, or is jealous and says that you have given it away to someone else? You know I am not. I will buy you another one and we will not think of it anymore. But all the same I wish that you would give up this Daffodil business. You do not take me seriously when I say there is something dangerous about it, but two people have been killed—isn't that enough to make you think it is serious?"

Gabrielle looked at me apologetically, as if she were at fault in allowing the evening to end on so sombre a note.

"I had some bad news when I returned to my office, Hilary—I told Michel of it earlier—a colleague of ours, our Jersey advocate, died in an accident on the day we left Sark. Well, of course I am very sad about it. But if I had heard the news yesterday, I would have thought dreadful things, and now at least I know that it really was—only an accident."

Cantrip, on the following morning, displayed no such confidence.

Rising rather late, I had found myself impeding the duties of the gipsy-eyed chambermaid who arrived to clean my room, and had accordingly joined Cantrip for breakfast on the balcony of his. We looked out, as we drank our coffee and ate our croissants, at the neat rectangular harbour, glittering in the sunlight and crowded with the yachts of those too rich to afford to live elsewhere.

"I didn't say anything last night," said Cantrip, "because I didn't want to upset Gabrielle, but the way I see it is that if old Wellieboots is loopy enough to lock me in a cellar, then he's loopy enough to have pushed poor old Malvoisin off the cliff. And if he did, he's a pretty dangerous customer."

Reluctant as I was to encourage his suspicions—for I had no doubt that the more serious the danger, the more difficult it would be to persuade him to leave Monte Carlo —I could not in fairness and friendship withhold from him the information I had gathered in the previous two days. I did not mention, however, the possibility that Gabrielle was Welladay's daughter and thus herself a beneficiary of the Daffodil Settlement. I saw all too well that to breathe the faintest suspicion of her would result at best in our ceasing to be on speaking terms.

As I had feared, he concluded instantly that the case was proved against Mr. Justice Welladay.

"Mind you, I reckon he's probably loopy as well—I expect he thinks that bumping off tax planners just doesn't count as murder. But that doesn't make him any safer to have around." He began to canvass my views on a variety of schemes to frustrate the judge's supposedly homicidal intentions, all characterized by a certain alarming robustness.

"My dear Cantrip," I said, "I do beg you to do nothing precipitate. I will reflect on the problem in the hope of devising some less hazardous solution than those you have so far proposed. I suggest that we meet again after your lunch with Gabrielle."

"All right," said Cantrip. "How about four o'clock in the Casino?"

"By all means," I said, "if it is open at that hour and does not require evening dress or anything of that sort."

Hearing noises within of domestic activity, Cantrip went indoors to seek guidance from the chambermaid on the opening hours of the Casino and the degree of formality in dress expected of its customers. I heard her assure him, with a certain amount of flirtatious giggling, that it would indeed be open and would be content with any costume satisfying the ordinary standards of decorum.

"It is good," she said, "that you are going to the Casino. You will win much money."

"Or lose it," said Cantrip, with uncharacteristic realism.

"Ah no, monsieur, I am sure that you will win. I see it in your face, I have the gift from my grandmother. Trust me—I am as sure that you will be lucky at the Casino as I am that you are lucky in love."

"Oh," said Cantrip, in a tone which Ragwort would have thought altogether too forward and encouraging, "what makes you think that, mam'selle?"

"Ah, monsieur, I have told you, I have the gift. You love a lady with auburn hair, and her perfume is Raffiné by Houbigant—and she is very fond of you, I think. Ah, it's true, isn't it? You see, you cannot deceive me."

She was still laughing when Cantrip returned to the balcony.

"Dear me," I said, "what a remarkably perceptive young woman. I wonder how she knew that?"

"What do you mean?" said Cantrip, blushing.

"Gabrielle has auburn hair, and she uses Raffiné—I noticed the scent spray in her handbag last night."

"Oh rot," said Cantrip; but continued to blush.

CHAPTER 14 ══════

At about midday I began the steep but relatively brief ascent of the steps which lead up from the northwestern corner of the harbour, through shrubberies of cacti and bougainvillea, to the summit of the Rock. Upon reaching the plateau, I averted my eyes, in accordance with the advice of one of the more austere contributors to the Guide, from the Disney-esque grandeurs of the Palace and turned somewhat at random into the network of narrow streets which constitutes the old town of Monaco.

The area is not a large one, and although almost every establishment that was not a souvenir shop seemed to be an eating place of some kind, I had little difficulty in identifying the restaurant where Cantrip and Gabrielle were to meet. Some twenty yards down the street, and on the opposite side, was a pleasant-looking bistro. I entered and chose a table close to the window.

Gabrielle was the first to arrive, coming from the direction of the Cathedral several minutes before the appointed hour, wearing a black-and-white dress and a hat of glossy black straw. She sat down at one of the tables on the pavement outside the restaurant.

Soon afterwards I saw approaching from the same direction the tall figure of Mr. Justice Welladay. Though he was dressed in the flannel trousers and cotton shirt which are the customary apparel of the Englishman seeking pleasure abroad, they seemed in the nature of a disguise: there was little in his bearing to suggest the holiday spirit. After an unconvincing pretence of contemplating the purchase of a garment bearing the motto "Kisses from Monte Carlo," he entered the bistro and sat down a few feet away from me.

Of the three of us Gabrielle was the first to see Cantrip, who must have been approaching from the direction of the Palace. She stood up and called out to him, waving her straw hat, and he went quickly towards her, manoeuvring his way adroitly through a group of jostling sightseers.

The judge, on observing this, half rose from his chair, his expression one of surprise, anxiety, and something like anger—he seemed almost to be considering some physical intervention in the encounter. Evidently perceiving, however, the absurdity of such a course of action, he sank back into his chair. I rose and went across to his table.

"Sir Arthur," I said, "may I join you? You will perhaps not remember me—we met a few months ago when you were dining on High Table in St. George's, where I am a Fellow. My name is Hilary Tamar—Professor Hilary Tamar."

"I'm afraid," he said, "that I don't remember the occasion." I saw that he thought it tasteless of me to presume on so slender an acquaintance, but the civility usually prac-

tised between members of the legal and academic profes-
sions permitted nothing closer to an outright rebuff.

"I fear that I am contributing," I said, with a smile
which I hoped was disarming, "to one of the hazards of
judicial office. It must be difficult for you to take a private
holiday without meeting someone who knows you in your
public capacity."

"It does seem," said the judge, "to be becoming increasingly so."

"Here you are, for example, in a little back street in
Monaco, thousands of miles from Lincoln's Inn, and you
find yourself within a stone's throw of at least two people
who can claim a professional acquaintance with you."

"Two?" said the judge. "I have seen no one but yourself, Professor Tamar."

"The dark-haired young man at the table over there is
at the Chancery Bar—his name is Michael Cantrip. He is in
Basil Ptarmigan's Chambers in 62 New Square. I don't
suppose that he has appeared before you sufficiently often
for you to recognise him, especially without a wig and
gown. But he, of course, would recognise you."

Welladay drew back a little from the window, as if
realising that any more than a casual glance from Cantrip
might reveal his presence; but he continued to stare in-
tently at the boy, apparently trying to verify what I had
said.

"Now that you say it—yes, I believe I may have seen
him in Lincoln's Inn. Are you quite sure, Professor Tamar,
that he is who you say he is? It is a matter, as it happens, of
some interest to me."

"Quite sure," I said. "He is well known to me."

He sat in frowning silence, evidently weighing up the

significance of what I had told him, but showing no disposition to discuss it further.

"But I do not think," I said after a few moments, "that there is any danger of his seeking to engage you in conversation—he seems very well content with his present company. Understandably so—a most charming and attractive woman. Would you say, Sir Arthur, that she much resembles her mother?"

He made no sudden movement or exclamation of surprise; but he betrayed his astonishment by that instant of perfect immobility which is the one undisguisable sign of emotion in those accustomed to conceal it.

"What an extraordinary question, Professor Tamar—how on earth should I know?"

"I cannot imagine," I said, "that you will disclaim the acquaintance of Rachel Alexandre."

"I find you, if I may say so, Professor Tamar," he said, with a certain grimness, "excessively well informed on matters which seem to me to be no concern of yours."

"To an historian, Sir Arthur, that can hardly be a reproach."

"May I know, if you please, for what purpose you have engineered this meeting? After what you have said, you cannot expect me to believe that it is accidental."

"I will not attempt to persuade you that it is—it was, I readily admit, in the hope of having some conversation with you that I came here this morning. My knowledge of your friendship with Rachel Alexandre is indeed accidental. I learnt of it by chance in the course of some research I was engaged in relating to the last year of the Second World War." I hoped that he would not remember that I was a mediaevalist. "I believe, however, that the accident may prove to have been a fortunate one. Cantrip, you see, has been telling me a rather extraordinary story, to the effect that during the past three days you have been following the Contessa di Silvabianca across France and that during that time you caused him to be locked up in a wine cellar." The judge said nothing, but his heavy eyebrows gathered themselves together in a manner which Julia would have found extremely alarming. "He has drawn the conclusion," I continued, "that you intend some harm towards her."

"That I . . . ? Oh, that's preposterous."

"Knowing what I do, I have no doubt that it is, but he is convinced of it. You, I suspect, entertain a similar notion with regard to him. If you continue in your mutual misapprehensions, I fear that the matter may end in a good deal of embarrassment to both of you, not to speak of the Contessa herself. Sir Arthur, I understand that the reasons for your conduct may well be of a personal and confidential nature and that you would not wish them to be disclosed to Cantrip. Since, however, I already know so much of the story, can there be any grave objection to telling me the rest—in, I need hardly say, the strictest confidence? If I were able to tell Cantrip that I knew your motives and that they were in no way inimical to the interests of the Contessa, I believe that he would accept my assurance."

The judge was silent, gazing down the sunlit street to where Cantrip and the Contessa were now engaged in a very animated and apparently entertaining conversation over a bottle of champagne. Neither of them looked, at present, to be much weighed down by anxiety. He was plainly inclined to tell me to go to the devil, but he was also reflecting, I suppose, that his conduct of the previous few days had been of equivocal propriety and that I might be a means of extrication from a potential embarrassment. Moreover, a man in his sixties does not easily decline an opportunity to speak of his youth.

"It's rather a long story," he said at last, "though I gather that some of it is already familiar to you. We'd better order something to eat."

I had reason to be glad of the suggestion, for the story was indeed a long one. It began with an account, similar in substance to that I had heard from Colonel Cantrip, of the events which on that moonless night in 1944 had brought him, wet and shivering, to the cliff tops of Sark.

"There's nothing like cold seawater for washing the heroism out of you, Professor Tamar. By the time I got back to the guard hut I was cursing myself for a fool for having gone. I was pretty sure it was too late to be any use—after all the noise, I was expecting to find the place full of German soldiers. But there were no Germans—just a girl in a white dress kneeling by the dead man's body, with her hair shining in the light from the oil lamp."

There was a warmth in his voice that I had not previously heard, and a note of remembered astonishment.

"I must have been a grim enough sight, dripping wet and with my face blacked, but she didn't show any sign of being frightened. She asked what I was doing there and I told her about the raid and why I'd had to come back. She said she'd help me, but it wasn't enough simply to undo the ropes—we had to dispose of the body altogether. She was worried about reprisals—if the Germans found one of their men shot dead they were likely to react fairly brutally against the civilian population. They might not even have believed there'd been a raid at all—the girl and her brother were the people living nearest the guard hut, and she thought they'd be the first to be suspected. He was a big man, the man I'd killed—it took the two of us to carry him. We threw him over the cliff at a point where we could be sure of him being washed out to sea—Rachel knew the currents and found the right place. In spite of everything, she was a good deal calmer than I was—she was a remarkable girl."

"And afterwards she kept you hidden from the Germans?"

"For three months. Luckily for us, there was no great search made for the missing soldier. I suppose the Germans thought he'd deserted, stowed away perhaps in one of the fishing boats. Still, it was desperately dangerous for her—if they'd found out she was hiding me, they'd certainly have sent her to a concentration camp, if they hadn't shot her outright. Her brother, too, I'm afraid, although he was only sixteen. Well, finally the news came through that St. Malo was in the hands of the Allies. As soon as we heard that, she set about finding someone to take the three of us across, and one night in July we were landed from a fishing boat on the coast of Brittany."

"And you, I suppose, fell in love with her?"

"Oh of course—what else would a boy of nineteen do under such conditions? Head over heels in love with her, and making myself no end of a nuisance about it, I daresay. I must have pestered her almost to death trying to persuade her to marry me, but she wouldn't have me."

"Not even," I said, having no choice but to venture the assumption, "when she knew she was going to have a child?"

"Not even then, though life wasn't easy in those days

for a woman with a child and no husband—it wouldn't have occurred to her to marry for the sake of convenience. But things turned out well for her, I'm glad to say—she married a Breton businessman, and he made her very happy, I believe, until his death a few years ago. He brought Gabrielle up as his daughter."

"But you have never met her?"

"No. Rachel thought that it would be disturbing for her to meet me, even when she grew older—it would hardly have been possible, even if it had been right, to prevent her finding out who I was. But Rachel and I kept in touch—chiefly by letter, though we met from time to time. So although Gabrielle knew nothing about me, I knew a great deal about her. Rachel's letters were of almost nothing else—how pretty she was, how clever she was, how well she was doing in her studies, how successful she was in her profession. Her husband wasn't good enough for her, of course, but then no one could have been. And then, a few months ago, there was something quite different—a letter suggesting disquiet."

Gabrielle's mother, it seemed, no less than her husband and Clementine Derwent, had noted the lowering effect on her spirits of events at recent Daffodil meetings and had eventually confided her anxieties to the judge.

"Did you," I asked, "regard the notion that the Contessa was being followed as one to be taken seriously? Did you not think it more likely that she was simply imagining things? Her work is demanding, and she may be subject to considerable stress."

"I could not be sure, Professor Tamar. I certainly did not think that our own Department of Inland Revenue would go to such lengths as she appeared to believe—or

even the French Revenue authorities, though their methods of investigation are perhaps more vigorous than our
own. I thought it not impossible, however, that her profession might have brought her into contact, and potentially
into conflict, with persons very much more dangerous—if
your clients are the sort of people who are anxious to hide
their funds away in Jersey or Liechtenstein, then you are
fishing in deep and murky waters."

"But surely," I said, "there is nothing necessarily criminal about keeping money in such places. My understanding is that the purpose may be perfectly legitimate tax
avoidance."

"In some cases avoidance. In most, in my opinion,
downright evasion—why else the secrecy? Even if the
money itself is honestly come by—and that is by no means
always the case—I do not consider that a crime to be
treated lightly. In my view a man who enjoys the privileges
of living in a country, and yet is not willing to make his just
contribution to that country's exchequer, is no more an
upright or honourable man than one who spends a week at
a first-class hotel and leaves without paying his bill. Still,
you must not allow me to bore you on the subject—some of
my colleagues would say that it is a hobbyhorse of mine.
Suffice it to say that I am sorry Gabrielle has chosen to use
her talents in assisting such people, and should not be surprised if there are those among them with whom it is dangerous to have dealings."

Rachel Alexandre had done more than confide in him.
She had asked him to go to Jersey at the time of the next
meeting and to try to discover if her daughter's fears had
any foundation in reality. Gabrielle herself was to know

nothing of his presence or its purpose. I remarked that it sounded like a difficult task.

"Difficult? It was a hopeless task, Professor Tamar, an impossible task. But what could I do? Rachel Alexandre had saved my life, and it was the only favour she had ever asked of me. Moreover, I still feel a sense of responsibility for Gabrielle. I told her that I would do my best, and so I did. I have been following Gabrielle since she left her mother's house in Brittany eight days ago. That part wasn't so difficult—I knew in broad terms about her travel arrangements, and some tomfoolery of dressing up as an old countrywoman when she crossed the French frontier. I don't mean that she was constantly in my view—that would indeed have been impossible, but I always knew, at the very least, what building she was in, and I would have been, I think, within earshot if she had needed help. But as to knowing whether anyone else was following her—it was hopeless. Any one of a thousand holidaymakers could have been watching her, and I would have been none the wiser."

And then, within hours of being obliged to report to Rachel Alexandre the abject failure of his assignment, he had seen Cantrip—behaving in a way he had found unquestionably suspicious. He had of course observed that, in the Channel Islands, Cantrip and Gabrielle had been much in each other's company. Why then, in the Place Chateaubriand in St. Malo, had Cantrip been at such evident pains to conceal his presence from her? The judge could imagine no reason that was not sinister. When he saw Cantrip again at Dourdan, suspicion had some near to certainty, and when on the following day it became clear that Cantrip was still following Gabrielle southwards, he had no doubt that he had found the man he was looking for.

"And it began to look as if luck was on my side. There's an old friend of Rachel's and mine who has a restaurant and vineyard just south of Beaune—I was reasonably sure that Gabrielle would lunch there, if only for the sake of politeness. I telephoned him from Beaune and asked him to arrange a little reception party." The judge's eyes, I regret to say, brightened at the thought of this, and he seemed untroubled by any interesting questions of his jurisdiction to behave in the manner he had described. "The plan was to leave your young friend to cool his heels in the cellar for a few hours, until I was sure that Gabrielle was safely back to Monte Carlo, and to question him on my return. But yesterday morning I learnt that he had escaped, and I did not feel, in those circumstances, that I could consider my task as being at an end."

I attempted to explain, as tactfully as I could, the reasons for Cantrip's conduct in St. Malo and Dourdan, but I saw with some dismay that the judge was not wholly convinced. His suspicion, it seemed, had taken too firm a hold to be easily dispelled, even by the knowledge that Cantrip was a member of Lincoln's Inn.

"But apart from your suspicions of Cantrip," I said, "you have seen nothing to confirm the Contessa's fears? On Sark, for example, where a stranger might perhaps have been more conspicuous than in Jersey—you observed nothing unusual?"

"Thinking it a piece of exceptional good fortune that so reliable and conscientious a witness should have been in Little Sark on the night of Edward Malvoisin's death, I was anxious to draw from him an account of what he had seen and heard there. When at last I succeeded in doing so, however, it was something of a disappointment—he had been asleep. He had resisted the temptation to reveal his presence to Philip Alexandre, who would certainly have offered him a comfortable bed, and had instead spent the night in a barn a little distance from the main building; but fresh air and unaccustomed exertion had had their way with him, and he had slept as soundly as in the most luxurious four-poster. He had remained awake long enough to see Gabrielle, with Cantrip and Clementine, return after dinner to the Witch's Cottage. Of any event occurring after that he would evidently have been oblivious. Not even the commotion of Albert's homecoming, it seemed, had roused him from his slumbers.

"I did notice something in the morning that struck me as a trifle odd. I woke early, as one does after a sound night's sleep, and took the chance of looking round before there was anyone about. There's a porch at the side of the farmhouse—the hotel as it is now—which we used to use as a kind of lookout post. It provides a certain amount of cover, and it's a good place to watch out for anyone coming along the road from the Coupee, or indeed from the cottage. It seemed to me that someone might have been using it quite recently for that purpose. It looked as if it was cleaned and dusted fairly regularly, but there were traces of damp mud on the floor and half a dozen cigarette butts."

His heavy eyebrows gathered again in a frown.

"But there are any number of possible explanations—I don't think it's of any significance. No, Professor Tamar, I'm afraid I still think that if Gabrielle is in danger from anyone, it's your young friend Mr. Cantrip. I don't doubt your own belief in the explanation you've given me of his

motives, but I have to say that I find it less than convincing.
Nor does the fact that he has evidently gained the trust of
Gabrielle herself serve to reassure me—quite the reverse.
In academic life, Professor Tamar, you do not have the
opportunities which I have unfortunately had of learning
how easily a personable appearance and an engaging manner may conceal a plausible scoundrel. I do not pretend to
know precisely what young Mr. Cantrip is up to—I would
be only too happy to believe that it was nothing sinister.
But I should feel that I was failing in the responsibility I
have undertaken if I were to leave Monte Carlo while he is
still here."

Glancing across the street, I saw that Cantrip and
Gabrielle, having consumed enormous quantities of pancakes and champagne, were now drinking coffee. I began
to think the situation a trifle desperate.

"But I rather fear," I said, "that Cantrip may adopt a
similar position—that is to say, he will refuse to leave
Monte Carlo while you are still here. Sir Arthur, the legal
term has already begun and you cannot, I imagine, absent
yourself indefinitely from your judicial duties. Cantrip also
has responsibilities, albeit of a far humbler nature, which
require his presence in London. Surely you will agree that
something must be done to resolve this impasse? If I can
persuade him to be at Nice airport tomorrow in time to
take the first plane to London, will you undertake to be
there and to take the same flight?"

It was with some difficulty that I convinced him of the
sense and practicality of my proposal; but his conscience, I
fancy, was troubled by the thought of his neglected judicial
duties, and he could think of no other means to reconcile

his conflicting obligations. By the time Gabrielle and Cantrip rose from their table, the arrangement was agreed on.

I saw that nonetheless he was once more preparing to follow them, having evidently no intention of abandoning as yet his watch over Gabrielle. It occurred to me that after all, quite apart from any concern he might feel for her safety, it was natural enough for him to be interested in her.

"It must be," I remarked, "a matter of great regret to you, Sir Arthur, that you have never been able to meet your daughter. She is a delightful woman."

He stared at me with every sign of astonishment, and then gave the harsh snort of laughter which I had found to be characteristic of him.

"My daughter? Oh, my dear Professor Tamar, is that what you thought? I confess I had thought your researches to have been more thorough. My daughter? Oh no, Professor Tamar, that isn't why Rachel wouldn't let me meet her —Gabrielle is not my daughter."

"I'm sorry," I said, considerably discomfited. "I was under the impression—"

"She's the daughter of the man I killed. I told you, Professor Tamar, that Rachel Alexandre was a remarkable woman."

CHAPTER 15

There was a breathless hush in the Casino as all eyes turned towards the suave figure in impeccable evening dress of the daredevil young barrister who that evening had already won a fortune at the roulette table and was now preparing to stake it all on a single spin of the wheel. Beautiful women sumptuously attired in gowns of gold and silver and adorned with gems of fabulous value gazed at him admiringly, their lovely bosoms heaving with emotion.

"Sair," hissed the white-faced croupier, "zees is madness. In all my years at ze Casino, I 'ave never seen a man 'oo would dare to reesk so much."

"Risk?" cried Martin Carruthers with a contemptuous laugh. "Do you suppose this is the worst risk I have taken? Let me tell you, my good fellow, that to-morrow I go to meet my deadliest enemy, the fiendish Mr. Justice Heltapay—what risk can I take tonight to compare with that? Do your duty, my good man, and spin the wheel."

Those familiar with the Casino will infer that Carruthers, with characteristic recklessness, had begun the evening by paying the sum of five pounds required to secure entry to the Salles Privées. Cantrip, on the other hand, had judged this too high a price to pay for the privilege of joining the handful of gamblers, dressed with respectability rather than distinction, who amid an expanse of deserted green baize were gathered there in mournful silence round a single roulette table. I found him in the Salle des Jeux Américains—that is to say, the room devoted to what I believe are called fruit machines—moving eagerly from one cacophonous device to another in search of one responsive to his skills. It was accordingly under conditions of some difficulty that I told him of my conversation with Mr. Justice Welladay, explaining that on certain matters, having undertaken to respect the judge's confidence, I was obliged to silence.

His efforts were from time to time rewarded with clattering showers of coins, eventually amounting to a sum almost equivalent, at the prevailing exchange rate, to eighty pounds sterling. While not seriously imperilling the solvency of the Casino, his winnings seemed to him sufficient to vindicate the chambermaid's prophecy and to justify the purchase of a celebratory bottle of wine among the ornate mirrors and pink and crimson draperies of the Salon Rose.

It was here that his muse came upon him. He motioned for silence with the true imperiousness of the creative artist and for several minutes wrote without pause, looking up only to enquire my opinion on the spelling of *sumptuous*. At last he leant back wearily in his pink velvet chair, gazing with admiration at the ceiling, upon which

222

were depicted a number of lightly clothed young women reclining on rose-tinted clouds—of tobacco smoke perhaps, since all were smoking cigars. He remarked, with sentimental tenderness, that one of them looked just like Julia. I could see too little of her face to judge of the resemblance.

"My dear Cantrip," I said, "I perceive that for the purposes of fiction you still regard Mr. Justice Welladay as the villain of the piece. You do understand, I hope, that I am now satisfied that in real life he is not?"

"Oh rather, Hilary, I quite understand that *you're* satisfied."

"Would you care," I said, "to explain your emphasis on the second-person pronoun?"

"Well, what I understand is that old Wellieboots has spun you a yarn and you've fallen for it. And he's told you to keep the whole thing under your hat, the way chaps do when they're trying to get some mug to invest in underwater motels or Venusian railway shares, so you won't have a chance to talk it over with anyone who might have a bit more sense."

"My dear Cantrip," I said, "I may claim, I believe, to be not quite so lacking in judgment and worldly experience as your comparison might seem to suggest."

"You can claim what you like, old thing, but you can't say that pootling to and fro between libraries and senior common rooms and giving the odd lecture or two on novel disseisin is exactly a training in the tough school of life. You're jolly good at picking up juicy bits of gossip, I give you that"—he seemed to think this a most generous admission —"but the trouble is you don't much care if it's true or not as long as it makes a good story. So when some con artist pitches you a yarn, you swallow it hook, line, and sinker."

"If I say that Sir Arthur Welladay impressed me as a person of almost unshakable integrity, you may perhaps be reluctant to rely on the impressions of a person so naive and inexperienced as myself. I would remind you, however, that since he has been appointed to be one of Her Majesty's judges, he would appear to have made a similar impression on the Lord Chancellor."

"There you are," said Cantrip triumphantly, as if I had proved his point. "That's the impression successful con artists always make on people. I mean, let's face it, if everyone can tell at first sight that you're as crooked as a cross-eyed kookaburra, it's not much use going in for being a con artist, is it? Better give up the idea and be an old-fashioned burglar—ask any careers master."

"Moreover," I continued, thinking it right in the circumstances to exercise the utmost patience, "the explanation which he offered of his behaviour was consistent with other evidence available to me of which he could not have known. It is inconceivable that it should have been a spur-of-the-moment invention."

"That's what you think. What you're forgetting is that before you get to be a High Court judge you've got to spend about thirty years in practice at the Bar, and you've got to be jolly good at it. And one of the things you've got to be jolly good at it is thinking on your feet and coming up with a convincing explanation when the evidence comes out all different from what you expected. So for old Wellieboots thinking up a good story in ten seconds flat would be a piece of cake. After all, he'd know you wouldn't have any experience in cross-examination, so he didn't have to worry about you picking holes in it."

"I questioned him," I said rather coldly, "with as much rigour as the circumstances permitted."

"Oh yes? All right then, what does he say he was doing that night in Sark when poor old Edward Malvoisin got pushed off the cliff?"

"He told me," I said with some reluctance, though I did not regard this part of the judge's narrative as being confidential, "that he spent the night in one of the outbuildings on Philippe Alexandre's farm and saw you all retire for the night to the Witch's Cottage. After that he slept until daybreak."

Cantrip's hooting merriment echoed round the Salon Rose.

I spent, I confess, a somewhat troubled night. Though I myself had every confidence that Sir Arthur Welladay had told me the truth, I had been obliged to admit that his account of his movements on the previous Monday night did not, strictly speaking, provide him with what is termed an alibi. If he had in fact stayed awake rather longer than he had claimed—long enough, that is to say, to observe the departure from the farmhouse of Edward Malvoisin, to follow the unfortunate advocate to the Coupee, and there to encompass his death—it would indeed have been beyond the limits of reasonable truthfulness to give me a wholly accurate account.

I did not for a moment believe that anything of the kind had occurred. On the other hand, if I were in error, I could not disguise from myself that the arrangement I had made would require my young friend to travel back to London in inescapable proximity to a murderer. Such thoughts conduce ill to sleep.

His belief in Sir Arthur Welladay's homicidal inclinations had not at all deterred Cantrip from giving effect to the arrangement. On the contrary, he had embraced it, I suspect, with far greater enthusiasm than he would have done if I had persuaded him of the judge's innocence. His spirits, when on the following morning we set out for Nice airport—I could do no less than accompany him so far— were high to the point of effervescence; mine were weighed down by doubt and apprehension.

"Cantrip," I said, when we had been driving for some ten minutes along the Middle Corniche, "you know that I would not for the world expose you to any personal danger."

"Oh, I wouldn't worry about that, old thing," said Cantrip cheerfully. "I mean, you didn't when you set the thing up, so why start now? I shouldn't think old Wellieboots is loopy enough to stick a knife in my ribs in the middle of a planeful of passengers."

"I'm sure he isn't," I said. "I mean, I am sure that he is perfectly well-balanced and law-abiding. But at the same time—"

"Anyway, if he does, that'll jolly well prove he's as nutty as a fruitcake and ought to be put away somewhere he can't do any harm—House of Lords or somewhere. So at least he'll stop bothering Gabrielle. I say, you'll be seeing Gabrielle, won't you?"

"Yes," I said. "We are lunching together on Monday."

"You'll explain why I've left Monte Carlo, won't you? I wouldn't want her to think I'd just gone off and left her in the lurch."

"Yes," I said. "Yes, of course."

"And the other thing you might do is give something

to that rather jolly chambermaid for me. I know she talked a lot of rot about me being keen on Gabrielle, which was all bilge, of course, but she was right about me winning at the Casino, so I sort of feel she ought to get a slice of the winnings. If I give you a tenner when we get to the airport, will you pass it on to her?"

"Yes," I said. "Yes, certainly." His requests fell on my ear with a dismally testamentary ring.

Having delivered the motorcar to a representative of the company from which he had hired it, we joined the line of prospective travellers waiting for boarding cards. I saw, a few places ahead of us, the tall figure of the judge. He glanced briefly towards us as he strode away towards the departure gate, and for the first time that morning I perceived in my young friend's eyes a flicker of apprehension.

"My dear Cantrip," I said, "perhaps after all it would be better not to take this flight."

"Don't talk rot, old thing," said Cantrip. "If I don't go on this one, Wellieboots won't either, and we'll be back at square one."

"But if you really think—"

"I'm not worried about him trying to bump me off. It's just that I'd forgotten how he looks at you, like one of those things that turn people to stone—you know, an obelisk."

He meant, I suppose, a basilisk, but I had not the heart to dispute with the poor boy.

It consoled me but little to reflect, during my return journey to Monte Carlo, that if he were now travelling in the company of a murderer I would not myself be lunching with one in two days' time. Admittedly, if Gabrielle was not Welladay's daughter—and it would hardly be logical to accept his evidence on all other issues and reject it on that—

she was not a descendant of Sir Walter Palgrave and accordingly not a potential beneficiary of the Daffodil fund. I had believed from the outset, however, and saw no reason now to alter my opinion, that so far as motive was concerned the professional advisers to the settlement were as worthy of suspicion as the beneficiaries. And what of Gabrielle's fountain pen? All those who had been in her company on Sark and might have found an opportunity to steal it seemed now to be excluded from suspicion. It appeared then that she herself must have dropped it: for her to have done so by any innocent accident at the very place where Malvoisin had fallen would surely be . . . a most remarkable coincidence.

A telephone call on Saturday afternoon assured me of Cantrip's safe arrival in London, unmolested by any homicidal attention from Mr. Justice Welladay. I was sufficiently relieved to be able to spend the remainder of the weekend in almost unalloyed enjoyment of the pleasures of the Mediterranean. On the Monday morning, however, I woke with a sense of apprehension, which I realised after a few moments was attributable to the prospect of lunching with the Contessa.

Shortly after breakfast I encountered, for the first time since Cantrip's departure, the gipsy-eyed chambermaid, and made haste to honour my undertaking to give her a suitable share of his winnings.

"I do wish," I said, "that you would tell me how you knew of my friend's attachment to an auburn-haired lady who wears Houbigant's Raffiné."

"Oh," she said, with a teasing smile, "don't you wish I would tell you how I knew he would win at the Casino?"

"No, mademoiselle, I don't think I need to ask you that. I would rather suppose that you tell all visitors of a certain type that they will be lucky at the Casino. If they are not, they will hardly venture to reproach you. If they are, they will think it just to give you a share of their winnings. Inexperienced as I am in the ways of the world, I can guess so much of the art of prophecy."

"Oh," said the girl, "I am afraid you are a very cynical person, Professor. Well, if you can guess my secrets so easily, I do not see why I should tell you any more."

"Mademoiselle, I beg you," I said. "Take pity on the curiosity of a poor harmless Scholar."

She could not at once be persuaded to relinquish the pleasure of teasing; but she was a good-natured girl at heart, and well disposed to me on account of Cantrip's present.

"Well, Professor, it is very simple after all—I am surprised that you could not guess. When one finds three pretty auburn hairs on the jacket of someone's pyjamas, and it still smells just a little of Raffiné, it is not so difficult to tell his fortune."

"Mademoiselle," I said, "are you quite sure about the brand of perfume? Could you have made a mistake?"

"I am from Grasse, Professor. I do not make mistakes about perfume."

I left in excellent spirits for my lunch with the Contessa, knowing that whatever her failings she had not murdered Edward Malvoisin.

She had suggested a restaurant in the Condamine, at the junction between the Rue de Millo and the Rue Terrazani, within five minutes' walk both of my hotel and of her own office. Its Provençal cooking and an admirable wine list are mentioned with approval in *The Guide to Comfortable Tax Planning.*

Though she seemed to me to have a little less sparkle in her large eyes than when I had last seen her, she was nonetheless charming company. Having considered the menu with the care it deserved and ordered a bottle of pale pink Provençal wine, we somehow fell to exchanging small items of harmless scandal—on her side of those residents of Monaco sufficiently noted for their wealth or other distinction to be of interest to me, on mine of various friends and colleagues whose names were known to her from her professional reading. She seemed to feel that she had the best of the bargain.

"I am afraid," she said sadly, "that Monte Carlo gossip is not so interesting as the gossip of Oxford and London. It is a very small place, you see—one is always meeting the same people and hearing the same stories. And always about how much money they have spent—how much on the new yacht, how much on the new mistress, how much on the new Picasso. It is so parochial, I sometimes think I shall suffocate—I have to walk across the border to Roquebrune just to feel that I can breathe."

"But, Gabrielle," I said, "your skills are of an international nature, and the Edelweiss Bank has offices all over the world. Could you not arrange to be transferred to somewhere more congenial?"

"I don't know." She shrugged her shoulders. "Perhaps it could be arranged. But Giovanni feels at home here, you see—he would not like to move."

"At least," I said, "your work provides you with opportunities to travel."

"Not so many as you would think—with the telephone and the telex and the tele-this and the tele-that, it is hardly possible nowadays to find an excuse to leave one's office. Oh, all this technology, it's taken the fun out of everything. I travel in connection with the Daffodil Settlement, as you know, but that is rather exceptional—oh, my darling Daffodil, what should I do without you? I should go nowhere and meet no one."

"You cannot meet many new friends in connection with that. I gather that all those connected with it have known one another for many years."

"Yes, of course that is true, but sometimes one makes new friends. This time there was Michael."

I recalled my promise to explain to her the full reasons for Cantrip's departure, making it clear that he had not heartlessly abandoned her to the persecutions of Mr. Justice Welladay.

"Oh no," said Gabrielle, the sparkle returning to her eyes, "I know he would not do that. Wasn't it wonderful how he followed me all the way across France to protect me from his Mr. Justice Wellieboots? Of course he is quite mad."

Since the remark seemed intended in a complimentary spirit, it did not seem to be incumbent on me to offer any defence of Cantrip's sanity. I contented myself with remarking that I myself was very fond of the boy, but thought him perhaps a trifle lacking in discretion.

"Discretion?" Her face dissolved into a charming arrangement of upward curves. "Oh, I am afraid you are right, he has very little discretion. Do you perhaps know a friend of mine, Julia Larwood, a tax lawyer in London?" I acknowledged that I did. "Well, the first time I saw Michael he was with Edward Malvoisin in the Grand Hotel in St. Helier—they did not know I was there, I was wearing my old-lady clothes—and he was talking about poor Julia, the most personal things, quite at the top of his voice. And he meant it so nicely, because he wanted to show Edward how passionate she was and how fond of men. But I sat behind my potted palm tree and remembered that Julia had been to great trouble to make Edward think she was not at all passionate and not at all fond of men. Poor Edward, sometimes with women he could be a little bit of a nuisance. So I knew at once that Michael was not at all discreet."

"He is, of course, very young," I said. "Naive and lacking in experience of the realities of life. He has not been reared in that sceptical tradition which teaches one to doubt whether things are always what they seem. He could not otherwise have been deceived by thick stockings and a black shawl into thinking that a beautiful young woman was an aged crone." She smiled and refilled my glass in recognition of the compliment. "And to take another example—he is probably unfamiliar with the plot of *All's Well That Ends Well.*"

"Oh," said the Contessa thoughtfully, and for several minutes devoted her attention to the gobletful of fruit and multicoloured ice cream which the waitress had just placed in front of her. I in turn kept myself occupied with cheese and biscuits, thinking it tactful to remain silent until she spoke again.

"I should like you to understand," she said at last, "that I am truly very fond of my husband. I would not hurt his feelings for anything in the world. But one needs, you understand, a little variety, a little amusement. Giovanni would not understand—he would be upset. So you see, discretion is important to me."

"Yes, I quite understand. And knowing that Cantrip did not possess that quality, you made a plan with Clementine for him to spend the night with you but be under the impression that he had spent it with her. Gabrielle, I should not like you to think me censorious, but do you not feel that that was just a little heartless?"

"Oh dear, Hilary, do you think so? We thought it was such a nice idea—and I knew that Clementine was very discreet. At least—I thought so."

I hastened to reassure her that my only source of information was Cantrip himself, and that he was still under the firm impression that his companion that night had been Clementine.

"But then—how did you know?"

"My dear Gabrielle, for the Scholar the reasoning was very simple. When one finds that two manuscripts have a number of curious features in common, one is disposed to conclude that one is a copy of the other or that they are copies of the same original. A liaison, however brief, conducted in complete silence and total darkness can hardly be considered usual—I could not fail to be reminded of the scheme by which Helena secured the consummation of her marriage to the Count de Roussillon." I thought it unnecessary, and perhaps indelicate, to make any mention of the chambermaid.

"Once I learnt of your connection with Sark, I saw how easy it would have been for you to make the necessary arrangements—to persuade Albert to desert his post, so that you were all obliged to stay overnight, and to engineer a convenient light failure."

"Well, that is very clever of you, Hilary. Clementine owes me a bottle of champagne—she bet me that Michael would find out somehow. Of course, if he had, I would have asked him not to tell anyone, and I think that really he would not have done, but it is much better that he does not know at all. You won't tell him, will you? I think it might upset him somehow—I am much older than he is, you know—I think he looks on me as a sort of favourite aunt."

"It does not seem to me," I said, "that he regards you in quite that light. But I agree that it is better for him not to know the truth."

We ordered coffee, content with the understanding between us, but Gabrielle had no chance to drink it. A neatly dressed girl, who proved to be her secretary, arrived with news of a telex message from Clementine convening an urgent meeting of the Daffodil advisers at the Grand Hotel in St. Helier at nine o'clock on the following morning. There had been, it seemed, a further development.

"Hilary, I am very sorry—I must leave you. I know we have not talked at all about your research, but if I am flying to Jersey tonight I have so many things to arrange before I leave. Oh, poor Giovanni, he will be so upset at me going away again so soon. Please, stay and finish your coffee—I will leave a cheque with you to cover the bill. No, no, I insist—you are my guest."

It happened to be the last cheque in her chequebook. She did not trouble, having signed it, to detach it from its counterfoil but left the whole chequebook lying on the table beside me. I have wondered since whether in some recess of her unconscious mind she remembered and intended me to learn the secret that it contained. At the time, however, though it struck me as a piece of uncharacteristic carelessness, I thought it of no consequence. After settling the account for our meal I put away the little book of counterfoils with the intention of at some convenient time returning it to her.

It occurred to me after a few minutes that a similar summons from Clementine might be awaiting me at my hotel. I accordingly returned there in some haste, but found no message from her. With a curious sense of restlessness and unease, I walked back to the corner of the harbour and took the *ascenseur publique* to the Exotic Gardens. Any hope, however, of being soothed by the beauties of nature was doomed to disappointment. The grotesque and distorted shapes of the huge cacti imitated all too well the confusion of my mind concerning the death of Edward Malvoisin.

I could find no way of construing the facts known to me that did not lead to some absurd and irrational conclusion. Every theory that I proposed to myself, whether fanciful or commonplace, left some vital element in the problem mysterious and unaccounted for: Gabrielle's conviction, long before Sir Arthur Welladay appeared on the scene, that someone was watching her at Daffodil meetings; the finding of her pen on the Coupee; above all, perhaps, the part played in the affair by the woman in white—the formless, faceless figure who had appeared from the darkness on Walpurgis Night within a few yards of the place where Malvoisin had met his death.

It was not until late that evening, after dining at my hotel, that I recalled being in possession of Gabrielle's chequebook.

There are many, I daresay, who would have thought it pointless, perhaps even improper, to subject such an item to any careful scrutiny; but it is not in the nature of the Scholar to neglect the study of any documentary evidence that comes to hand, however unrewarding the task may at first sight appear. It was almost by instinct that I read through the counterfoils, noting with idle interest how clear a record they provided of Gabrielle's movements in the Channel Islands.

The penultimate entry related to a withdrawal on 1st May from a bank in St. Malo. When I saw it my blood seemed to turn to ice.

16

From the entrance to the Grand Hotel there is an admirable view across St. Aubyn's Bay to Elizabeth Castle, named by Sir Walter Raleigh in honour of his formidable sovereign and built on the islet where the hermit Helier, patron saint of Jersey and its capital, was martyred in the sixth century by marauding Norsemen. Alighting from my taxi on the following morning, however, I spared the historic fortress no more than a glance before turning to make my way towards the reception desk.

Weary though I was from rising before dawn and from the rigours of my journey, my steps were quickened by an anxiety more urgent than the desire for rest. My attempts to communicate by telephone with Cantrip, directly or through any of our mutual acquaintance, had all proved fruitless. Eventually, finding that I chanced to have in my possession a letter bearing the telex number of Julia's Chambers, I had prevailed on the telex operator at the Clair de Lune to transmit a message to her; but I had been obliged to express myself in terms more guarded than I would have wished, and in any case had little hope of its being read in time to be of the slightest use.

I had no need to enquire the whereabouts of Clementine Derwent, for she was standing at the reception desk, engaged in what seemed to be a mildly acrimonious conversation with a member of the hotel management. She looked flustered, like a schoolboy who has been overoptimistic about the time required for his homework, and despite the civility of her greeting I was not entirely sure that she was pleased to see me.

"It's awfully good of you to come, Professor Tamar, but I really didn't mean to drag you all the way back from Monte Carlo. That's why I didn't send you a telex about the meeting."

"My dear Clementine," I said, "that was most thoughtful of you. The fact is, however, that I am not here solely for the purpose of the meeting. There is something I have to discuss with Cantrip, as a matter of some urgency, and I was expecting to find him here. Perhaps, however, you thought his presence unnecessary at this particular meeting?"

Her answer dashed such slender hopes as I had that the boy might still be safely in London.

"Oh no, I asked him to be here and he is. Well, here in Jersey. He's invited Gabrielle to go out for breakfast somewhere."

"Do you happen to know where?"

"No, Professor Tamar, I don't," said Clementine with a certain peevishness. "And I don't quite know why everyone expects me to act as some kind of keeper. Oh dear— I'm sorry, but Gabrielle's husband has turned up and he's in a bit of a stew because I don't know where she is. He says awful things keep happening at Daffodil meetings and he's had a sort of premonition of something that she's in some kind of danger. So I'm feeling a bit—"

"Your telephone call from Geneva, Miss Derwent," said the switchboard operator behind the reception desk.

"Oh lord—Professor Tamar, will you excuse me? Would you like to go and join the others in the coffee lounge? I'll be with you as soon as I can."

In the coffee lounge three men were sitting round one of the low tables: Patrick Ardmore, Gideon Darkside, and Count Giovanni di Silvabianca. My last encounter with Ardmore and Darkside having taken place, as my readers may recall, in somewhat unconventional circumstances at the Remnant Club, it was with some degree of misgiving that I renewed the acquaintance. My explanation of my presence at the Grand Hotel—namely that I had been retained by Clementine to trace the descendants of Sir Walter Palgrave and had thought my attendance to be of some possible value—met with a mixed response: Ardmore expressed his pleasure at meeting me again and enquired warmly after the Colonel; Darkside made various observations with which I need not trouble my readers—"nosy-parkering academic" was among the least offensive of the expressions he employed. I treated these, I need hardly say, with the dignified indifference becoming to the Scholar.

"I am afraid that Mr. Darkside must think me also an intruder," said the Count apologetically. After giving me a courteous greeting he had kept a troubled silence. "And Gabrielle, too, will say I ought not to have come. But last night I had suddenly a feeling that she was in danger here, and I do not think one can ignore such feelings—you will think perhaps, Professor Tamar, that I am too superstitious?" I shook my head, having found that such apparently irrational presentiments are often the product of some perfectly efficient process of unconscious reasoning. "Well, perhaps I am, but I could not stay in Monte Carlo when I thought she was in danger—I have been travelling almost all night. And now she is not at the hotel where she was staying, she has not arrived here for the meeting, and no one knows where she is."

"Giovanni," said Patrick Ardmore with gentle impatience, "she's simply having breakfast out somewhere. Our meeting's not due to begin until nine o'clock, and it's only just after half past eight."

"It's nearly quarter to nine," said the Count, "and she knows everyone is here. And she is always so conscientious about her business engagements."

"Young Michael Cantrip's with her—he'll take good care of her."

"I know he will do his best," said the Count, but the anxiety remained in his dark eyes.

After glowering in silence for a while Gideon Darkside found further food for his displeasure. He pointed to the far corner of the room.

"What's that girl doing here? Haven't we even got this room to ourselves? This is supposed to be a private meeting, even if we are keeping open house for freeloaders from Oxford."

Looking in the direction he indicated, I saw that there was indeed another person present, though sitting in a large armchair in such quiet and timid obscurity as readily to escape notice. It was Lilian.

"She is employed as a secretary at 62 New Square," I

said. "Since it cannot be supposed that she is here by coincidence, presumably Miss Derwent has some reason for thinking her presence desirable."

"A secretary? What do we need a secretary for? We've never needed a secretary at Daffodil meetings before. And if we do, why can't we hire one here in Jersey instead of flying her in from London and putting her up at the most expensive hotel in St. Helier? Oh, I know what it is—62 New Square. That's young Cantrip's Chambers. She's his little bit of fluff, I suppose, and the Derwent girl's let him bring her over here at the expense of the trust fund. Well, he's not getting away with it."

"Do be quiet, Gideon, she'll hear you," said Patrick Ardmore.

It appeared indeed that she was aware of being an object of discussion, for her cheeks had grown pink and she was studying a magazine with the intensity of one who wishes to be thought unaware of her surroundings. Plainly, however, it was a pretence—the instant that Clementine entered the room she looked up and smiled as if at a potential rescuer. Clementine went straight across to her, stooped and squeezed her hand, and seemed to be uttering words of encouragement.

When the young solicitor finally joined us at the coffee table, Darkside renewed his objections to my presence at the meeting.

"Well," said Clementine a little wearily, "I don't quite see what it is you're worrying about, Gideon, but if that's how you feel about it, I don't suppose Professor Tamar will mind leaving us once the meeting's properly started."

"My dear Clementine, not in the least," I said. "I

merely supposed that it might be helpful to those attending to hear what progress I have made."

Clementine looked embarrassed.

"Well, actually—actually, Professor Tamar, this latest development means it's not really necessary for you to go on with your investigation. I'm awfully sorry you've come all this way for nothing—if I'd known you were thinking of coming, I'd have tried to let you know."

"I see," I said, reflecting on the significance of this unexpected turn of events. "You will recall, my dear Clementine, that there were two aspects of the matter which you wished me to consider. The identity of the descendants now living of Sir Walter Palgrave and—a further question which you believed might be related. Am I to understand that you now regard both aspects of the enquiry to be otiose?"

"Well, yes," said Clementine. She looked uncomfortable, but at the same time slightly belligerent. "I'm sorry, Professor Tamar, but when we first talked about this I was in a bit of a state. In view of what's happened since, I know I was just imagining things. So I'd really be awfully grateful if you'd just forget the whole thing—subject to our settling your account for the work you've already done, of course."

It was perhaps fortunate, since I was in some uncertainty how to proceed, that at this point a waiter entered the coffee lounge to enquire whether we included among our number a Miss Larwood, a Mr. Cantrip, or a Professor Tamar—a Miss Jardine telephoning from London wished to speak to any one of those named. I rose and left my companions with, I confess, some relief.

Despite the distance which divided us, I detected in Selena's voice an uncharacteristic note of agitation—she seemed to be accusing me of having encouraged Julia to elope with the Colonel. I protested in bewilderment that I had done nothing of the kind.

"About ten minutes ago," said Selena, "I arrived in Chambers and found on my desk a note from Julia, apparently written in some haste in the early hours of the morning. She says that she and Colonel Cantrip are going to Jersey and she has no time to explain why, but that the items of correspondence enclosed will make everything clear to me. By 'enclosed' she seems to mean 'attached by means of a paper clip,' and by 'clear' she seems to mean 'totally obscure'—I suppose one can't expect a very high standard of precision at five o'clock in the morning. The correspondence to which she refers consists of the following items. Item one—a telex message from Clementine to Cantrip, sent at lunchtime yesterday, asking him to attend a meeting at the Grand Hotel this morning and to telephone to confirm the arrangement. Item two—a telex message to Cantrip from the Contessa di Silvabianca, transmitted in Monaco yesterday afternoon, inviting him to have breakfast with her. Item three—item three, Hilary, is a telex message from you to Julia, apparently dispatched from Monte Carlo late last night, indicating that if Cantrip goes to Jersey he will be in danger of a murderous attack from the same person who is responsible for the death of Edward Malvoisin. I really can't imagine what you expected Julia to do about it."

"I certainly didn't expect her," I said, "to come to Jersey herself. In any case, there's no sign of her here, or of the Colonel. I daresay the plane was full and they're still at Heathrow or Gatwick. I really don't think that you need to worry about her."

Sarah Caudwell

"Don't you? Well, in that case I can concentrate on worrying about Cantrip. Have you seen anything of him?"

"I have only just arrived, and he has not yet returned from breakfasting with the Contessa. Selena, is there anything in her telex to indicate where they were to meet?"

"I will read you the full text. 'Dear Michael—there is something in connection with the Daffodil Settlement which I would like to discuss with you in private before the meeting, but I arrive in Jersey too late to talk to you this evening. Can you get up very early and have breakfast with me at St. Clement tomorrow? I will bring some coffee and rolls from my hotel and hope to see you at quarter to seven at the place where we met before. Warmest wishes— Gabrielle di Silvabianca.' Hilary, are you serious about someone wanting to attack Cantrip? Is St. Clement the sort of place where he might be in any danger?"

"It is the place, according to Julia, where the witches danced and the sirens sang. But I don't think," I added with foolish complacency, "that Cantrip can be in any danger there. The person who murdered Edward Malvoisin is here in the Grand Hotel."

Although it still lacked a few minutes to nine o'clock, I returned to the coffee lounge to find Gideon Darkside complaining of the delay in opening the meeting. Gabrielle and Cantrip both knew perfectly well, he said, that everyone else was already there and that to wait any longer was a waste of time and money. How much longer were they going to be, and where were they anyway?

"I have been speaking," I said, "to a colleague of Cantrip's in London. I gather that they have gone to a place

244

called St. Clement—they were to meet there at quarter to seven."

The information seemed to move the Count to renewed anxiety.

"I know where they will have gone if they have gone to St. Clement. There is a rock there that Gabrielle calls the Sirens' Rock. It's a favourite place of hers—one of those you can reach only at low tide. I don't like her going there, it's too dangerous—I've heard of people being cut off by the tide and drowning. But what can I do? When I say she should not go there she laughs at me." He spread his hands in a gesture of hopelessness.

"My dear man, of course she does," said Patrick Ardmore. "She's a sensible woman, Giovanni, and she knows the Channel Islands—she isn't some silly day-tripper who doesn't know about the tides. She's as safe at St. Clement as by the swimming pool."

"If we knew what time low tide was," said Clementine, "we might have some idea of when to expect them back. Is there any way of finding out?"

"Nothing easier," said the Irishman. "It'll be in the *Evening Post.* I'll see if they've got a copy at the reception desk."

We waited in silence for his return, as if we had all begun to feel more disquiet than we cared to speak of aloud. I observed that Lilian had drawn unobtrusively closer, as though fearing to miss some news of grave import, and was sitting, pale and serious, in a straight-backed chair at the edge of the group round the coffee table.

Returning from his errand with a copy of the local paper in his hand, Patrick Ardmore seemed to me to look a trifle less carefree than when he had left us. He spoke, however, with his customary optimism.

"Low tide was at six-twenty this morning, so it must already have turned by the time they set out. Assuming it takes three quarters of an hour or so to walk out to the rock, they'd have been there by half past seven, and I'd say they'd have to start back again by about quarter to eight to be sure of getting back safely. That gives them just time to eat their breakfast. Allowing twenty minutes or thereabouts for the drive back here, my guess is that they'll be here any moment now." Something in his expression, however, made me think that he found the timing imprudently fine.

"And wanting more breakfast, I expect," said Clementine. "Yes, Patrick, I'm sure you're right."

"Excuse me, Mr. Ardmore," said Lilian, "but what happens if you're not?"

The Irishman seemed disconcerted by the question, or perhaps by the identity of the questioner.

"If I'm not—I'm sorry, my dear, I don't quite understand what you mean."

"You said they'd have to leave that rock place by quarter to eight to be sure of getting back safely," said Lilian, blushing at her own persistence. "What would happen if they hadn't?"

"Well, by the third hour after low water, the gullies between the rocks and the shore start filling up with water fairly quickly—the tide's at its fastest, you see, in the third and fourth hours after it turns. If they left it much later than that, they'd be cut off."

"So they'd get wet," said Darkside. "Don't suppose it

would do them any harm. They can both swim, can't they?"

"You don't know what you're talking about, Gideon," said Ardmore, provoked by the irritation which the accountant seemed always to inspire in him to say more than I think he had intended. "The tides here are among the most powerful in the world, and the currents correspondingly dangerous. You'd have to be a very strong swimmer indeed to have any chance of making it across St. Clement's Bay when the tide is in." He meant, it seemed to me, that it could not be done. "It would be better to stay put on the rock and hope to be rescued—but it wouldn't be very long before you were underwater."

"O dear God," said the Count.

"But it couldn't conceivably happen to Gabrielle," said Ardmore, becoming aware that these last remarks were less than reassuring. "It can only happen to people who don't know about the tides or are silly enough to forget about them. It's out of the question for Gabrielle to do such a thing."

"Suppose . . ." said Lilian timidly, "suppose they fell asleep."

"My dear girl, that really is nonsense, you know. On a hot summer afternoon, perhaps, with a couple of hours to spend out at the rock before they had to come back, I suppose it could happen. But first thing in the morning, knowing they'd only got twenty minutes out there—no, my dear, the idea's absurd."

I did not doubt that he was right. And yet the image having once entered my mind would not easily leave it of a dark young man and an auburn-haired woman, asleep as if

247

spellbound on the Sirens' Rock, while the sea crept in to surround them in its implacable embrace.

The Count rose suddenly from his chair.

"I am sorry, but I can't bear it, simply to go on sitting here. So many terrible things have happened, and Gabrielle is my wife. How can I sit here and do nothing when she may be in danger? Please, Patrick, I know that you will think me very foolish, but will you drive me out to St. Clement?"

"If that's what you want, Giovanni, then of course I'll drive you there. But I'm sure there's nothing to be afraid of, nothing in this world."

"But you see, Patrick," said the Count sombrely, "I am not sure that it is anything in this world that I am afraid of."

CHAPTER 17 —

I have endeavoured throughout my account of the Daffodil affair to present the evidence to my readers in the order in which it became available to me, neither concealing any facts of which I was aware nor anticipating those of which I was as yet ignorant. It would be difficult, however, to understand clearly what occurred during the next half hour without knowing of certain other events which took place outside the range of my observation. I have accordingly thought it right—all the more readily because the contrary decision might perhaps have been attributed to a vulgar and meretricious desire to create what is termed suspense—to interpolate at this point in my narrative a letter, written by Julia, which I did not in fact see until some time later.

Sarah Caudwell

Dearest Selena,

Although it seems far from certain when, if at all, I shall be able to send this to you, or whether, if and when I am, it will represent the most expeditious means of communication, I shall not on that account deprive myself of the consolation of writing to you and the benefit, if only in fancy, of your always invaluable advice. I am beginning to feel that I may have acted unwisely.

When Cantrip rushed into my room yesterday afternoon, saying that he was obliged to go instantly to Jersey and asking me to stand substitute for him in the arrangements made for the entertainment of his uncle, he gave me little opportunity for reflection or refusal. Taking my compliance for granted, he rushed out again, pausing only to thrust into my hands two telex messages, one from Clementine and one from Gabrielle, which he claimed would enable me to explain everything to Henry. You will have found these enclosed with the note I left for you.

The Colonel's idea of a real evening out, apparently, is one which begins at about eleven o'clock at night and continues until dawn. I accordingly took the precaution of having two or three hours' sleep beforehand, and was sufficiently invigorated to share his disappointment when the nightclub which enjoyed our custom decided to close at the absurdly early hour of 4 A.M. I persuaded him to leave, however, without any unduly vigorous protest, and we set forth in search of breakfast.

It is extraordinary how difficult it is to find breakfast in central London at four o'clock in the morning—
one would have thought, with all the initiative and
enterprise that is supposed to be about nowadays, that
the area round Covent Garden would at that hour be
full of charming little cafés eager to offer refreshment
to the passing reveller. This proving, however, not to
be the case, we were eventually obliged to walk back to
Lincoln's Inn and make coffee for ourselves in Chambers.

It was thus that I found much earlier than could
reasonably have been expected the telex message from
Hilary which I also enclosed in my note to you—the one
which seemed to imply that if Cantrip went to Jersey
he would be in some serious danger. I read it with great
anxiety, shared, when I showed it to him, by the Colonel.

We drank some strong coffee to clarify our minds,
wondering what we should do, and it occurred to me
that it might be helpful to look again at the two other
telex messages which Cantrip had given me. It struck
me, when I looked more closely at the one purporting
to be from Gabrielle, that there was something distinctly odd about it.

Gabrielle, as you know, has spent most of her adult
life in the employment of a Swiss bank, and on matters
of secrecy and confidentiality she has become, if I may
so express it, more Swiss than the Swiss. And yet there,
where any Swiss banker I have ever met would have
written "in connection with the matter we were speaking of," was the phrase "in connection with the Daffodil
Settlement."

I told the Colonel that in my opinion the message
was spurious, and we were at one in concluding, in the

light of the telex from Hilary, that it had been sent for some very sinister purpose.

"Dirty work at the crossroads," said the Colonel. "We'd better get over there and put a stop to it."

Left to myself, I am bound to say, I should not have thought of so energetic a course of action, but I would not have liked the Colonel to think—nor indeed would I have wished to think it of myself—that if Cantrip were in serious danger I would be deterred by mere indolence from doing anything to assist him. I reflected, moreover, that the Colonel, by virtue of his profession, had long experience of what to do when people are trying to kill people, whereas I had the good fortune to have none, and accordingly it was right that I should defer to his judgment. I pointed out, however, that the early morning plane to Jersey, even if we could obtain seats on it, was unlikely to arrive in time for us to play any useful part in whatever dirty work might be in progress.

The Colonel spoke dismissively of aeroplanes and said that what we wanted was a helicopter. I at first found this remark somewhat lacking in realism, since I saw no prospect of our being able to obtain such a thing, still less of our finding anyone to fly it.

"Nonsense, my dear," said the Colonel, "I was flying choppers before you were born. And I know where to get hold of one easily enough—still got a few contacts from the old days, you know. The problem's getting to it—pity we've got no wheels."

This observation brought to my mind three facts which taken in conjunction seemed material to our dilemma: (i) that since Timothy went away his motorcar had been parked in Lincoln's Inn; (ii) that the keys to it were in his desk next door in 62; (iii) that the key

which gives me access to your room would also provide
access to Timothy's.

I hope that Timothy will not be unduly vexed
about the motorcar. It has suffered no damage, apart
from one or two scratches, and is really quite safely
parked in a field somewhere about an hour's drive
south of London. Admittedly I do not know the precise
address of the field, but it can be distinguished from
other fields in the vicinity by the fact that it has a high
wire fence round it and contains a number of helicopters. It also contains a large shedlike structure pro-
claiming itself to be a heliclub.

Arriving there shortly after daybreak, we found
the place deserted, save for an elderly man sitting in a
sort of booth or kiosk beside the gateway. He greeted
the Colonel with cordiality and deference—I gathered
from their exchanges that the Colonel had at some time
been his commanding officer—and admitted us to the
field. To my surprise the Colonel made no reference to
the urgency of our business or to the helicopter which I
understood to be available for his use, but implied that
our expedition was for the simple purpose of my
amusement—a notion to which my still being in evening dress no doubt lent a certain credibility. He enquired what chance there was of my being able to
enjoy the spectacle of a helicopter actually taking off,
and was told that one of the members of the heliclub
would be arriving shortly and flying to Le Touquet.

Evidently pleased by this information, the Colonel
led me into the shedlike structure and asked me if I
would care to powder my nose. Having acted on this
suggestion, I returned from the cloakroom to find him
in conversation with a tall man whose face was vaguely
familiar to me from the financial pages of the newspa-

pers—his name, if my memory serves me, is frequently mentioned in connection with takeover bids and so forth. The Colonel was showing a friendly interest in the technical details of his flight to Le Touquet—the amount of fuel he would need and the kind of equipment he was using and matters of that kind—and being unable to make any useful contribution to such questions, I took no part in the conversation. After a few minutes the financier withdrew to the cloakroom and the Colonel followed his example.

The Colonel was the first to reappear, saying briskly, "Time we were on our way, m'dear." Taking me by the arm, he led me outside and across the field towards one of the helicopters. He assisted me into it with his usual old-fashioned gallantry, and himself then climbed into the pilot's seat. Various knobs and levers were twiddled and pressed, the blades above us began to rotate at ever-increasing speed, and we rose rapidly into the air.

Turning my head for a last look at the building we had left, I saw the financier waving to us from the window of the cloakroom and thought it courteous to wave back.

The flight so far has been, I suppose, uneventful, save that from time to time the machine gives a sort of hiccough and descends, before recovering itself, to within twenty feet or so of the waters of the Atlantic. I am still attempting, since I know of no other way of coping with the situation, to sustain my imitation of my Aunt Regina, and this precludes any overt display of nervousness; but the phrase "Whoops, sorry, m'dear," which is the Colonel's habitual comment on such occasions, does not altogether serve to reassure me. I do not doubt his assertion that he was flying helicopters before

I was born; but you will perhaps think that it would have been prudent to ask him whether he has flown any since that date. It may be, of course, that flying a helicopter is one of those skills, like swimming or riding a bicycle, which when once acquired is never lost; on the other hand, it may be that it isn't.

My mind is at present anxiously divided between the following questions: (i) is Cantrip really in danger? (ii) does the Colonel know how to land the helicopter? (iii) why did the financier remain so long in the cloakroom? There was something about the way he waved at us which somehow—but surely not even the Colonel . . .

We are approaching a coastline which the Colonel believes to be that of Jersey—I suppose, therefore, that my doubts on all these matters, if not indeed others of a more eternal nature, will shortly be resolved. In the meantime I remain, dearest Selena,

Yours, as always,

Julia

It would have been sensible, no doubt, if at least one of our number had remained at the Grand Hotel to explain to Cantrip and Gabrielle, should our misgivings prove ill-founded, the reasons for our sudden excursus. Patrick Ardmore's motorcar, however, was of sufficient size to accommodate five passengers, and none of us, not even Darkside, least of all Lilian, could resist the compulsion which drew us towards St. Clement.

"There are several places that they might have started

from," said Ardmore as we drove eastwards along the coast road out of St. Helier. "I'm afraid we'll simply have to stop and see if there's any sign of them at any of the places one can park a car. I suppose Gabrielle has hired a car? She usually does."

"She told me on the phone last night that she'd hired a little Fiesta," said Clementine. "But I don't know the registration number or even what colour it is."

"Patrick," said the Count, "you will go quickly, won't you?"

"As quickly as I can, Giovanni."

He continued eastwards, with neat granite houses and colourful gardens to our left and to our right an expanse of damp brown sand, scattered with rocks and seaweed, stretching down to a deceptively smiling sea. Once or twice we stopped at what seemed a possible parking space but found no sign there of those we were seeking.

"Clementine," I said, struck suddenly by a discrepancy in what I had been told, "didn't you say earlier that it was Cantrip who had invited the Contessa rather than vice versa?"

"That's what she told me on the phone last night," said Clementine. "She said he'd left a message for her at her hotel."

"But I understand," I said, "that it was she who invited him—by telex from Monte Carlo."

Clementine shrugged her shoulders, as at some point of tedious triviality.

The uneasiness which my supposed rationality had hitherto kept at bay laid a chilling hold on my spirits. I had thought of nothing save a direct attack, and it had not occurred to me how easily some soporific might be introduced into a flask of coffee provided for a guest by her hotel.

A little before half past nine, at the beginning of the fourth hour of the tide, we came to a place called Green Island, a beach between two small headlands, one topped with grass and the other with oak trees. Overlooking it was a little esplanade, showing signs of a modest popularity with the tourist trade: a café, at present closed, and a parking area, at present unoccupied save for a pink Fiesta motorcar.

On the backseat of the Fiesta was a coat which Clementine recognised as belonging to Gabrielle.

We stood looking out across the sea to where two or three minute arrowheads of rock on the far horizon were still uncovered by the incoming tide. One could not have guessed how rapidly the water was moving, for it seemed to creep inland only by inches, each successive wave breaking hardly closer than the one before; but I recalled that we were in the same area as the island of Mont St. Michel, where I had heard that when the tide is flowing the sea moves faster than a galloping horseman.

"She's out there," cried the Count, with a wild gesture towards the horizon. "I'm sure of it, she's still out there."

I felt a dreadful certainty that what he said was true, that on one of those tiny and still diminishing crests of rock were Cantrip and Gabrielle, perhaps in a drugged and oblivious sleep, perhaps now awake and too late aware of their danger, while the insatiable sea advanced hungrily upon them. As the sea gulls circled above us I saw dawning in the eyes of my companions the same terrible conviction.

Then, just above the horizon, there became discernible the rapid whirring of helicopter blades.

The hope that it offered must have seemed too fragile to risk speaking of. We pressed in silence against the railing which bounded the esplanade, straining our eyes to watch. The helicopter looked in the distance no larger than a flying insect, and when it seemed to slow and alter course we could feel no certainty that we were not deceiving ourselves. Beside me was Clementine, very pale, her left hand gripping the railing, her right arm protectively round Lilian's shoulders.

It was some moments before I realised that the Count was no longer on the esplanade but running down the stone steps which led to the beach, tearing off his jacket as he ran and flinging it down behind him. I saw also that Patrick Ardmore had set out in pursuit. Knowing what I did, I had no choice but to follow them.

Seeing the tall dark figure running swiftly across the damp brown sand and remembering the athletic prowess of his youth, I had thought that the Count would easily outdistance his pursuer. He slipped, however, or perhaps caught his foot in one of the tangled piles of seaweed, and took some seconds to recover himself. It seemed also that the tawny-haired Irishman was a faster runner and in better condition than one might have expected of a man of easygoing temperament. He overtook the Count before he reached the water and seized hold of him. The dark man broke away and turned again towards the sea, but Ardmore brought him to the ground and held him there.

They were locked, when I came up with them, in what looked like mortal combat, the one man twisting and turning in every direction to escape the unyielding grip of the other. The Count struck out furiously in his efforts to free himself, but Ardmore, though the shorter by three or four inches, was the more powerfully built, with some advantage in weight, and the blows were too wildly directed to oblige him to release his hold. Their words, when I came close enough to hear, were painful and breathless.

"Damn you, Patrick, let me go. I must try to get to them. I must try."

"It's suicide. You don't understand, Giovanni—the water will be coming through the gullies by now at a rate that would knock a wall down. It's no use—if they're there, you've no chance of saving them."

I looked out again to the far horizon. The helicopter had settled, gently and steadily, on one of the tiny arrowheads of rock.

"And no chance," I said, "of preventing them being saved."

Startled by my intervention, Ardmore relaxed his grip. The Count, had he chosen to do so, might perhaps have made his escape. He, too, however, seemed at that moment to lose heart for the struggle. The two men remained motionless, staring at me, as if turned to stone in the attitudes in which I had found them. For a long time, as it seemed to me, the silence was broken only by the crying of the sea gulls.

"What do you mean?" said the Count at last, his voice hardly audible.

"I mean," I answered, "that I know you, Count Giovanni, to be the murderer of Oliver Grynne and Edward Malvoisin, and that you have today attempted to procure the deaths of your wife, Gabrielle, and my friend Michael Cantrip."

"Professor," he said, fixing me with his dark tormented

eyes, "suppose I were to tell you that you are talking nonsense?"

"It would be no use," I said. "The evidence is conclusive. Your wife used the pen after her return to France, and the fact could be proved in court."

"Ah, the pen," he said musingly. "Yes, of course. I should have known the pen was a mistake."

"Dear God, Giovanni," said Ardmore, staring down at the man he still held pinned to the ground, "you can't mean it's true? It isn't possible." But I saw that all at once he knew it was.

"Of course it's true, Patrick," said the dark man. "As Gabrielle would tell you, one can't deceive a professor from Oxford. Now will you let me go?"

The Irishman did not instantly comply. He looked for a moment at me, as if half thinking that the decision ought to be partly mine, but then looked away again without meeting my eyes, evidently judging it one not to be shared. At last he released his grip and allowed the other man to rise to his feet.

"Why, Giovanni? In the name of reason, why?"

"She had dishonoured me," said the Count. "For my dishonour I must be revenged or die."

And still not knowing, I suppose, that people do not say or do that sort of thing any more, he walked steadily out into the implacable sea, which in due course closed over him.

Far away on the horizon, the helicopter began to rise and move towards the shore.

CHAPTER 18 ═══

On the evening before her departure for the Bahamas—she had been advised that it would be prudent, in all the circumstances, to take up residence outside the United Kingdom—Lilian had invited all those who had been, as she expressed it, so kind to her while she was working in Chambers, to join her for a farewell glass of champagne in the Corkscrew. She stood at the bar, blushing slightly at the competition between Cantrip and Henry to refill her glass and responding with charming smiles to the congratulations of Timothy, the improving advice of Ragwort, and the dulcet laments of Basil Ptarmigan for the loss of so decorative and skilful a telex operator. A month before she would no doubt have been embarrassed to find herself at the centre of such a circle; but to become the sole beneficiary of a trust fund worth nine million pounds sterling has a remarkable effect on a young woman's self-confidence.

Withdrawing a little from the throng surrounding her,

I found myself sharing a candlelit table with Clementine and Julia.

"My dear Clementine," I said, "do tell me how exactly you discovered that it was Lilian's uncle who established the Daffodil trust. She has been thanking me very prettily for all that I have done for her, but I felt obliged to say that so far as I am aware my own investigation played no part in the discovery."

"I suppose you could say," said Clementine, "that it's Cantrip she's mostly got to thank for it—I mean he was the one who got me to stir up our Probate Department about the books her uncle left her. You see, Oliver Grynne got the news of her uncle's death just before that last meeting in the Cayman Islands, and he didn't have time to do much about it except bung all the files across to Probate Department, with a note saying he'd discuss it with them when he got back. It's perfectly normal procedure," added Clementine rather defensively, "where we're appointed executors of the will."

"And no doubt," I said, "everything would have gone quite smoothly if Oliver Grynne had in fact returned from the Cayman Islands."

"Absolutely, but of course he didn't. So Probate Department just went into their standard routine, which doesn't include going through the correspondence files for the past umpteen years. They got as far as finding that the estate was worth twelve thousand quid—of course the whole idea of the settlement had been that the settlor wouldn't have anything in his own name—and they sort of lost interest. I mean they put the case at the bottom of the pile, and when a case gets put at the bottom of the pile in

THE SIRENS SANG OF MURDER

Probate Department, it tends to be a century or two before it's heard of again."

"And when you were unable to find anything in Oliver Grynne's files which seemed relevant to the Daffodil settlement, I suppose it would not have occurred to you . . . ?" I paused, fearing the question to be tactless.

"To ask Probate Department? Of course it occurred to me," said Clementine with asperity. "I rampaged up and down the office like a lunatic trying to find out whether Oliver had passed any of his files on to anyone, and they were the first people I asked. But you know what Probate Departments are like. I told them the files I was looking for were connected with a nine-million-quid trust fund and it didn't cross their tiny minds that a fund that size could have anything to do with an estate worth twelve hundred. So it wasn't until they had to fish the papers out again to deal with Lilian's bequest that someone noticed a letter referring to a settlement and the penny finally dropped."

Julia had been sitting in anxious silence, looking frequently at her watch and as often towards the doorway.

"I can't understand," she said, "why Selena isn't here yet—I hope it doesn't mean that things have gone badly."

It was the day of Colonel Cantrip's trial, and Selena had been prevailed upon to undertake his defence. The arm movements which Julia had observed at the cloakroom window on taking off from the helicopter club had not been the friendly waves of valediction with which one amateur of aviation bids Godspeed to another; they had been the gestures by which a financier locked in a cloakroom and from there observing the theft of his private helicopter expresses his intention to instigate criminal proceedings at the earliest opportunity. Thus it was that the

263

triumphant landing of the Colonel and his three passengers on a beach just west of St. Helier had been slightly marred by their immediate arrest, and that he was today being tried by a bench of lay magistrates somewhere in the Home Counties on a number of charges arising out of the incident.

"I think it's frightfully mean to go on with the prosecution," said Clementine. "After all, if the Colonel hadn't turned up with the helicopter, Gabrielle and Cantrip would have been drowned."

"The financier," said Julia, "appears to regard that as a matter of trifling importance by comparison with his meeting in Le Touquet, and has insisted on pressing charges."

"I didn't know," said Clementine, "that Selena ever did any criminal work."

"She doesn't. But the Colonel showed a touching determination to be defended by a member of Cantrip's Chambers, and Selena did once do a common-law pupillage. She didn't seem to think it would be helpful for Cantrip and me to give evidence—indeed, she has expressly forbidden us to go anywhere near the place. Clementine, you don't think they'd send the Colonel to prison, do you?"

"Oh no," said the young solicitor, "I shouldn't think so. Not at his age. Well, not for very long, anyway."

A further bottle of champagne had appeared as if by magic on our table, but it failed to distract Julia from troubled thoughts of the Colonel. She continued to glance anxiously at the doorway in which Selena still persistently failed to appear.

Between Clementine and myself there was perhaps a certain constraint. In the hours following the death of the Count di Silvabianca I had had no opportunity for any private conversation with her. She had been occupied with the task of arranging Gabrielle's return to the comforting refuge of her mother's house in Brittany, while Patrick Ardmore devoted his energies to securing the release on bail of Julia and the Colonel. (He was fortunately on terms of friendship with a senior Jersey police officer, to whom he explained that they were both personally known to him and were of the highest character and respectability.) She still felt some embarrassment, I suppose, at the suddenness with which she had asked me to terminate my investigation and now seemed to think it appropriate to give some hint of her reason.

"You know, Professor Tamar," she said, refilling my glass, "there was suddenly a ghastly moment, after I'd asked you to investigate the Daffodil case, when I thought you might suspect me of bumping off poor old Oliver and Edward myself. You didn't ever, did you?"

"My dear Clementine," I said, "not for a moment." The period during which I had done so had been so brief as to make any mention of it an excess of candour.

"Because we knew, of course . . ." Julia paused in time to save herself from what she supposed an indiscretion. Since Cantrip was not to be undeceived as to the identity of his bedfellow on Walpurgis Night, I had thought it unwise to enlighten Julia. She was accordingly still under the impression that Clementine had an alibi. "Of course we knew, Clementine, that you would never dream of such a thing."

"Well, I'm glad you didn't think it was me. But I can see that in a way it might be quite a logical thing to think—I mean, I am engaged to one of the default beneficiaries under the settlement, so I'd have had a motive."

"But if," I said, "you had decided to commit murder for the motive which you suggest, you would certainly not have done so in circumstances which would direct attention towards the provisions of the settlement—a meeting of the Daffodil advisers was the very last occasion you would have chosen. The same was also true, of course, of the other beneficiaries. I therefore reached the conclusion—much later, I confess, than I ought to have done—that the fact of the deaths occurring at meetings of the Daffodil advisers made it virtually certain that they were quite unconnected with the provisions of the settlement."

"I say," said Clementine, "how frightfully subtle."

"My dear Clementine," I said, "it is kind of you to say so, but to one versed in the art or science of textual criticism it is a very simple piece of reasoning—one learns to distrust the reading which seems at first sight to be the most obvious. The question which remained was whether the deaths were, after all, merely coincidental or whether there was some other distinctive feature of the Daffodil meetings, quite apart from their subject matter, which might make them occasions for murder. One feature, of course, was that they were the occasions when Gabrielle di Silvabianca travelled abroad without her husband."

"Hilary," said Julia, "this is the twentieth century."

"Quite so, my dear Julia, but the fact weighs more with some than with others. An attractive married woman, of adventurous temperament, is travelling away from home. She has the impression that someone is watching her, and two of the men in whose company she spends her time meet possibly violent deaths. A hundred years ago many people would have thought it obvious, some might think it so even nowadays, that her husband was the person responsible. If it does not seem so to us, it is not merely because we do not think of matrimonial jealousy as a sufficient motive for murder. It is also because it would not occur to us to describe what took place in the terms I have just suggested. We would tell an entirely different story—a story of trust funds and companies, in which the husband has no significant role. I was as misguided, in the initial stages of my investigation, as a person who tries to decipher an inscription in Latin believing it to be in English."

"If one knew no Latin," said Julia absentmindedly, "it would be difficult to perceive one's error."

"Certainly, but I cannot claim so complete an ignorance of human passion as to justify my obtuseness. If I had considered the possibility that the story was one of passion rather than tax planning, the truth would very soon have become clear. You had told me, Clementine, when we first spoke of the matter, of Oliver Grynne's admiration for Gabrielle, and I already knew that Malvoisin had from time to time made advances to her. You mentioned also that her husband resented her travelling abroad on business. I chose, without conscious reflection, to treat these things as irrelevant to my inquiry. Nor did I ask myself, as I should have done, why, out of all the Daffodil advisers, it should be Gabrielle who was singled out for surveillance. And I failed, above all, to reflect on the oddness of her being alarmed about it. She had not struck Cantrip, nor when I met her did she strike me, as a woman who would be unduly anxious about being watched by the Inland Revenue or anyone of that sort—one would have expected her to find it rather stimulating."

"Oh, look here," said Clementine, "you're not saying she knew all along it was her husband watching her?"

"Consciously, certainly not. He employed, no doubt, some quite effective form of disguise—false beard and dark glasses and so forth—and took care to keep at a safe distance. Such devices, however, can seldom deceive a person who knows one well, and the unconscious mind, as we know, often observes and reasons far more efficiently than the conscious. I do not doubt that at some quite early stage she observed something about the person following her which to her unconscious mind unmistakably identified him as her husband. Her conscious mind, however, would quite naturally have rejected this conclusion as unthinkable, and the conflict between the two would be more than enough to account for her nervousness. It must have been much worse, of course, after the death of Oliver Grynne."

"The idiotic thing is," said Clementine, "that she wasn't having any sort of affair with either Oliver or Edward. Oliver adored her, of course, and she quite enjoyed flirting with him a bit, but I'm pretty sure that's all there was to it. Anyway, she'd been going to Daffodil meetings for years—why did her husband suddenly go off the deep end?"

"It's clear enough that she married the Count for his looks, and perhaps finding something glamorous about his success as a sportsman. After some years of marriage she remained fond of him and reluctant to hurt his feelings, but his company provided her neither with intellectual stimulus nor with that element of excitement which someone like Gabrielle requires as a seasoning to everyday existence."

"You mean he bored her," said Clementine.

"Quite so. The interruptions to her customary routine afforded by the Daffodil meetings must have become, in these circumstances, increasingly agreeable, and her husband no doubt noted all too well how her eyes brightened and her spirits rose at the prospect or recollection of them. The inference that they were opportunities for her to meet a lover must have seemed to him almost irresistible, and so he began to make plans to keep watch on her. The suspicions of jealousy can be confirmed but seldom allayed—once he had reached this point it was almost inevitable that sooner or later he would see something which seemed to him conclusive of his wife's infidelity. Something happened in the Cayman Islands which convinced him that she and Oliver Grynne were lovers, and for him it followed that Oliver Grynne must die."

"Of course," said Clementine, "foreigners do tend to overreact a bit about things like that, don't they? Latin temperament and so on."

"I think," I said, "that it is less a matter of temperament than of literary tradition. People do what books have taught them to do and feel what books have taught them to feel—it is curiously difficult to do otherwise. There is a tradition in Romance literature which regards jealousy as a requirement of honour."

Julia's glances at the doorway were at last rewarded by the appearance there of Selena. Our table being at the furthest end of the room, we could not judge, in the murky light of the Corkscrew, whether her expression was downcast or triumphant. I supposed we would know soon enough what sentence the magistrates had imposed; but Julia rose, champagne glass in hand, and began to manoeuvre her way, with difficulty and apologies, through the intervening groups of gossiping lawyers and journalists.

"But look here," said Clementine, "if the Count

thought Oliver was the one she was having it off with, why did he go on following her after he'd got rid of him? And how on earth did he get the idea she was having an affair with Edward?"

"The appetite of jealousy is insatiable. No sooner had he disposed, as he imagined, of one lover than he began to fear a successor. So when his wife went to the Channel Islands for the next Daffodil meeting, he followed her again, and again kept watch. He watched as she wandered round Jersey with Cantrip. He watched as she made her way to Sark disguised as a Breton peasant woman—of course he knew all about that. He watched as she retired to the Witch's Cottage for the night in the company of Cantrip and yourself, and he was still watching an hour or so later when a woman of similar build, wrapped up, I suppose, in a white coat or raincoat, came out of the cottage again and went to meet Edward Malvoisin. My dear Clementine, I do not wish to seem critical, but it would have been helpful, you know, if you had told me of your assignation with him."

"Oh dear. I'm very sorry, Professor Tamar, I know I ought to have told you. But you see . . ." She looked round to make sure that none of those nearby was paying any heed to our conversation. "You see, I thought you'd be bound to be discussing the case with Cantrip, and if he knew I was meeting Edward, he'd know it must have been Gabrielle who was with him in the cottage. So I thought it would be a bit unsporting of me to say anything about it without talking it over with her, and then—well, everything happened before I had a chance to. But she says you'd worked it out anyway, about us switching places after the lights went out."

"Later, I fear, than I ought to have done. I knew of the wager you had made with Edward Malvoisin that he would not walk across the Coupee at midnight, and I should have inferred from that that you had a rendezvous with him."

"I just meant it as a joke at first, but then Edward said he was game to do it as long as I came with him as far as the Coupee to cheer him on his way. So of course I said I would. It turned out a perfectly beastly night—black as pitch with a gale-force wind—but I was blowed if I was going to be the first to cry off, and I suppose Edward felt the same, so we went ahead."

"He went across the Coupee and you sat and waited for him, I suppose, on one of the benches at the approach to it?"

"That's right. There's a sort of antique cannon on the far side, and the idea was that he'd unscrew the brass plate on it and bring it back to prove he'd been all the way across. We'd have put it back next day, of course. Anyway, he was gone much longer than I'd expected, and I started getting a bit—well, not worried exactly. More like miffed, really—I thought he was doing it on purpose to see if I'd come after him. Then I heard the carriage coming across the Coupee and the noise of it crashing, so of course I went down to see if I could help, but Albert didn't seem to appreciate it. I could see that if Edward was on the other side he wouldn't be able to get back, but I just thought—well, I'm afraid I just thought it served him right rather for playing the fool and keeping me hanging about in the dark. So I went back to the Witch's Cottage and went to bed."

She bit her knuckles and looked disconsolately at the flickering candle which provided our illumination.

"Poor old Edward, I quite fancied him in a silly sort of way, and I suppose you could say I sent him to his death."

"My dear Clementine," I said, anxious to dispel any notion so lowering to the spirits, "you could not possibly have foreseen that there was any danger. I do not doubt, moreover, that if you had not emerged when you did from the cottage, the Count would later that night have found some means to gain entry to it. If he had found Cantrip and Gabrielle in each other's arms—"

Warm as the evening was, Clementine shivered.

"How do you think he found out about them in the end?"

"I'm not sure," I said, "that he ever guessed the truth about the night in the Witch's Cottage. But surely it must have been Cantrip whom he initially suspected—consider the amount of time that he and Gabrielle had spent together in Jersey. And afterwards in Monaco—one could see all too easily that Gabrielle found Cantrip more entertaining company than her husband. Moreover, the trap which the Count eventually set for them—the spurious invitations to meet at St. Clement's Bay—would have seemed self-justifying. To have declined the invitation would have been evidence of innocence; to accept, in his eyes, conclusive of guilt."

"But it was the first time he'd tried to do any harm to Gabrielle—do you think he'd always meant to or was he just getting worse and worse?"

"Pathological jealousy is no doubt a progressive disorder, but I suspect that he always intended her to die in the end. He wished her to live long enough, however, to feel pain for the loss of her supposed lovers. That, as I understand it, is the classic pattern of the jealous revenge. The rival must die: the faithless spouse must suffer and die."

A crescendo of cheering and exploding champagne corks among those gathered at the bar had already indicated that Selena bore victorious tidings and was lingering there to relate the particulars of her success. I had little fear of missing them; it is seldom that any member of Lincoln's Inn is reluctant to repeat a story of forensic triumph. In due course she and Julia made their way to our table.

"I can't really claim," said Selena, demurely sipping her champagne, "that it was anything to do with my skill in advocacy. I had quite a nice little speech ready, based on a plea in mitigation I once did for some juvenile delinquents when I was a pupil in the Temple—all about the Colonel being the inevitable product of a society which encouraged aggression and glamourised violence and not being morally responsible for his actions and so on—but I didn't have to use it. The financier had a change of heart. Just before the case was due to be heard he told Counsel for the prosecution that he thought he might have said something in his conversation with the Colonel which the Colonel might have understood as permission to fly the helicopter. So all charges were dismissed and the Colonel left the court without a stain on his character."

"How extraordinary," said Clementine. "Did the financier have a specially nice lunch or something?"

"Possibly," said Selena. "Actually, it seemed to happen just after I mentioned to Counsel for the prosecution that I naturally intended to cross-examine his witness about the meeting in Le Touquet—after all, if it was part of their case that we'd made him miss an important meeting, we were entitled to know what it was about and who was there. It's possible, I suppose, that he didn't want the details to be generally known, and with the legal affairs correspondent of the *Financial Times* sitting in the press benches . . ."

"The *F.T.* correspondent?" said Clementine. "What on earth was he doing covering a criminal case in a provincial magistrates court?"

"Oh," said Selena, "I always let him know when I have a case he might be interested in. It's very important to maintain good relations with the press, don't you think?"

It was several minutes—a surprisingly long time, considering the company I was in—before it occurred to anyone to suggest that it was my fault that the Colonel had stolen the helicopter: Why had the truth not occurred to me until eleven o'clock on the night before the last Daffodil meeting? If I had thought of it sooner, the whole helicopter adventure would have been quite unnecessary. I explained patiently that it was not until eleven o'clock on the night before the meeting that I had studied Gabrielle's chequebook.

"I expect," said Selena, with an air of indulgent generosity, "that you would like to explain to us about the chequebook."

"Until I saw the chequebook I had assumed that the fountain pen which Gabrielle had lost was the same one which Patrick Ardmore had found—it would have seemed perverse to imagine otherwise. That meant either that Gabrielle herself had dropped the pen on the Coupee or that someone had stolen or borrowed it from her before she left Sark."

"Yes," said Selena, "of course."

"The chequebook included the counterfoils for the period of Gabrielle's visit to the Channel Islands, and they had all been completed in ink, with a fountain pen rather than a ballpoint. The next counterfoil after these recorded a withdrawal from a bank in St. Malo on the first of May—the day that Gabrielle left Sark. It was in the same hand, in the same ink, and beyond all shadow of doubt written with the same pen—as a student of ancient and medieval manuscripts, I am not without experience of such questions. It was clear then that when Gabrielle reached St. Malo she still had with her the fountain pen she had been using in the Channel Islands. Once I knew that, I could have no doubt of her husband's guilt."

"I suppose you mean," said Selena, frowning slightly, "that he was the only person who had the chance to steal it between the time she used it in St. Malo and the time she discovered it was missing?"

"I couldn't be absolutely sure of that, though it would have been easier for him than for anyone else—no doubt he took it while she was changing for dinner. But if Gabrielle still had the original pen in St. Malo, then the pen which Patrick Ardmore found on the Coupee must have been a duplicate. As Ragwort pointed out earlier, the pen was not an item which any jeweller who valued his reputation would duplicate without the authority of the original customer. The Count was the original customer."

"I say," said Clementine, "do you mean he had a copy made in advance to frame Gabrielle for the murder?"

"I don't suppose," I said, "that when he ordered the duplicate he had any precise plans for its use, but I have little doubt that he expected it to be in some way of use to him in perfecting his revenge. He would not have intended, I think, that she should actually be charged with the murder—merely that she should be exposed to a sufficient degree of suspicion to compound her distress for the loss of her lover."

Julia renewed her complaint that the pen was a deplorably old-fashioned clue. No doubt she was right; but we had been dealing, as I pointed out, with a deplorably old-fashioned murder.